Totally Bound Publishing books by L A Tavares

Consistently Inconsistent
One Motion More

Consistently Inconsistent

ONE MOTION MORE

L A TAVARES

One Motion More
ISBN # 978-1-83943-957-5
©Copyright L A Tavares 2021
Cover Art by Louisa Maggio ©Copyright March 2021
Interior text design by Claire Siemaszkiewicz
Totally Bound Publishing

ONE MOTION MORE

Dedication

Kati,
Before this book had a title, it had its biggest fan.
Thank you for you supporting me endlessly and
loving Xander wildly.
You rock SO hard.

Acknowledgements

Of all the words I've ever written these will absolutely be the hardest. I've had so much support and so many great people in my corner that I can't possibly include everyone. If you've ever taken the time to say 'what are you working on now?' or 'tell me about your books', please know that in those few syllables you became part of the reason I made it this far and I thank you from the bottom of my heart for being a part of my story.

First and foremost…My parents. I write romance and have believed in true, unwavering love my entire life because I had the best example of it every single day. Thank you both for being the most incredible display of love, loyalty and laughter there is.

Brad and Jacoby,
I love you both 'to the moon and back'. The best part of this entire journey is having you both to share it with. Brad, I could write a thousand more love stories but ours will always be my favorite. Love you every day and always. Jacoby, you are the thing I am the most proud of in this world. Please don't ever lose your love of art and books. I made the decision to pursue publishing as my work shortly after I had you. I hope someday you read this and understand that you are the reason I did this and the reason I made it this far.

My agent, Stephanie: I didn't believe in me until you believed in me. Thank you for everything you've taught me, every chance you've given me and most importantly never letting me give up on this story.

My TEG content editor Jamie: Thank you for taking my story and perfecting it in a way I never could have achieved on my own. I have learned so much from you in such a short time and can already feel my other works in progress garnering strength as I frequently ask myself 'WWJD—what would Jamie do?' while I write. Thank you for tolerating me while I write exclusively in made-up words, fragmented sentences and an abundance of randomly placed commas.

Totally Entwined Group: Having you believe in my story and give me this opportunity changed my life. You gave me a gift when you gave me the ability to change 'I write sometimes' to 'I'm a published author.' Thank you, beyond words, for taking a chance on me.

I grew up with two sisters who taught me everything I know. I look up to them in so many ways and I know that most of the good in me comes from wanting to be like them. Love you Michelle and Nicole!

My mother in law, Darlene, has been so invested in this journey and her support means the world to me. Thank you for being my person, allowing me to be 'the chosen one' and for always being so interested in this process and supporting me every step of the way.

There are people from family members to friends to critique partners to coworkers who had a huge hand in ensuring I stuck to my goals. Kati, thank you for knowing these stories better than I do. I couldn't have done this without you pushing me to never quit. Kristen D, Elizabeth M, Marissa H and my "Author Queens" — CL, KW, RH and R2 — every one of you have taught me something about reading and writing and inspired me over and over again. Keep writing. Keep reading. Follow your heart and never give up. Jennifer and WBC: for reading every word I've ever written and always asking for more, I thank you. It's your constant support and always asking what happens next that makes me keep writing. My coworkers at my day job: thank you for always keeping me persistent, on track and caffeinated.

Last but certainly not least: Normand. It pains me to write this knowing that you're not here to see it. Thank you for being one of my biggest fans and supporters. Even when things got hard for you, you always went out of your way to make sure I was still writing. The efforts you put in to ensure I was following my heart and trying to make my dreams come true drove me to keep going, and for that, I'll be forever grateful.

Chapter One

The locked, guarded door and shiny new mark on my already scarred record are laughable penalties. The real punishment is the *smell* in these small quarters — body odors, stale alcohol. One thing is for sure... There are no VIP suites in New York police stations.

More like a bench than a bed, the slab of flat ceramic I lay on is uncomfortable and determined to punish me with back problems that will last longer than this overnight hold.

My eyes snap shut each time I try to open them — an involuntary response to block out the outdated fluorescent light overhead. I press the palms of my hands into my eye sockets and run my fingers through my overgrown hair. Sure, the lights don't help my already throbbing head and the sleeping arrangement is a far cry from comfortable, but the atmosphere is 'welcoming'. I purposely bent the rules just far enough to win myself a one-night, all-inclusive stay at the nearest precinct.

Quiet. No crowds. No screaming fans. Nowhere for me to be, no way for me to screw up. Most people would find the locked doors, silence and lack of company alarming. Not me. For me, it's tranquil. A vacation. Maybe that's why I frequent the sin-bin so often.

"Hey there, sunshine," a plump guard says, opening the thick-paned glass door so it swings into the hallway. He leans into the metal door frame, holding a large stick of beef jerky in one hand, tearing off a chunk between his teeth and chewing so I can hear it.

"The doors are a nice upgrade," I say through a yawn as I knock on the glass. "They were bars when I was here last."

He gnaws on the dried meat, unamused. "There's someone here to pick you up," he says as he chews, spewing small chunks of meat and saliva as he speaks.

"Aw, so soon?" I bring myself to my feet and stretch — every muscle protests. "Guess I'm not twenty-one anymore, eh?" I ask.

"Maybe you should stop trying to be," he says. His stone expression remains as such.

"Noted," I add, and salute him as I step away from the cell, turn around and head toward the station's lobby to retrieve my sunglasses and cell phone before heading out of the doors.

Blake — my bass guitarist and lifelong best friend — leans against a car I've never seen before, opens the back door and gets in without waiting for me to approach him. He slides to the opposite side of the hired car and I slide in next to him, closing the door as the driver pulls away from the curb.

"How bad this time?" I ask, one side of my mouth lifting at the corner.

"You really don't remember?" he asks.

12

"No. That was the whole point." I drop my phone into the breast pocket of my shirt and place my sunglasses over my eyes.

Blake tilts back the top of a box of Marlboro Reds, a flagrant disregard of the *No Smoking* sticker adhered to the car's dash. The lingering tobacco smell of the car tells me he's already broken that rule.

"Never fear," I say, elbowing him in the arm. "Social media and the news will remind me, I'm sure."

"If Cooper doesn't kill you first," Blake adds, cracking the window and fishing for a Bic in his breast pocket. His words come out draped in a mix of his slightly faded South African accent and the dialect he has picked up during his years in the States.

Blake moved into my house at a time when his mother couldn't provide for him anymore — right as we started tenth grade and, truthfully, his appearance hasn't changed much since I met him in junior high. He looks almost the same way now as he did then, down to his stupid blond-tipped faux hawk and slightly spaced teeth. Only now, the tall, slender physique he boasted back then has morphed into a 'definitely enjoys beer'-type body. Though, the same could be said for me.

The car arrives back at the venue where we are set to have our second show in a back-to-back schedule.

We enter the building and Blake walks ahead of me by about five strides. I am in no condition to keep up. He turns a corner, disappearing from view. As I turn the same corner, Cooper, our band's manager, is standing there waiting for me. Startled, I jump out of my boots and my stomach takes a drop it can barely handle. I swallow back whatever threatens to make a reappearance.

"Jeez—" I start, but he has no intention of letting me talk.

"Leave," he says, his eyes an even deeper brown than they usually are, enhanced by the dark bags beneath them. "Go find food, water and a shower. Whatever it is you need to do to clean up and be ready for today."

"I'll be ready, Coop. I always am."

"You should be grateful we have a show today because I can tell you—no, I can *promise* you—if I didn't need you today, you would still be sitting in that cell." Cooper paces the width of the hallway, pausing every few moments to make a hand gesture my direction, as if he can't walk and shake his fist all at the same time. "You're lucky the cops here are fans of yours, you know. There will come a day where just *being* Xander Varro doesn't get you what you want. Your status won't get you out of everything forever. The sooner you understand that the better."

"I had a few drinks. I was having a good time—"

"Drunk and disorderly, disturbing the peace, resisting arrest." Cooper starts listing off, using his fingers to keep track of all the misdemeanors. "This band can't keep a publicist because they're tired of covering for you. You can't keep yourself out of the negativity and the spotlight. You're dependent on drama. You're going to be a father, for crying out loud. When do you plan to grow up, Xander? When is enough, enough?"

He's right, but I'm too proud to admit it. Cooper's growl shifts to a hushed pause, allowing me to say my piece or apologize, but I don't do either, so he continues, filling the silent void.

"This isn't just about you, you know. Your band counts on you. Your fans count on you. *I* count on you.

Someday your kid will count on you, and you are becoming the kind of guy who can't be counted on." His pacing comes to a halt and his eyes soften. His voice quiets, falling so calm that I would almost prefer the yelling. "You have it all, Xander. Everything. Stop *trying* to throw it all away."

I nod, a silent response, even though I know Cooper wants more from me. It's all I have to offer.

"Just go, Xander," he says. "Come back when you're ready to be on that stage and not a second sooner."

"Can you send a car to take me back to the hotel?"

"You can walk."

I laugh at his joke, but the sound becomes a scoff when I realize he's serious. I nod without enthusiasm and turn toward the door, slamming my bodyweight into the metal push bar though the signs clearly indicate Emergency Exit Only.

The hotel is only just over a mile away, but I'm still annoyed. These boots definitely were not made for walking. My feet are throbbing by the time I arrive at the lavish hotel doors. The lock clicks as I hold the key card to the door of the hotel room that I was supposed to be long-checked-out of. I lay on the bed longer than I should, ignoring the clothes and other items strewn across it. A red light blinks at the base of the landline phone the hotel provides, most likely a wakeup call ordered by Cooper or a message about the late fees incurred as a result of the ignored check-out. I almost delete it without listening, figuring whatever message it holds is either now irrelevant or I just don't care what it has to say.

But I click it, and my girlfriend's voice is on the other end. I smile at first, listening to her words.

"Hey, it's Mariah."

But the smile fades to a flatline. Why would she call the hotel and not my cell phone?

"I have something to tell you."

* * * *

The brilliant spotlights above the stage beam hot against my skin as if the sun itself made a front-row appearance at the show. Sweat soaks my long hair, my shirt sticks to my skin.

Thousands of people are packed wall-to-wall into the venue. A mosquito would put us over capacity. The crowd is just feet from me, yet their profiles are indecipherable. The bodies become blurred as they jump and dance at the front of the stage. The crowd melts together to form one jumbled image.

With a wrinkled forehead and my eyes shut tight, I will my vision to clear, but it's not enough. The words she left me with can't be unheard.

'I lied to you.'

Stumbling back across the bowing floorboards of the stage, I stagger, but fight to keep myself upright.

'I'm sorry. I was holding on to something that wasn't there and hasn't been there for quite some time.'

The band still plays, strumming their guitar strings and keeping time on the drums, but I can't concentrate on the words I am supposed to be singing while hers still play wildly in my head.

'I knew if I called your phone, you'd answer, but if I hear your voice, I know I'll never tell the truth.'

This feeling—the chest tightness, the rapid pulse— it's foreign to me. I don't recognize this kind of distress.

'When I told you that I was pregnant with your baby, I was just trying to give you a reason to stay. But it's not true.'

My mouth goes dry again, paralyzing my tongue against the back of my front teeth. Everything around me moves in slow motion, like quicksand.

I should be entertaining this crowd. The only thing I'm entertaining is spiraling thoughts.

The baby that never was.

The conniving woman who screwed me over.

The fastest way to get out of playing a show tonight and be anywhere but here.

The members of the band shout to me — maybe *at* me — but their muffled voices sound miles away. A high-pitched ringing sounds at both ears, overpowering the thousands of voices that fill the venue. Blake stands in front of me, asking if I'm okay.

I'm *not* okay.

The lights are glaring, the music is flawless, the crowd is thunderous but I am broken. The microphone falls through my clammy palm, hitting the stage and bouncing with harsh echoing thuds and horrid feedback. I make my way toward the wings of the stage. I can't look back — and I don't.

Proof of this disaster is better than likely already uploaded to every available social media platform shared by one person, then the next — gone viral.

Like a disease.

The magazines and tabloids, they will slander my name with assumptions of drug use. *Xander Varro Performs While Inebriated at New York Venue.*

They think they know me.

They don't know a damn thing.

The truth is…. Well, it doesn't matter what the truth is. The truth doesn't sell like the bullshit does. This isn't drugs. This is a feeling that tears through my chest cavity like rot in old walls. This is unrelenting anger that robs me of my breath. The lyrics to a song I wish I had never written in the first place, had dismantled me in a way that I never would have anticipated. Blindsided me, much like Mariah had.

This is panic.

Everyone tried to warn me about her.

All the signs were there.

Warning. No lifeguard on duty. Swim at your own risk.

And I did.

I dove in head-first every damn time, catapulting myself into deep, troubled waters — a treacherous mix of her crooked lies and mouth full of deceit. I filled my lungs with air and held it as I treaded the waves of fables she was known for.

And now, I'm sinking like an anchor in waters I never should have navigated in the first place.

There is no mistaking the sound of the crowd beyond the stage now — their disgruntled outcry a mix of boos and jeers, openly expressing their demands for our return to stage. I don't blame them for being this vocal. Had we been nearing the end of the show, we could have passed this off as a cutoff point and returned to the stage for an encore, but we had just started our set. "What do you want to do, Xander?" Blake asks, sweat beading across his brow. "Are you okay? Do you want to try to get back out there?"

Blake's eyes are trained on mine. Without blinking, I stare at him. He's my best friend, my brother, really — but there wasn't much going on between his ears.

More often than not he wears this absent expression with his eyes frosted over and his lips parted like someone asked him a question he doesn't know the answer to. That's the face he wears now, only no one asked him anything, and I wish he would just shut up.

"I need to get the hell out of here," I mumble. Leaving the band behind me, I stand and half jog the length of the backstage area. Eager to escape, I slam my bodyweight into the first door I see, with no idea what sits on the other side.

Hundreds of pairs of curious, demanding eyes await. I stand frozen in the doorway. There are only two things separating me from the crowd—a thin fabric barrier and a few security guards who may not even be tall enough to ride large rollercoasters.

A guy who stands about six feet tall or so—only about an inch or two shorter than me—steps around the barrier with two other men flanking closely beside him. The two security guards closest to me step forward, posing about as much threat as a Nerf gun in a bad neighborhood.

"I paid for a show. I came to see a show. I expect a show," the disgruntled fan says, flaunting a pierced tongue. His friends yell a resounding agreement.

"Fuck off," I hiss, turning away from them. That should have been the final word. At least, that was my intention, but he spits in my direction. I urge myself to keep walking and forget this jackass exists—but I can't.

Not tonight.

My conscience is as lopsided as a seesaw with only one passenger, encouraging me to turn and give this guy a piece of my mind. The security detail instructs me to 'Let it go', which I kindly disregard, shaking free of his grasp on my arm.

Security is on my heels as I approach the man, who somehow seems bigger than he did a few moments ago. His back is to me, but he yells over the house music, bragging to a group in the crowd as if his disgusting behavior were something heroic.

I tap him on the shoulder and he turns toward me.

"How's this for a fucking show?" I say through clenched teeth and throw my body behind a well-timed right hook. Either my knuckles or his jaw emits a distinct *crack* as the two connect, but there is no time to think about which it was. He lunges back at me, grabbing the front of my shirt.

The security staffed by the venue floods the area, separating me from my opponent and the gathering onlookers.

A salt-and-pepper-haired security guard pushes me backward a few steps as the other guy is escorted from the venue. He looks back at me with fury in his eyes. I curtsy, holding the edges of an invisible skirt, then give him the middle finger as the security detail drags me backstage.

Chapter Two

The flashes are instant and blinding — the camera clicks audible, despite the reporters and media yelling their unanswerable questions in my ear as I leave.

Our personal security guides me forward, the short walk to the tour bus feeling as if it has no end. My eyes had adjusted to the dark venue atmosphere, but now scattered spots from the cameras cloud my vision.

Finally onboard the bus, I collapse into my favorite seat nearest the liquor shelf.

My head is pounding. Night after night of drum solos just a few feet behind me may be to blame, but this was more than likely a hard fall from a good buzz. Though both the lights in the bus and the night sky are unlit, I drop my sunglasses over my eyes. I press the heels of my hands against my temples and grab the roots of my overgrown hair in my hands. A single bead of sweat releases from my hairline and drips to the toe of my boots as I lean forward with my face in my hands and the weight of the world on my shoulders.

The odd blue-and-orange carpet that runs the length of the bus catches my attention. It looks like it was stolen from the floor of an outdated movie theater. I'm lost in the loudness of the heinous carpet pattern I somehow never noticed before when I hear the unmistakable rustle of body verses leather as someone takes the seat next to me.

"Do you want to talk about it?" Blake asks. His tone offers no emotion. He doesn't seem mad that I ruined the show, but he's not laughing about it either. He leans the chair back as far as it will go and rests his leather high-tops on the footrest in front of us.

"Not particularly." My voice is so quiet I can barely hear it over the ringing in my ears from tonight's partial set.

"Okay," he says as he leans to the side, pulling an unopened bottle of whiskey and two cups from the shelf closest to him. He opens the bottle and pours the amber liquid, handing me one of the glasses. In one large gulp, I swallow the contents.

"How about now?" Blake asks. Thankfully, these sunglasses mask my expression. He wouldn't appreciate the narrowed glare I wear behind these tinted lenses.

"That was a sold-out crowd in there tonight," Blake reminds me as if the size of the crowd and the 'Sold Out' banner across the marquee were lost on me. "New York has been very kind to us. We sell out every time we're here. I don't even know what happens in this instance. Do they get their money back? Because that's a massive loss for us."

I feel like a second grader being scolded by a schoolteacher.

"You are the lead singer of this band, Xander," he continues.

"You don't say." The bite in my words is intentional. I reach for the whiskey bottle, but he moves it just beyond arm's length.

"Are you okay?" Blake asks. "Physically, is the hand okay? You need that hand to play. I mean, I'm a good musician. I am *great*, in fact. I can do all the guitar parts myself, but it makes the music better and my job easier when you play," he jokes, pouring himself another glass of whiskey, then giving in and filling mine too.

"Yeah." A light smile crosses my face. It feels transplanted, like it doesn't belong to me. "My hand is fine," I add.

"Good," he says, "'cuz it was a hell of a punch." He laughs and taps his glass off mine. The liquid splashes and the clink of the glasses echoes through the otherwise-silent tour bus.

"Listen… Whatever it is that you're going through, put it into the music. You are a talented singer known for the lyrics you write. Smear on some black eyeliner and turn this pain into *gold*. Put your feelings into one of those sad, dark, borderline scary songs you write so well and lay it out on the stage," he says around a sip of whiskey. The way he slurs his words makes me think he has already had too much tonight.

"I have never worn eyeliner a day in my life," I dispute over the squeaks and whistles of the tour bus as the driver pulls away from the venue parking lot, leaving the cameras and reporters in the distance. The occasional camera flash can still be seen at the rear of the tour bus, as if the photographers think they might catch one last picture of me as we drive away.

Leaving my sunglasses perched on the bridge of my slightly crooked nose, I lay my head back and close my eyes. The night replays again and again in my head like an inflight movie until sleep finally finds me.

* * * *

After what feels like only a few moments but was close to four hours and change, Blake elbows me and whispers quietly.

"Xander, take a look," he says with his forehead pressed to the nearest window. I slide my sunglasses onto the top of my head and look out the same pane. In the distance, the perfectly illuminated outline of the Boston skyline interrupts the otherwise pitch-dark backdrop.

"Home has never looked better than it does right now," I say through my exhale, leaving my breath on the window in a circle of fog.

The bus screeches and the air-pressure brakes sound off their familiar hiss as we come to a full stop. Cooper approaches us. Cooper has a first name, but we have called him by his last name for so long that his first name has become obsolete. *Greg? George? Gary?* Something with a G, I think, but I don't really know.

What I do know is he takes care of everything for us—public relations, schedules, merchandise, rehearsals, money. He does it all. I can say, with confidence, that this band would not be as successful as it has become without him at the helm.

"You guys can go. It's been a long day," Cooper says. "I will be in touch with the plans for the next few days leading up to the next show." He throws a thumb over his shoulder. Blake wastes no time and jumps from the top stair of the bus door to the parking lot without looking back. Dominic, our drummer, and Theo, the band's keyboardist, both stand and stretch before exiting the bus with some 'Good nights' and 'See you tomorrows'.

Cooper lifts one hand, effectively holding me back the way a crossing guard would halt oncoming traffic. I fall to the chair again.

Spectacular. Lecture time.

Truthfully, this was expected. In fact, it's a damn miracle we made it out of the venue parking lot before Cooper had one of his infamous speeches prepared and delivered.

He takes a seat directly across from me and runs his fingers across his jaw line a few times before speaking.

"Cooper?" I ask, to which he holds up one finger in response, still avoiding eye contact with me. If I've ever seen Cooper this mad, I can't recall the moment now.

His Adam's apple trembles beneath a hard swallow as he closes his hands so his palms touch, and taps his fingertips to his tight-lipped mouth.

"Is it drugs?" he asks, a hollow question revealing no emotion.

"No," I reply, but he closes his eyes and his nostrils flare. He doesn't buy it.

"Is it *drugs*?" He repeats with more volume this time, but his deep brown eyes are staring directly at me, into me, looking for the answer my eyes give and not the one my mouth offers.

"No, it's not drugs, Cooper. I'll be fine. I *am* fine." The words pour out like water through a broken dam. "I just had a bad night." His eyes soften, a defeated surrender, and guilt sets in as I realize what he is thinking.

"I cannot…" he begins but chokes on the words. "I will *not* lose another member of this band to drug use. Do you understand me?"

There it is, the words I knew were coming but didn't want to hear. Cooper has been the only father figure I've ever had, starting the day he accepted a position with this band. Even now, just shy of thirty years old, I hate hearing any form of disappointment in his words.

Consistently Inconsistent, now a four-man band, began with a fifth member, Julian Young. A uniquely talented musician, he birthed brilliant guitar riffs and harmonics that were nearly impossible to imitate. A born guitarist, sure — but he could keep up on the keyboard with the best of them and had even been known to take over the drums on occasion. He was, as the saying goes, a jack of all trades, but offered a twist on the old trope as he was, indeed, master of all.

He was an original member. Blake and I had planned to play in a school talent show, and he showed up to a rehearsal. Blake's and my two-man act became a three-person performance. Before long, we had added Dominic and Theo and had a band name and a set list.

Julian, however, could fit all his positive qualities in a handbag while he dragged his suitcases full of negatives behind him. He had struggled on and off — more *on* than *off* — with drugs over the course of the last two years. Of course, that was all that we *knew* of.

We tried to help him. Cooper pushed to be in Julian's corner as often as possible to help him get and remain clean, but Julian couldn't do it. He didn't want sobriety bad enough.

He started showing up late for shows, skipping practices, ignoring calls and texts all together, and we knew we couldn't have that kind of instability going into the tour.

Though our band name paired with my antics tonight would suggest otherwise, Consistently Inconsistent was a group of musicians as reliable as they were talented, a description that no longer fit Julian. Before hitting the road, we released a statement saying Julian Young was no longer a member of

Consistently Inconsistent and he would not be appearing with us going forward.

As a band, it was the hardest decision we had ever made, but it was the right thing to do. Maybe, just maybe, if he weren't exposed to the lifestyle this career offered, he would finally get the help he needed — but from what I've heard, that wasn't the case.

Cooper must think I'm going to make the letdown of tonight become a routine thing, because that was what he was accustomed to, thanks to Julian — and now, me. Worrying about Julian over the last two years had aged Cooper in a way that I'd never noticed until he was sitting this close to me, worrying about me now too.

"Go home, Xander," Cooper surrenders, his shoulders releasing from their tensed state. "Go home and go to bed. Go *directly* to bed. Do not stop at any bars. Do not pass go, do not collect two hundred dollars. Got it?"

"I make no promises." I raise my partially filled glass of whiskey his direction. I wink, and he sighs. Following Blake to whatever shit-hole bar he has found for the night isn't on the to-do list, but plans change. Cooper pats a hand on my shoulder and we stand at the same time.

As we exit the bus and walk toward the waiting town cars, he looks at me and says, "You know we're here for you, right? The band, me... If you need us, whatever it is, we can figure it out together. We always do."

"I know," I say, as a driver opens the back door of the car set to take me to my apartment — an empty apartment where I have no desire to go.

* * * *

Overlooking the cityscape below me, my reflection stares back at me from the pristine glass of the floor-to-ceiling windows of the high-rise apartment. The smell of my home, my life and my belongings enter my lungs for the first time in almost seven months as I breathe in. The crystal glass from the tour bus remains in my hand, and if I were a betting man, I would say it never finds its way back. It will find a home among all the other glasses and plates I've stolen from various limos, room services and bars.

Back and forth, back and forth... I pace at the window in silence for a few moments longer before I turn on the TV. I know this is a terrible idea, but I've spent my whole life ignoring my instincts and I've survived this long, so I roll the dice and click on the entertainment news channel.

A blonde female news anchor with overly Botoxed lips and long hair set in large, flowing curls speaks to the camera.

"Just a few hours ago, fans got more than they bargained for when Xander Varro, front man of the well-known rock band Consistently Inconsistent, left the stage not only mid-concert but mid-song. Concert goers report that a fan confronted the lead singer as he tried to exit the doors, telling him they 'paid for a show and expected a show.' Varro didn't take to kindly to the confrontation and punched the man, as you can see here in this video that was submitted by a witness to the altercation."

My head falls so my chin touches my chest and my dark hair drops like a curtain over my peripheral vision. I don't want to watch this, but I don't want to turn it off. I shift my gaze slightly so I can see out of the corner of my eye, checking every few seconds to see if it is over.

"I don't think that is quite what the poor man meant when he asked for a show, Tanya," a balding, male co-anchor wearing a revolting shirt-and-tie combo adds as he laughs at his own joke.

"Agreed, Jonathon. Fans have taken to social media outlets to post both their concern for the singer as well as their concern for the upcoming scheduled show. The topic is trending on the Internet right now. Consistently Inconsistent is scheduled to play in Boston this weekend. Not only is the show sold out, but Varro is from here. The band was born and raised, so to speak, in Boston. They went from playing local shows to becoming an enormous success practically overnight. We can only hope Xander gets his head on his shoulders and remembers where he came from before Saturday's show in Boston rolls around.

"Everyone is wondering, what has gotten into Xander Varro? Could it be that he's following the dark path band mate Julian Young took not too long ago? I certainly hope not. Varro has too much talent to waste."

With that, I turn and release the crystal glass from my grasp. As it leaves my fingertips, it hurdles across the apartment, stopped by the gray-painted wall at the opposite side of the room. Shards of glass rain down over the hardwood floor, leaving the remainder of the whiskey now dripping down the wall.

What the hell have I done?

This echoing apartment with only my thoughts to keep me company is the very last place I want to be.

Thinking back on what Cooper said, I know staying home is good advice. Naturally, I disregard it entirely, slamming the door behind me as I head to the nearest place that serves liquor.

* * * *

At some point, I made it to my bed last night, not that I have any idea how.

What I do know is this. I'm hesitant to roll over to see if there's someone sleeping next to me. An alcohol-scented sigh of relief escapes when I see I'm alone.

On one hand, I'm glad I don't have to call a cab for some nameless chick who I have no intention of seeing again and go through the well-rehearsed '*I'll call you later*' and '*Let's do this again soon*' charade. On the other hand, a body to occupy some space wouldn't have been so bad. The king-sized mattress feels empty and foreign. Many people who travel for work will list their bed among the things they miss the most when they are away from home, but I don't.

Not anymore.

My mattress isn't used to only having my weight on it. Before I left for the tour, my girlfriend, Mariah Delani, had spent most of her nights here.

Before we'd fallen apart.

Before we'd fought.

Before I'd found out about the baby.

Before I'd found out there never had been one.

Now I lie here, staring at the ceiling, trying various positions hoping to find one that's comfortable, without success.

The memory foam mattress doesn't even recognize me anymore.

Chapter Three

My desire to be anywhere except my apartment outweighs my desire to sleep. I pull on an old pair of jeans and a long-sleeved dark gray T-shirt. My eyes dart around the room looking for a hat to partially hide my face, a futile attempt at getting a coffee in peace, but I set my bar low on that hope.

Paparazzi are bound to be waiting to swoop in like vultures on roadkill—the way they always are when a celebrity is in the spotlight for something negative. A hat seems like a wasted effort, but I sport my sunglasses, which have become something of an eccentric addition to my appearance, day or night, indoors or out.

Much to my surprise, I make it to the small coffee shop, Chance's on the Corner, without drawing too much attention to myself. Thankfully, Jana, the one and only person I want to see right now, is working behind the counter.

Jana is a barista at Chance's who is a handful of years younger than me and has become one of my closest friends. She knows my order by heart, usually has it ready by the time I reach the counter and never makes a big deal of my presence here—or any other time or place. Jana is one of the few people I had in my seemingly decreasing circle of friends that still treats me like a normal person.

"Xander!" she exclaims, exposing a toothy grin. "I'm slammed here. I'll chat when I can."

Her coworker, a young lanky boy, starts a coffee grinder, which echoes through the café.

"Roy, who does this belong to?" Jana yells over the rattle of the beans in the grinder, pointing to a red cup on the counter. Roy, who I just realized has cordless headphones in, throws a thumb over his shoulder but never speaks.

"Don't worry, Roy. I'll do it!" she snaps. "It's not like we have a line here." Jana throws her arms out to the side, but Roy doesn't budge. "Employee of the freakin' month, I swear," Jana jokes, reaching for the cup.

"I can take it to her, if you want," I offer.

"You're a gem, Varro." She winks, handing me the cup.

The beverage is hot against the palm of my hand. I place it in a cardboard sleeve and grab a few napkins for good measure.

"Uhh...*ma'am?*" I announce myself as I walk up from behind her, but my voice catches and I clear my throat.

She doesn't respond.

More than likely, she has headphones in that I don't see or maybe has a Bluetooth earpiece in for a phone call, so I lean forward to see more clearly. That's not the case, though. She's not listening to anything at all. She is just staring out of the window, daydreaming as beautifully as I have ever seen someone do such a mundane thing. Her hair is this mess of tightly wound black curls pulled back by one of those thin elastic headbands.

As I stand here noticing everything about her, she notices me too.

She jumps inches out of her chair and claps her hand to her chest. When she's comfortably seated again, she takes three deep, steadying breaths behind a partly frazzled, somewhat embarrassed smile. Her gaze finally finds mine and I'm staring again — knowingly, but unable to stop.

Her eyes are two completely opposing colors — the left as blue as where the ocean meets the sky, the right a deep hazel — and I just can't look away.

"I'm... I'm so sorry," I mumble. "I didn't mean to sneak up on you. I think this might be yours?"

'I think this might be yours?' I mentally self-critique. *Moron.*

Sweat beads at the nape of my neck. I haven't felt this graceless since high school.

She nods with an uneasiness that parallels mine and reaches for the cup, her fingers brushing mine as I hand it to her.

"Uhh, well, enjoy, I guess," I say as she takes her first sip. *A+ timing, rock star.*

Frantically pulling the cup away from her lips and placing it on the table, she wipes her mouth with a napkin in one hand as she half-waves with the other.

With my hands shoved in my pockets, I turn to walk away before any further humiliation ensues. About ten tiles away from her table I pause, only for a moment, and look back at this girl who in five seconds shattered all the confident, borderline cocky image I had built for myself. She doesn't look my direction, doesn't recognize me, which is rare.

I'm not used to being ignored. It's both unnerving and relieving.

"*Smooth*," Jana jokes, her words accompanied by a slow, mocking applause, taunting me with each step as I walk the length of the counter. "What did she say?"

"Nothing. Literally nothing."

"I'd bet my tip jar it's the celebrity thing. *Oh my gosh, it's Xander Varro...*" Jana fans her face and waves her fingers, her voice changes to a high pitched, teasing tone.

She hands me a fresh, piping-hot latte. "How is the hand this morning?" she adds, returning to a serious voice. I cock my head to one side, my face stamped with a confused expression. It only takes me a second or two to register she's talking about the altercation at the show.

"Fine," I say, handing her a twenty-dollar bill for my drink. She punches in the keys on the register and hands me my change, all of which goes into her tip jar.

"Liar," she scoffs as I flex my stiff fingers. "What happened?" she adds.

"*That* is an incredibly long story and I don't want to take up your whole workday and some of tomorrow too," I exaggerate, taking a sip of the hot, foamy drink and savoring it as the warm liquid sinks into my taste buds. I travel to a lot of cities, in a lot of places, with a lot of coffee shops, but somehow Jana has mastered the perfect cup.

"I am off in ten minutes. You want to take a walk? Breathe in some fresh air and get out of your head for a little while?" she offers.

"Off in ten minutes? Already? What is it, nine a.m.?" I ask, looking at my watchless wrist.

"Xander, it's almost two p.m.," she says through sarcasm and a laugh.

"I'm a little...out of sorts today," I reply, "but a walk sounds nice. I'll see you outside in ten," I say. With my back against the door, I steal one last, long look at the girl seated on the other side of the coffee shop, but as I push the door open and the bells hanging from the door knob jangle wildly, she doesn't even flinch in my direction.

Pacing around the patio area outside of Chance's, I sip my coffee and breathe in the familiar scent of Boston—of home.

Small stones roll away as the toe of my boot kicks them up in my path, and I can hear the echo of the cars and trucks and city traffic in the distance. More than half of the band's songs were written exactly in this way—walking around unoccupied areas with unique background noises and suddenly someone is jotting down ideas on cafe napkins.

Blake penned one of our more popular songs, *Not Quite There Yet,* on the back of an old, greasy fast-food paper bag when we were driving through a crowded parking garage trying to find a vacant space. Sometimes one of us finds inspiration in the strangest place. How he got such an energetic song out of an echoing maze of cement with flickering lights and too-tight corners is still a mystery to me, but something inspired him and he ran with it.

I stare at the sky until the sun is too much to take and hope a song idea falls from it. The creative spark Blake found in the parking garage that night is avoiding me. The light bulb in the lyrical portion of my mind burned out a while back and I don't have a spare.

Jana opens the coffee shop door and waves to Roy as she exits. She holds a lightweight jacket over one arm and a coffee in her opposite hand. There is so often a coffee shop counter or a cross-country tour between us that I forget how petite she is. She's little, but far from fragile. She can hold her own—both physically and mentally. Her strawberry-blonde hair is braided over one shoulder and her piercing green eyes are always ready to sympathize with me when I need it—or judge me when I deserve it.

"Hold this," she says with a smile as she hands me the red disposable cup and slips on the olive-green jacket.

We walk the sidewalks through a residential part of the city along the water by the South Boston Yacht Club.

"How's school?" I ask, mostly to avoid talking about me.

"Difficult. *Really* difficult. Then again, if being a surgeon was easy, everyone would do it, right?"

"Is that what your end goal is?" I ask, taking a sip of coffee. "I knew you were in medical school. I just wasn't sure what direction you were going."

"I think so. I mean, I still have a lot of years to go, but we'll see, I guess. It's a lot of studying, a lot of work. On top of that, I have work at Chance's too. I have to go to school to be a doctor, but I have to work to pay for school to become a doctor—and work gets in the way of studying." She extends one hand and draws a large circle in the air. "It's a vicious cycle."

"I guess so," I say. I barely graduated high school, so I have nothing to offer as far as encouragement or study tips. My problem certainly wasn't a lack of intelligence but more so a lack of motivation. The courses my high school offered were hardly entertaining, and in my junior year, they cut the music program. It became increasingly difficult for me to care about anything after that. Now, in hindsight, I wish I had a degree in *something*. Education is forever, but unfortunately, as much as I would like to be, music is not. If my career came to a crashing halt, I was unsure what I would do next.

"So, are you going to tell me what's going on with you?" Jana asks, slipping her arm through mine so the crook of our elbows meet.

"Why does everyone keep asking me that? There's nothing to talk about," I snap back.

"Xander, you are one of the most laid back, mellow people I have ever known. You are not the kind of guy who goes around punching people," she says. She comes to a stop and leans against the cement wall overlooking the water. "I know you, Varro." She elbows me ever-so-lightly in the rib cage. "You don't have to lie to me."

Though I do my best to bury the things that bother me, I appreciate Jana's friendship now more than ever. I've recently concluded that I'm not an easy person to get along with. To be honest, I don't lose sleep over it. I have the band, and they're more than enough. Jana cares about me in a different way than the band does. It has been that way since the day we met. Four or five years ago I sat down at Chance's and I got an excellent cup of coffee and even better conversation. Jana has this way of making me feel like I'm not noticeable — but in a *good* way.

If she's listened to my music, she's never told me. She never mentions it or asks about it. She talks to me like she would talk to anybody — about life and current events and the latest *Game of Thrones* episode. Her wit and intelligence keep our conversations light and easygoing. At the end of the day, she's become like family — the sister I never had.

"Is it Mariah?" she presses.

Both my jaw and my fist clench simultaneously at the sound of her name.

"She's not draped off your arm right now like she's an annoying extra appendage like she usually is when you grace us with your presence. And I haven't seen her in a while. She was an everyday customer then stopped coming in right about the time Consistently Inconsistent left for the international schedule." She keeps talking, her voice decreasing in volume, as if she's tiptoeing into the question I know she is going to ask. "I'm really good at math. I can put two and two together. So, what happened?"

I pause for a good while and stare out over the water.

Talking to Jana is enjoyable, and even more than that, I trust her, which is a rarity for me. It wasn't that I didn't want to talk, but more so that I had no clue where to begin. I hadn't even told Cooper or the guys yet. Not even Blake, and we tell each other everything. Taking the final sip of coffee and a deep breath, I begin the story. It is a long one, but she asked for it.

Mariah and I had stayed together for most of the tour. We knew it would be challenging, but we thought we could make it work. Getting on the bus this time was harder than any other time I'd left. For one, this was our very first tour without Julian. That was a drastic change—something he might never forgive us for. The weight of that decision pressed heavily on my chest. Having to get on the bus without him was like trying to do a puzzle without having seen what the final picture looks like—stressful and damn near impossible.

Then, of course, there was Mariah.

She was headed to California for a project she was directing, I was leaving for the tour, and I just had this feeling life was going to get in the way of the normalcy and stability we had before music and movies had crept their way back in.

But we tried, and for a long time, things were perfect. We kept in touch, we talked a lot and we made it work until just about mid-May. A photo of her standing much too close to some guy in a hooded sweatshirt circulated and got back to me. I assumed he was the male lead of the movie she was directing, and I asked her about it. I tried not to be *that* guy. But I couldn't get the swirling negative thoughts out of my head. She kept feeding me the usual '*It's not what it looks like. It wasn't what you think*' trope that people lean on so often—but nine times out of ten it is *exactly* what it looks like.

What's even worse is I have been on that side of the camera. There have been pictures of me that catch a still frame of something that makes it appear I'm doing something I shouldn't be—or, even worse, something Photoshopped or edited then posted all over the Internet, just to cause problems.

So, I should have understood it better than anyone. I *should have* – but I *didn't*. I just didn't have a sliver of confidence that she was telling me the truth. My brain was screaming at me not to fall for it, to be smarter than that, but my heart yelled louder.

We stayed together, but it wasn't the same. That nagging feeling at the back of my mind kept telling me something was wrong.

A few weeks later when we arrived in Los Angeles for our show, she and I met out there.

I was going to end it.

Things weren't getting better and I was going to tell her we should see other people.

But I didn't.

I saw her, and I went back to her hotel room. Before I knew it, our clothes were on the floor and we were in the bed. I couldn't do it. I couldn't end it like that, not after sleeping with her. But when I left LA, that nagging, undying feeling of suspicion set back in and I knew it was over.

After a month of trying to convince myself to stay in the relationship, the voice in my brain muscled out the one in my heart and I knew I had to end it.

One night I had a few drinks — liquid courage — and I called her and told her we should back off, take some space and see other people.

"And she told you she was pregnant," Jana said, finishing my thought. I glance sideways at her and press my teeth into my bottom lip as I nod a slow, exaggerated yes.

"Oh, shit, really?" she says, quickly swallowing back her sip of coffee she had taken. "That was kind of a joke, but I guess it's not funny."

"Yeah. She said she was pregnant. Mathematically, it would have had to have been that night in LA. At first, I didn't believe her, because something deep inside me was screaming not to let her in again. But then there were positive tests and pictures, and I mean…what the hell was I supposed to do? I've done stupid things," I add. "I have been in the spotlight in a negative way more than once over the last number of years, but I'm not a *bad* guy. Even if I didn't love her at that point, I did once. I wasn't going to let her go through that alone. The thing is, I let my guard down. I fell for her shit and fell in love with the idea of being a dad. Me, a father. I would have had something more than the music. I would have had a reason to start making better decisions."

"Starting with an overnight hold in New York?" Jana says. "That doesn't seem like a step in the right direction."

"That was... That was a last hurrah, I guess" — I swallow hard — "before I knew the truth."

She tilts her head, her eyes full of sympathy, waiting for me to speak.

"Before the show the other night, she left me a voicemail...a voicemail, Jana." My voice is growing tired as I struggle to surpass the emotions and spit out the story. "She said the whole thing was a facade to keep me around."

Hearing myself say the words out loud are just as painful as hearing her saying them. Repeating the words keeps the wound open and fresh.

"Do you know how I planned to end that show? Because I certainly didn't plan to have knocking some guy's teeth out as the grand finale."

Jana can sense the toll this story is taking on my mental state as I say the words. She places one hand on my arm and squeezes tight.

"I was going to tell the band, then the audience, that my touring days were over — that the upcoming Boston show would be my last appearance as the lead singer of Consistently Inconsistent. I was going to give it all up for *my* child. The only thing I ever learned from my father was how not to be one. I sure as hell wasn't about to be in my kid's life part time. I was going to give up my first dream of being a musician to live out my new dream of being a good father. I could have changed, I think. She shredded those feelings and completely turned my world upside down all in a voicemail shorter than a verse in a song," I say, bringing the saga to a close.

"Oh, Xander, that's horrible. She's awful. I don't even know what to say," Jana rambles.

For the better part of the last twenty-four hours I have been pushing everyone away, but now that it's out there, I feel ten pounds lighter.

"I mean, I should be grateful, right? I should be happy I get to go forward with my music career and do what I love for just a bit longer, yeah?" I run my hands into my hair and let out a loud breath that I can hear in both ears and see against the crisp air.

"You are now and will always be a person before a musician, Xander. You make the music. It doesn't make you. You can be upset and have bad days. I mean, I wouldn't recommend punching people every time you have an off night, but you don't have to try to act so tough *all* the time. You get to be mad when lying bitches try to screw up your life," she says. I look at her and smile a bit.

"You sure you want to be a surgeon and not a therapist?" I joke.

"One hundred percent positive. And just so you know, I never liked her anyway," she adds, and we both laugh—a sound that echoes through the cool air over the ocean waves.

Jana leans her head into her hand and looks up at me as I push myself into a sitting position on the cement wall.

"She's going to text you, you know—Mariah—now that you're back in town."

I raise an eyebrow her direction.

"That's what my ex-girlfriend does anyway," Jana continues. "She texts me one of two times—either when she's single or when I'm not. She dates someone else, she tries to move on and the very second things go south she contacts me. Or she won't text me for a while, and she finds out I'm seeing somebody and instantly she misses me, *needs* me and there's no one else, *blah blah blah*. It's just a game, Xander. So, when she texts you, and she *will*, do yourself a favor and don't play into it."

"I will keep that in mind, but I really don't think she's going to message me," I say, thinking back to the voicemail. Her words were so final, ending something I should have ended months ago.

The thing of it all is that I knew what kind of woman Mariah was. From the beginning she was a person who altered and twisted every story so she was either the hero or victim but never, ever the villain.

Jana sighs dramatically. "I bet you your Sunday morning coffee that she contacts you by the end of your show Saturday night."

"You are on," I say, and we shake hands firmly.

She's quiet for a moment, looking out over the water, then, speaking into the open air in front of her, she says, "Sometimes you have to let the past go and know that not all forfeits are losses."

"So, you *do* listen to my music," I say, hearing the words she says and knowing exactly where she was going with it before she finished the lyric.

"Sometimes, when it comes on the radio or whatever," she says casually. "Actually, speaking of your music, I have a favor to ask you and it goes against every single rule of this friendship," she says as she spins her empty cup on the cement wall. The cup makes a hollow, echoing sound.

"We have rules?" I say, leaning over and placing a finger on the cover of the cup, stopping it from spinning like a top.

"Total disclaimer, you can one hundred percent say no."

A goofy, knowing grin grows across my face. "You want concert tickets," I say, and her cheeks grow as red as the cup she's fiddling with.

"I usually wouldn't ask, but this girl I have been seeing is a massive fan, she really wants to go and I didn't get tickets in time." Jana rambles again, and even though I had already planned to offer her tickets, I let her keep talking because I find it amusing. "You're enjoying this, aren't you?" she says.

"Every single second."

"It would just score me mega cool points if I could get her to the show." She spins the cup one more time, but I grab it mid-spin and toss it free-throw style toward the trash can.

I miss.

"Can you be there by one?" I ask.

"Doors don't even open until six," she states.

"Yes, but if you want cool points, you can bring her in for sound check. Then you can hang out with us or go walk around the city or whatever and come back for showtime."

"Don't screw with me, Xander. Are you serious?" she asks, and I nod. She's given me more free and discounted coffees than I could ever pay back. A little pre-show tour is the least I could do.

"Okay, one more favor," she says, holding one finger up. "Could you actually show up and play a whole show? Because this whole thing will fall apart if you walk out mid-song."

"Oh, I don't know. That's a lot to ask," I say, rolling my eyes and pushing myself down off the wall. She leans into me, and I wrap one arm around her small frame as we walk back toward the shop.

Chapter Four

The hot, steaming water of the shower soaks my hair and runs down my body. My fingers find nothing but tile as I reach one hand to the vacant shelf of the walk-in shower. The procrastinator in me chose not to unpack, which means my toiletries are still in a bag on my floor. I turn the water off and open the curtain, planning to wrap a towel around myself and get my necessities from the bag I traveled with, but quickly realize I never grabbed a towel either. *Well, shit.*

Coming home and settling in is always a challenge. Living in close-quarter hotel rooms where everything was within arm's reach or living out of a bag is such a norm now that it throws me off to be in a stable environment. A trail of wet footprints follows me the length of the apartment, but I reach my bags and dig through them, tossing the contents aside until I find the toiletries leftover from the trip. *Go figure... The body wash is almost empty.* I had made a mental note to get myself some more, but that method of reminders has proven to be unreliable.

I return to the shower and turn the knob once more, preparing for a lengthy, hot shower, but the once-hot water is gone. I always feel as if the water is washing away all the negative energy, and often times, showers are where I have my best thoughts — lyrics, intros, merchandise and promotional ideas, set lists for upcoming shows. Anything, really. The heat and steam seem to clear my mind and stir my imagination.

The water cools, and I turn the knob once more to cut it off, then use the towel to dry. Wearing nothing but a full sleeve of tattoos, I walk to the fridge and open it, though I'm not sure what I was expecting. I have been gone for almost seven months. The only things left in this fridge are an open box of baking soda and half a bottle of barbecue sauce. There is so much space around me that I struggle with what to do with it. The idea of selling the place crosses my mind often. Then again, this space was perfect when there were two of us here.

When I bought the apartment, Julian was my roommate. He and I always were a good pair. We weren't around often enough to warrant us having separate spaces and the place was plenty large enough to accommodate those times we were both here. But eventually, I started dating Mariah, and when she moved in, he moved out. I never understood that. They always got along great. But he gave me some pre-rehearsed bullshit monologue about giving us our space, then packed his things and left.

Now, the apartment felt as empty as the refrigerator. The space around me is the vacant shelves and I am the half-used bottle of barbecue sauce. The space and openness are intimidating. It gives me more room to think, wonder and feel the hollowness — and difference.

An extended homestretch is on the itinerary, so I suppose it is time to make the house a home again. My shopping list essentially starts and ends with toiletries, but the fridge is looking a little pathetic, so a trip to the store is in my immediate future — no matter how much I would rather avoid it. I jot a few things down on an envelope from a seven-month pile of mail I hadn't even sorted through yet — and let's be honest, I never will. Using an app on my phone, I book a transportation service and ask the driver to take me to a local grocery store.

Returning home and to the real world? Well, it is *strange*. After a tour, I feel more out of place in my own home than I ever do on the road. Most people don't have to think about cooking or grocery shopping or errands. These seemingly uninteresting, mindless tasks aren't something most people overthink, but I do. Coming back into a regular life is like awakening from being frozen in time or suffering from amnesia then remembering everything from your past life all at once.

We spend so much of our time on a bus, eating deli sandwiches or food that was prepped for us backstage at venues, that cooking or preparing foods is alien to me. At the hotels, the staff kept our rooms cleaned, stocked and would deliver food on command. It was bizarre to have to fit these things back into my schedule — to relearn them, so to speak.

I tip the driver and enter the grocery store. I thought going to the store this late in the evening might mean less people to run into, but I didn't even make it to the produce section, which is visible from the door, before the first person took out their cell phone and snapped a photo of me.

This just in. Xander Varro goes grocery shopping.

I laugh at myself because a more realistic headline would read, *Xander Varro goes grocery shopping. Forgets major ingredients. Gets takeout, even though he just bought food.*

The soles of my boots rub the white tiles as I walk, creating squeaks and screeches that echo through the aisles as I walk up and down, scanning the shelves and throwing things I don't need into the cart to make myself feel like I fit in there.

The cold air of the frozen food section bites at my skin and leaves raised bumps on my arms as I realize I never checked my list. I reach in the pockets of my jeans and pat my thighs as if that's going to make the list appear, but my pockets come up empty. Scanning the cart, I do a mental checklist and convince myself I have everything. Checkout is a breeze, and I dial for a ride once again.

The driver is a young kid — no more than twenty or twenty-one years old — who exits the car and opens the passenger door for me.

"Can I help you with those?" he asks, pointing to the grocery bags.

"Uhh, I guess so," I reply, but he's eagerly taking the bags before I can spit out the words. I climb into the passenger seat and he returns to the driver's side.

He stares at me long enough to make it uncomfortable. I am about to tell him to forget it, that I'll find my way home, and he finally remembers how to string words together.

"I am...a really huge fan," he says. "See?" He lifts his pant leg to his knee, revealing a large tattoo of a deep-purple-colored tiger that spans the length of his lower leg and wraps around the shin and calf. The art is from the album cover of Consistently Inconsistent's first album. It isn't the first time I've seen the album cover permanently inked to someone's skin. Julian has the exact same artwork tattooed in the exact same spot. This kid was probably disappointed with our decision to cut Julian out, but if he is, he doesn't show it or say a word.

He finally pulls himself together long enough to do his job, drives away from the curb and turns up the radio to something that was thankfully not one of my songs, and I realize I forgot the one thing I went to the store for in the first place. *Fucking body wash.*

We drive up to the main door of my apartment complex, he pulls out his cell phone and holds it out with the camera open.

"Do you mind?" he asks, pointing to the screen. I almost say no, no pictures. I'm just not in the mood. But my image right now is already tainted since the news is hell-bent on painting me as some kind of deviant, so I think twice about this and let him have his selfie.

Whatever jingles his bells.

"Thanks for the ride," I say, taking my bags in both hands and kicking the car door closed behind me. The driver waves as he peels out of the apartment driveway.

My phone pings as I enter my apartment. I drop the bags on the counter and look at the screen. I have one new message from Cooper. As usual, he is short and to the point.

Fans want apology. You will give them one tonight.

I text back a short message.

What? Like a press conference or something?

Three floating gray dots appear on the screen as he types out his reply.

No. Live on social media. All the cool kids are doing it. Blake, Dominic, Theo and I will be at your place at nine. Start practicing your most sincere mea culpa.

I type back a quick 'okay' and Internet search the phrase '*mea culpa*' because I have no idea what the hell I just agreed to.

I tap my foot against the hardwood floor as I drum my hands against the countertop, trying to decide what to do for the next hour. Having an awkward amount of time where it seemed like we were just wasting minutes but didn't have enough time to go and do anything was something I had grown used to. My career as a whole was a waiting game. We were busy in a way that involved doing a whole bunch of nothing — waiting on buses, waiting on interviewers, waiting on each other, waiting on venues to get us in and set up for sound checks, waiting until the clock hit nine p.m. and we got to play. Then, more waiting. Waiting on Cooper for the post-show meeting. Waiting on fans for meet and greets and photo opportunities. Waiting to get back on the bus. I was used to it, the waiting.

It takes no time at all to put the few groceries I bought away and pour my travel bags out onto the laundry room floor. After doing a few necessary tasks to help myself settle in, I open the doors to the balcony and take a seat outside. A cool breeze blows as I jot a few lyric ideas for a song I have been mentally working on. Since I have some unscheduled time, now is just as good a time as any to start making these thoughts into words, and words into sentences and sentences into songs that eventually may become an album.

I bring an older acoustic guitar outside with me and adjust the tuning pegs at the headstock of the guitar until the strings produce a perfect, in-tune sound as I pick them.

It is hard to believe how far we've come, that enough seconds have ticked by to combine eleven total years of recording and touring and selling records. I look back on a time when the music was the only thing that mattered.

No one knew our names or stories — or lack there-of. There was no drama or demand. Hell, the knock-off brand canvas sneakers on my feet were a size and a half too small and had mismatched laces. The guitar used to create the sounds that made us famous was a beat-up thrift store gem that had been on this earth longer than I had, but thankfully, it sounded a hell of a lot better than it looked.

As a band, we owned almost nothing. We were stuck at the bottom of a rungless ladder. We weren't going to make it to the top if we weren't pulled up by someone who was already there — and we were.

I still love making music, but I miss the simplicity of the process.

Back then, a breath could be taken without a photograph or story following quickly thereafter. Nobody cared what was going on in our lives. My name didn't appear in the headlines — truth or fake news.

Time flies by as I lose myself in playing and reminiscing. There is a light knock at the door as an announcement of Blake's arrival, but he never gives me the chance to open it. He usually just waltzes right in and makes himself at home. Tonight was no exception.

He turns the knob and uses his knee to push the door open. His hands are occupied holding a thirty-pack of beer cans in one hand and a large, handled bottle of whiskey in the other.

"I figured your refrigerator was probably even less stocked than mine, so I stopped at the store on the way. The essentials, you know." He smirks and places the whiskey on the counter and the beers in the fridge.

Before long, Cooper knocks at the door. Dominic and Theo are strolling down the hall not too far behind, so I hold the door open and wait for them.

They both offer strong handshakes and pat me on the back like they haven't seen me in months, even though we saw each other yesterday—and seven months' worth of yesterdays before that.

Cooper places his laptop down on the counter. In typical Cooper fashion, he cuts right to the point.

"Okay." He claps his hands like a soccer coach to get our attention. "This is how this works. We screwed a lot of people out of a show they paid good money for. So, Xander, first you are going to set up this laptop in front of you, press the 'live' button on the band's Facebook page, and as convincingly as possible, apologize to the New York fans and promise them a rescheduled show."

"When is that happening?" I ask over the annoyed mumbles of my band mates.

"I don't know yet, but it *is* happening. End of conversation. And secondly, you're going to apologize directly to the guy you punched."

I scoff and raise an eyebrow his direction. "An apology would indicate I think I did something wrong."

"Would it kill you to admit that?"

"I don't know, Cooper, but is it a chance we're willing to take?"

"You are lucky the guy didn't press charges. You could be paying him instead of giving him a free apology," Cooper adds.

"How much is he asking for? Does he take checks?" I ask, but Cooper's eyes narrow and his shoulders tense.

"Do I look like I'm kidding?" Cooper responds.

He's *not* kidding.

"All right, let's get this over with." I don't put any effort into masking my irritation.

"Xander, listen. You are a rock star. You put on a show every single night. You captivate crowds. Give us a little bit of that guy. Show them the Xander they know and love is still in there, will ya?"

"You got it, chief," I say, doing my best to mean it. His eyes make it clear this is important to him, and I've disappointed Cooper more than enough this week.

Blake sits on my right on the couch. Dominic and Theo stand behind us. Blake sets up the laptop on the table in front of us and we get into a position that allows all four of us to be in the picture. Still, more than seven months later, it feels wrong to see only four of us on screen after being a five-person band for more than a decade. Cooper stands leaning against the wall directly across from us so I can see him above the laptop screen. Blake presses the record button. The screen counts down in front of us. Five, four, three, two, one...

"What's up, everybody? I'm Xander Varro here with Blake Mathews, Dominic Trudell and Theo Walker. Together we make up the band Consistently Inconsistent."

Cooper gives me a thumbs-up and an encouraging nod. The tally on the bottom right hand of the screen continues to increase. The number of viewers is in the thousands already and quickly growing. Comments appear on the screen as people type in their questions, say a general hello or, of course, post something negative, just to try to get under our skin.

"This message is for our New York fans. I know you all came out to see a show. I failed to make that happen, but I will not allow that a second time. We owe you, and we will be in touch to let you know when the rescheduled show will be. We promise it will be bigger and better than ever before, because you guys deserve it, you rock, and we love you guys for standing by us."

I reach forward to click out of the live video, but Cooper glares at me. I take a deep breath and look back into the camera once more.

"Additionally," I add without enthusiasm, "there is a fan out there who I owe an apology to. He knows who he is. Listen, man. I shouldn't have reacted the way I did. I hope this is something you can look past and it doesn't ruin the music for you. I'm sorry things played out that way. It was uncool of me to do what I did."

"But it was equally uncool of you to spit at Xander...or anyone, really. *So* uncool," Blake chimes in. Cooper is drawing his fingers across his throat, indicating we should cut.

"All right, guys, that's it for now. We are Consistently Inconsistent, and we will be back for you guys soon!" I add, struggling to keep my grin and impending laugh to a minimum.

Cooper's face is redder than I've ever seen it. As Blake clicks out of the video, we all laugh and, eventually, Cooper joins in too.

"All right, all right," Cooper starts. "I'm going to get out of here. You guys have a fun night—but not too much fun. We have a show to play tomorrow. This is your home, boys. It'd better be the best damn show you have in you."

"Stick around, Coop. Have a drink," Theo insists. But Cooper raises his hand in protest.

"No, no. I'm too old to try to keep up with this lot. I will see you all tomorrow. Preferably on *time*." He looks directly at me as he emphasizes the words.

We have a few drinks and play a riveting game of 'best and worst headlines'. We have done this for so many years that it's become a tradition for us. Anytime the band or one of its members makes their way into the news, we scope out the stories, cut or print the best ones and pin them to an oversized corkboard at the back wall of the tour bus. The catch is that the more ridiculous or untrue the headline, the more likely it is to end up on the tour bus 'wall of shame'.

Blake clicks through the trending news articles under the *Music and Entertainment* tab, reading each headline out loud.

"*Xander Varro leaves stage mid show. Fans left without answers,*" he says.

Lame. They can do better than that.

"*Front man of Consistently Inconsistent proves to be only inconsistent.*"

Very punny.

"This one!" Blake says over a sip of whiskey, laughing so hard he can hardly swallow the drink. "This is going on the wall." Theo and Dominic laugh in unison. I lean forward and take a glance at the headline.

"*Varro institutionalized after mid-show breakdown. Will not appear for Boston performance,*" Blake reads, laughing between each word.

"Print it," I say through a sip of liquor.

The article is from a garbage site that nobody uses as a real resource. The guys print the article and read the story that stretches and alters the situation into a morbidly unrealistic tale, but it is prime 'wall of shame' material. I will look at this one on our next tour and laugh, even if I am not laughing yet.

"Gentlemen," I say as I look at the clock, "get the hell out. I would say *'I'll see you tomorrow'*, but I believe the correct verbiage is *'I'll see you in a few hours.'*"

"Holy *shit*," Blake adds, looking at the clock. "When did that happen?"

"Three a.m. comes fast when you're having fun," I reply.

I pat Theo on the shoulder and shake Dominic's hand firmly on their way out of the door.

Blake stops at the door frame and turns to me before leaving.

"You going to try to get some sleep?" he asks.

I nod a yes and look at him with a confused expression.

"These are our people, man. If there's one place we can't let a crowd down, it's here. I just wanted to make sure you are going to try to get some rest and not attempt to set a whiskey-drinking record once we leave," he says, pointing to the open bottle on the counter.

"I've got everything under control. I'll see you tomorrow," I promise him.

He heads down the hallway and punches a button on the elevator.

Chapter Five

The next morning, Jana has a coffee prepared for me before I reach the counter.

"You are coming to sound check, yeah?" I ask, taking a sip of borderline undrinkably hot coffee.

"Yes, but I haven't told her where we're going yet. She's going to be shocked. I can't wait," Jana says, leaning into the counter.

"Awesome, I'm looking forward to having you there. I visit you at work enough. It's about time you come see what I do."

"Can't possibly be more spectacular than this." She waves her arms around the coffee shop.

"We will see, I guess," I say with a half-smile. "I'm going to head that way. I'll see you in an hour or so?"

"I wouldn't miss it," she promises.

"Great. I'll meet you both at the side doors and let you in," I say as I push open the door. "And get to work, slacker," I add. She rolls her eyes, and I let the door fall closed behind me.

* * * *

At the edge of the stage, I sit and take in the sights, smells and views of the venue as I always do. I guess one would call it a nervous habit, though I don't get quite as anxious as I used to. Back in the day, my body convulsed in a shaking I couldn't control and tried to hide under on-stage movements. I couldn't eat for hours before a show.

Not anymore. Now performing is second nature. Still, this is part of my usual routine but here, on this stage, in this city, the view from the stage brings me back to the first time we'd stood on it.

A high school friend was working for this particular venue at the time and convinced the headliner to give us a chance. It was a hot, humid night and I was playing on a tattered six string that my over-worked and underpaid mother had picked up at a second-hand store.

We started that night as a band made up of friends who had become family and a dream that was getting too heavy to hold by ourselves. Fast forward through a few well-performed songs laced with intelligent lyrics and mastered instrumentals and you would find us — a group of eighteen-year-old nobodies — given an invite to open for a well-known, extremely successful rock band.

I remember feeling like the ground was shaking around us, separating us from the world we had grown used to. That universe shift took us from the band we used to be and catapulted us into the band we would become.

That moment was tangible. I could feel my life turning around drastically — for the better — all in that very instant.

I didn't expect it. I didn't see it coming. That was the night everything had changed.

I look over my shoulder at Blake as he walked to center stage and stood completely still. He's staring at me, wide-eyed, like something was wrong or out of place. He raises his hands, extending his arms to his side, and bellows through the empty space.

"Ladies and gentleman… Take a picture. Document this moment. Memorize what this looks like so you can say you were here when history was made and Xander Varro showed up to a sound check on *time!*"

His voice echoes, the remnants of his underlying South African accent in full swing as it travels the length of the auditorium as I shake my head and sip my coffee.

"On time and sober?" he says, taking a seat next to me. "Should I be impressed or worried? Unless, of course, there is whiskey in there."

"Coffee only. Scout's honor," I say.

"Scout's honor doesn't really hold much weight coming from somebody who got kicked out of Boy Scouts…*twice*." We both laugh as he claps a hand on my shoulder, pushes himself up and leaves me at the front of an empty venue — just the way I like it to sit and think before a big show.

My thoughts are my only company for a bit, going over set lists and song lyrics in my head. Someone in the distance yells out, "Ten minutes until sound check," and I nod in response, even though I'm sure they can't see me.

"Mr. Varro?" I hear a much closer voice ask. I turn to see a staff member of the venue with a headset on and a clipboard in his hand. He wears black from head to toe and has slicked back salt-and-pepper hair.

"It's just Xander," I correct him. "Mr. Varro is my jackass of a father."

"Oh. Okay then, Xander," he says, "There're two young ladies here. They say they're supposed to be on the list for the day, but I don't see their name. Are you expecting Miss Jana Hampton and a guest?"

"Shit," I mumble as I push myself off the stage. My pre-show ritual had consumed all my thoughts. I had completely forgotten I told Jana I would meet her outside.

"Yeah, they are good. I'll go get them," I say, semi-jogging to the side doors of the venue.

The door is cracked open with a stopper, and I peer around it but don't see anyone. I push the door open farther to look to the right and Jana is standing there with a girl whose short black hair boasts an array of assorted colors peeking out from the bottom. They are facing away from me, and Jana has her cell phone out. She's probably trying to reach me, but my phone is backstage.

"Doors don't open until six, you know," I tease as I hold the door open. Jana turns and smiles at me, her date's eyes and mouth go wide. As they near me she grabs Jana's wrists and says, "That's *Xander Varro*,"

"I know," Jana laughs. "We're friends on the days that I claim him."

"Hey now, be nice," I say. "I can just leave you out here if you'd prefer." Jana purses her lips and offers me a sarcastic glare. "Do you want to come to sound check or not? It's practically a private show..." I say, still vocally jesting with Jana.

"Hell yes!" Her date answers with an enthusiastic nod.

I hug Jana, and when she lets go, she introduces me to her date.

"Xander, this is Nellie. Nellie, this is Xander."

"Nellie. That's a great name," I say, taking her shaking, outstretched hand in mine.

"It's actually Danielle, but everyone calls me Nellie." Her cheeks blush as she speaks.

"Totally understood. My real name is Alexander," I say with a wink.

"Alexander Edwin Varro," Blake chimes in as he, Theo and Dominic step outside and join us on the sidewalk.

"Edwin?" Jana says, covering her mouth to stifle a laugh.

"Blake Mathews," Nellie says as he reaches his hand out to introduce himself to her, though I don't think she meant to say it out loud.

"Blake *Cornelius* Mathews," I say, and everyone starts laughing. Cornelius is not Blake's middle name, but before he can protest, Cooper leans his head out the door and yells for us to get our asses on stage and pick up an instrument. I walk inside and direct Jana and Nellie to the area of the venue where they can pick a seat or stand at the front of the stage.

We hit the stage and take our designated places. Dominic strikes the drum set a few times, but he's unhappy with the setup for reasons I can't hear over everyone else's instrument and mic checks. As the crew and Dom iron out the issues at the back of the stage, Blake and Theo strum a few notes on each of the separate guitars they use to ensure they are properly tuned, tight and ready to go. Theo, a dual instrument musician, follows his check of his guitar with a few strokes on the keyboard.

I take my place at the front of the stage and look at the setlist taped to the floor. My eyes scan it once…twice…a third time — and *Delayed Reactions* isn't on it. They've removed it since the New York show, and they didn't consult me on the decision. My mind is reeling, bringing me right back to the stage in New York — the stage where I left thousands of fans and my bandmates wondering what the hell had happened.

"Xander," Cooper yells from the center of the empty floor of the venue, "are you just going to stand there and look pretty or *what*? *Do* something!"

Blake leads me in for one of our newer songs. We hardly rehearse our old stuff anymore. We have played the same chords, riffs and harmonics for so long and gone over them so many times that our fingers and vocal cords can produce the sounds and notes without taking any signal from our brain at all. We still play them — our older, more popular stuff is a huge hit at every concert, so they stay on the set list — but we warm up with the newer songs we haven't grown tired of yet.

I stand in front of the microphone and smile, looking into the very small, very select crowd.

"Nellie," I say into the microphone. She sits up and leans forward, looking around with her hand pointed to her chest, double checking that I meant her. "What song do you want to hear? Preferably something off the newest album, but I'm not picky," I say.

"Oh…umm. I'm a really big fan of *Without A Doubt*," she replies.

"Good choice. This one's for you, Nellie," I say through a smile. Jana mouths me a thank you and I pick the guitar strings, playing the intro to the song Nellie chose.

About halfway through the first verse of the song we play, I cut myself off, but the band continues.

"Pick up the pace a little bit, will you?" I yell to Blake, who is off by about a beat and a half. He corrects the speed and I jump back into the lyrics to finish off the song.

For the most part, sound check consists of us being fitted for microphones and wires, making sure we are happy with the setup and sound and spending time screwing around and ridiculing each other before the crowd gets there and we must be serious for ninety straight minutes. We play our songs, get any issues squared away and return our instruments to their holders.

At the end of the pre-show routine, I invite Jana and Nellie up on stage. Nellie and Blake take selfies at the back of the stage, and Nellie poses with Blake's guitar as he snaps photographs of her. Her face is permanently stamped with a large grin.

"This was amazing, Xander, thank you," Jana says, standing beside me at the side of the stage. "She's having the best day."

"I'm glad I could help. She seems great."

"And how about you? All things quiet on the ex-girlfriend front?" Jana bumps her shoulder into my arm.

"So far, so good. I look forward to my free coffee I'll get tomorrow when I win our bet," I say through a half-smile.

"Where's your head at? Or your heart, I guess," Jana asks me.

I know how this sounds, but I don't miss Mariah. I wasn't upset that our relationship was over. I have been over her for a long time. I was angry at how I let her play me like a friggin' fiddle and how she had gotten my hopes up over something that had never been a reality. I was madder at myself for falling for her shit than I was at her.

"I'll make it through the whole show tonight, if that is what you're asking," I say, looking down at her with a smile.

"Thatta boy," she responds.

We stand in the wings of the stage watching and laughing while Nellie lives out her rock-star dreams at the front of the stage, dancing around and strumming Blake's guitar like no one is watching.

* * * *

The crowd fills in every square inch of The Rock Room, forcing the temperature to increase by at least ten degrees as soon as the doors open. Bodies fill the area in front of the stage, along the staircases and all around the balcony overhead. While the first opener gets set to take the stage, I analyze the crowd as they fill in the empty spaces around the venue.

Since we are playing for our hometown, we invited additional bands as opening acts for the night. We got our first big break when a friend of mine put in a good word for us with a well-known band eleven years ago. They invited us to play before them on this very same stage, so we like to do the same for the bands we believe have what it takes to make it in this industry.

In the wing off the stage, I lean against the wall and listen to the opening act play. The crowd is responsive—singing, dancing and clapping along. My eyes wander across the stage, down into the crowd and across the venue. I'm scanning the area, taking in all the sights and sounds and my eyes stop suddenly, my gaze falling on the bar at the far side of the venue. There is a female staff member behind the bar, smiling widely and moving her hands enthusiastically as she takes the order of someone at the bar.

Her deep brown, almost black curls fall loose from the knot at the top of her head and frame her face. She's beautiful and she's —

She's the girl from the coffee shop, and for the second time in as many days, she's left me completely beside myself.

As the stage crew tears down the set and changes it over to prepare for the next band, I make my way over to the main bar. As a general rule, I try not to make a habit of going to the bar myself at these shows, mostly because I usually get asked to take fifty-some-odd pictures and sign a bunch of napkin autographs that will end up lost or crumbled before I even get my drink.

Besides, we have people who do that for us.

But something in me urged me to go. Somehow, I thought facing the crowd would be worth the trouble to try to talk to her a second time — hopefully, with more success.

As expected, a few people stop me in my tracks and ask questions about the New York show, request pictures, scream excited, screeching yells in my ear — one guy even tries to fight me — but with a bit of extra effort, I make it to the corner of the bar where a security staff member steps in front of me, separating me from the crowd.

"Kelly!" I yell to the bartender closest to me. She rolls her eyes and saunters toward me.

"I have a line here. What? Do you think you get special treatment or something? What makes you so deserving?" Kelly has had a firecracker attitude since high school, where I'd first met her. She's a social butterfly, always flirting, dancing or making jokes. "I kid, I kid," she says. "Come here. I miss this face!" She places both of her hands on my neck and pulls me in closely, planting a friendly kiss on my cheek. "What are you drinking?" she adds.

"Oh, I'm not, actually," I yell over the music as the next band starts playing. Her eyes and mouth widen in surprise.

"I'm sorry," she yells. "It is really loud in here. I didn't hear you correctly. It sounded like you said you're *not* drinking." Her surprised expression doesn't change.

"I know, I know," I say. "Actually, I wanted to know what you could tell me about the new girl." I lift my finger lightly and discreetly point to the other side of the bar.

"I can tell you she's not interested," Kelly says, as if she expected my question.

"Did she say something?" I ask, too quickly, my words running together. Her comment had taken me by surprise.

"She said you look like you need to find sleep and Jesus." She's serious at first, convincing, but then her lips curl to a smile and she lets out a quick laugh. I nod, taking the hit. I can't say it's an inaccurate assessment.

"She didn't say anything at all," Kelly says through a mischievous, smile that suggests she knows something I don't. "She's my cousin," she adds. "More like a sister, though. She grew up with me and my parents."

"And I've never met her before? She's—"

"You choose your words very carefully now," she says, half joking, half threatening. "Remember… I have pictures of you when you were *Alexander* Varro — braces and all, marching with the band, way before you were *hot-shot-Xander-Varro-mega-star*. I'm not afraid to leak them."

"Understood," I respond through a grin. "I was just going to say she's beautiful."

Kelly's hard-pressed lips turn upward at the edges, revealing a hint of a smile. The music makes the conversation a challenge, but I want to know more about her cousin.

"Seriously though, how do I not know her?" I ask. "You and I went to school together for years."

"Right, but we weren't *friends* in high school," Kelly says, reminding me of a time when Kelly was class president, prom queen and had a large following of friends, and I was *just* Alexander.

'*Not friends in high school*' had been a gentle way for Kelly to describe it I'd asked her to that prom she had been crowned at. She'd said no — once she'd stopped laughing.

"Besides, she always went to different schools than us," Kelly continued.

As Kelly and I talk, her cousin catches me staring. Suddenly I wished I'd taken that drink Kelly had offered. "I, uhh… I tried to talk to her at the cafe by my apartment, but she didn't say anything to me," I say, tripping over the words. Kelly grins, but it's a different, unreadable expression. "Kelly, be honest," I say. "Is it the celebrity thing? She literally didn't say a word."

"No, Xander. It's not that," she says, looking over her shoulder at her cousin as she rings in an order on a register. "She's just not interested, okay?" She uses the bottle opener to pull back a few caps and places the drinks on the bar top for customers standing near us.

I stare over Kelly's shoulder at her cousin. She smiles and nods at a customer that I can't help but wish was me.

"She doesn't even know me," I argue, fractionally offended.

Kelly's eyes widen, closing the gap between her brow and hairline.

"You're Xander Varro," she says, emphasizing my name the same way the media does. "Have you opened a webpage lately? Turned on a TV? *Everybody* knows you."

"It doesn't matter how many good things I do. I'll never get credit for it in the media. But every wrong turn I take gets magnified exponentially and that's the reputation that precedes me? That's what people remember. Doesn't really seem fair." I'm frustrated, and I don't try to hide it as I speak to her across the bar. "Besides, it's not a marriage proposal. I just want to meet her."

"You're just not her type, okay?" she says, turning away from me to get back to work.

"In what way?" I ask, my final attempt before surrendering.

She turns back to me, placing her hands on the counter and leaning toward me.

"She doesn't date *hearing* guys," Kelly says, and for a moment, I don't understand. "She's Deaf," she adds.

All words escape me. I'm taken by surprise and yet, the revelation fits like the missing piece to an unfinished puzzle. I watch over Kelly's shoulder for a moment as the girl from the coffee shop pulls an aluminum beer bottle from the chest in front of her, opens the top and throws away the cap before handing it to the customer across from her. She smiles widely, revealing a set of perfectly white teeth behind red-painted lips.

She and Kelly have almost nothing in common physically. Kelly is tall, with brilliantly blonde hair and porcelain skin. Her cousin is considerably shorter and boasts dark features — her hair color a midnight black, her skin a shade of natural bronze.

"Are you screwing with me, Kel?" I ask, for as much as the answer makes perfect sense, I question if Kelly is trying to give me a reason to lose interest. If that's the case, she has already failed. "If you don't want me to ask her out, just say so."

"I don't want you to ask her out," she laughs, "but no, I'm not screwing with you."

I shoot her a semi-kidding glare and steal glances at the other side of the bar as frequently as I can.

"How does she take orders if she can't hear?" I wonder out loud, tasting the ignorance of the question as it leaves my tongue.

"Fair question. Watch." Kelly leans her back against the bar and puts her elbows up beside her.

The band on stage is loud and the crowd is screaming and cheering, adding to the already blaring sounds that reverberate through the venue.

A guy in a black backward baseball cap approaches the bar. She flashes her million-dollar smile at him and lifts her chin in his direction. He holds up an aluminum beer bottle and points to the brand on the label. She nods and reaches into the beer chest. Then she removes the cap, takes his card, swipes it and hands it back to him along with the bottle. He takes his card and she waves as he turns and disappears into the crowd. She moves on to repeat the process with the next customer.

"It's a concert venue, Alexander. Most of us can't hear shit anyway!" Kelly says, yelling over the music again. "That, and she reads lips. Well, in fact. Besides, she's a badass. She does whatever she wants. If she's interested in it, she makes it happen."

There's a lull in the music for a moment and I take advantage of the semi-reasonable volume.

"What's her name?" I finally ask.

"Xander," she says, but I intercept the comment,

"Really, huh. That's *my* name," I joke, and she throws a white towel in my direction.

"Her name is Natalie, if you must know. But seriously, Xander. It's just not going to work. Have a good show, okay?" She turns away and continues helping the customers at the bar.

Chapter Six

The lights go dark and the stage guys break down the current set, making the change to ours, exactly how we like everything. There is blue tape applied at various locations across the stage, and I watch as the crew sets Dominic's drums, so the legs of the drum matched perfectly with their mark. Theo's keyboard is placed carefully at the stage front with his guitar nearby. Blake's guitar and my own are handled with care and set on their holders at the opposite side from where I stand.

From the small stage exit I am standing in, I have a perfect view of the bar and its staff. I had grown used to people watching my every move. I have seen pictures of myself mid bite of food at a restaurant or candids of me coming out of various stores. It doesn't bother me like it used to, but I can't help wondering if it would bother her if she knew I was watching her so intently.

I don't know much about her, but I know I want to. She has all my attention, even if she doesn't want it.

"You ready?" Blake asks, appearing at my side. I nod but don't pull my gaze away from the bar — and now he is staring too.

"Who are we looking at?" he asks.

"The new bartender. Kelly's cousin," I say over the suddenly loud music used to get the crowd pumped up for our entrance.

"Izzit?" he asks, his accent ringing through a half-smile.

"Okay, new plan. You ask her out for drinks after the show, and tell her to bring Kelly along," he suggests.

"For?" I ask.

"For me. Work with me here, man," Blake says, "Kelly is a ten. She always has been."

"I'll think about it. Let's go. We have a show to play. Home court advantage and all." I place my hand on his shoulder and he smiles like he's laughing at a joke I missed.

"Actually, I need you to stay here for a minute," he says, and he runs onto the stage without me for the first time in our career.

The crowd erupts as he stops at center stage. He takes it all in for a moment, welcoming the applause and adoration. He picks up a microphone out of one of the holders and puts it to his lips.

"How are we feeling tonight, Boston?" he yells. The crowd shakes the venue walls with its collective noise and he waits for their united calm before continuing.

What the hell does he have planned?

"You all may have heard that our beloved lead singer has gone crazy. Clinically insane. Out of his *mind,*" Blake exaggerates. "You may even have read that he wasn't going to be available for tonight's show," Blake says. "Well, it's true."

I look around, confused as hell, trying to figure out what angle they are playing. The crowd's volume increases exponentially. Blake pats the air, trying to calm the crowd.

"At least, some of it's true, anyway! It's true that he's crazy, insane and maybe even a little out of his mind, but we love him anyway. Ladies and gentlemen, here he is, the lead singer of Consistently Inconsistent, Xander Varro!"

Theo and Dominic appear behind me from deeper in the wing and push me toward the stage. I'm a mix of confused, happy, laughing and plotting my revenge on Blake for the crazy comments, but I hug him at center stage, patting a palm heavy against the center of his back. Theo and Dominic take their places behind us. I raise both hands and face the crowd.

I *love* this crowd. I just love them. Their enthusiasm, their excitement—it never gets old. I'll never grow tired of the way it feels to be welcomed this way. It's not conceit. It's not greed. It's *humbling*. The cheers and the applause and the adoration—it's a reminder that we, as a band, have gotten lucky over and over again, but two times specifically above the rest. First, we were lucky enough to be born with the talents we have. And second, we were lucky someone believed in us enough to take us to this level.

Either way, we wouldn't be up here without the fans down there, and that's what I think about when they chant my name or yell for an encore to get just a few more minutes with us and our songs.

Blake strikes a chord on his guitar that resonates in a way that leaves his guitar and courses through every individual person in the crowd, as if they are conductors for the electricity he creates and suddenly the whole place is energized. Dominic engages in an overzealous drum solo that only amplifies the volume of the crowd. Theo duels with Dominic and hits a few keys of the keyboard, interfering with Dom's drum solo.

I stare into the lights and into the crowd, rocking back and forth on the balls of my feet. There are many nights where the borderline blinding lights ahead of me and the amplified music behind me trick me into feeling like I'm home. Because on the many stages where the floorboards creak beneath my boots and the sweat drips across my skin, I am home, in a way.

But this stage is where we got our first big break. The space in front us holds exponentially more people than it did at that first show, but this is where we are from. This is where we did our growing up. Every time I step back out onto this stage, every time I get to say '*How are we feeling tonight, Boston?*' before a show, my roots grow a little bit deeper. Being our home crowd, the applause we receive here is naturally the loudest of them all. The fans here bring us back to our early days. The way their shouts and whistles and claps welcome us to the stage makes it feel like the very first show all over again.

Blake plays so wildly yet so smoothly at the same time that it's as if that guitar is an extension of him, like it's an extra extremity. He leads us in with the guitar intro to one of our more popular songs and the crowd yells and claps with just the recognition of the very first note. They're so loud I can barely hear the music and I can't help but smile.

With the microphone close to my lips, I sing the lyrics without thinking about them. The words flow naturally from years and years of singing the same verses over and over in a way that allows me to sing without any conscious effort—like the words escape perfectly from my vocal chords without my brain directing them to. I sing about half of the song, and then, I don't.

Instead, I step away from the microphone and listen as thousands of strangers come together to sing and scream and shout the lyrics at me in unison, so collectively, so smoothly, that it's as if it were rehearsed. At the very edge of the stage, I lean forward, resting all my weight on one knee, reaching a hand to the crowd and they reach back. Our connection is instant and eminent without ever physically touching at all. This noise, these strangers that know the words to these songs as well as I do—they are far more intoxicating than the liquor ever could be.

As the show progresses, my mouth moves, my toe taps and my calloused fingers slide against the strings of my guitar but my eyes are fixated on the girl behind the bar, and I find she's looking at me too. Suddenly, my priority isn't the song or the guitar strings or the crowd, but ensuring I don't take my eyes off her, and she doesn't pull her gaze off me.

If I had not been told it were true, I wouldn't believe she doesn't hear. She stares back and moves her hips ever so slightly, swaying back and forth, tapping her foot along to the tempo of the song I am playing to her. She lifts a hand and tucks a stray hair behind her ear and for the second time in as many nights, I'm tempted to cut the song short and walk off the stage.

This time, though, *this* time it wouldn't be fueled by alcohol and anger but propelled by intrigue and curiosity.

We end the set and go backstage, the sound of the crowd screaming for our return following our footsteps. Drinks await us there. I take a sip of what I think is water but turns out to be the bitter bite of vodka. Shaking my head in a long, drawn-out no, I force it down and wipe my mouth with the back of my hand as the crew member returns with an unopened bottle of water.

The water bottle is still in my hand when I walk back to center stage, followed by Blake, Dominic and Theo. I take a lengthy sip of water then pull the bottle back, letting the last of the water flow freely over my face and hair and soak the stage beneath me. The crowd screams and continues to ask for an encore, and we oblige, playing a heartfelt, loud, energetic closing song – the very same song we closed with on this stage during our first big show at The Rock Room and have closed with every show since.

We stick around afterward to meet a few people who won a meet and greet through a social media outlet and have a quick post-show band meeting. Cooper encourages us to try to do this while the night is still fresh to see if we need to change anything before our next show, talk about what worked and what didn't and gauge interest and lack thereof of regarding the songs we played, which determines what we play and don't play at our next show.

When we finally wrap up, I make my way to the bar at the far side of the venue.

"What'd you think?" I yell to Kelly. My ears are still ringing, making my voice a few decibels louder than it needed to be.

She shrugs her shoulders. "It was okay, I guess. I've seen better."

"Ouch," I say. "I guess we'll just have to try harder next time."

She slides a glass of freshly poured whiskey across the counter to me and notices my gaze is elsewhere. Kelly looks from me to her cousin and back at me again.

"Alexander?" she asks, and I return my eye contact to her.

"Yeah?"

"Why do you care so much? Why are you trying so hard?"

"I honestly don't know," I say — and I don't. I can't explain it. Kelly's cousin piques my curiosity. Draws me in in a way I haven't felt since the first time I laid my eyes on a guitar and knew I wanted to learn everything about it.

"Aren't you with that Mariah Delani chick? I mean, I don't usually care about the celebrity gossip but that one was hard to miss. Local musician gone big-time star hooks up with young, talented movie producer?" she asks.

"Director, actually," I correct her, but I don't want to talk about Mariah. I clear my throat before I speak again. "That's over," I add.

"*Over* over? Or over until you run into each other at some big event and you get back together like all the other celebrity couples?"

"Jeez, Kel, for someone who doesn't care about the gossip, you certainly have a loud opinion on it," I say, immediately wishing I hadn't. I'm not helping my case.

She bites her lip, considering my words for a minute that aged like an hour.

"Okay, I'll introduce you, but don't do anything differently, okay? Talk like you usually would. Don't talk slower or anything. Just talk."

I raise an eyebrow and confusion takes over my face.

"She can't read your lips if you're not looking right at her or if you talk like an idiot," Kelly explains as if this should be completely obvious—and maybe it should be.

"Got it," I say, already overthinking, which is exactly what Kelly didn't want.

She shakes her head a few times before walking backward a few steps, turning away, and leaving me behind at the bar. She approaches Natalie and taps her on the shoulder. She turns and faces Kelly. Kelly's hands move in a fast blur of motions and I see her cousin's eyes flicker up to look at me, but only briefly. Her gaze is fixed on Kelly's hands once again, following each sign Kelly gives her.

I can sense the debate between the two. The looks Natalie steals every few moments aren't promising. Her eyes catch the tattoos on my arms and the length of my hair, but her expression remains neutral. She doesn't smile. She doesn't scowl. It's odd, being on this side of the judge's panel. I would be lying if I said I didn't notice beautiful women. I know what I like, but being looked over head-to-toe when you know it's happening makes me think twice about the next time I do it to a female. The emotions that cross Natalie's face say I don't have a chance—like I'd lost a battle I'd never even gotten the chance to fight in.

I can't say I wasn't warned.

I'm only a moment away from walking away when Natalie nods, Kelly wraps her fingers around Natalie's wrist and the two make their way over to me. I wipe my hands on my jeans.

Kelly translates our introduction, speaking and signing at the same time. I keep my eyes on Kelly's hands, though I don't understand even one motion. Natalie signs, her mouth moving, saying the words "Nice to meet you," though no sounds accompany the signs.

"It's nice to meet you, too," I say, looking at Kelly.

"Don't look at me. Look at her," Kelly reminds me, and my eyes dart to Natalie.

"So, listen. We're going to Prophecies tonight. You should come," I say, trying to speak toward Natalie but finding it difficult not to speak to Kelly, since she's interpreting.

Natalie signs to Kelly, and Kelly signs back a response too quick to be promising.

"What'd she say?" I ask.

"Umm, we'll think about it, okay?" Kelly says. "We have some things to get done here, but maybe we will meet you out after."

My stomach turns, an emptiness appearing at the pit of my chest. "Yeah, yeah," I say, swallowing back my disappointment, "maybe we'll see you there."

Natalie and Kelly wave a light goodbye as I head back toward the stage where I planned to meet Jana and Nellie. I keep my head down and my hands in my pockets. *That could have gone better.*

The backstage area has calmed. Only a few stragglers tying up loose ends remain back there. My footsteps cause the floorboards to creak, then suddenly I'm not alone anymore.

"Xander! That was amazing! What a brilliant show!" Jana says, running toward me, then rising on her toes to give me a hug.

"Seriously, that was the most unreal night," Nellie says, running her hands through her black and multicolored hair.

"You guys ready to get out of here? We're going to Prophecies," I offer, my words quiet, cloaked in chagrin.

"Actually, we're going to head out, I think," Jana says. "You have been beyond great, but you don't have to entertain us all night," Jana says, unable to control her grin, "Besides, I saw you talking to the cute bartender."

"Yeah, I don't think that's going to work out," I say, running my fingers into the roots of my hair, still wet with sweat from the show. "Anyway, thanks for coming. Today was awesome," I add, but Jana is looking through me, at something past where I am standing.

"Jana?" I snap my fingers jokingly. She opens her mouth to speak, but it's not her voice that I hear.

"Xander?" a honeyed voice sends a shiver down my spine, and I immediately know who it belongs to.

"Too soon for 'I told you so'? Jana whispers as I turn around and come face to face with Mariah.

"I'll see you later, okay?" Jana places her hand lightly on my forearm, but I just nod. All words have been stolen from me. Here I stand, a guy who makes a career out of words and wit and lyrical combinations and now? *Nothing*.

"Blake told me you had your eye on someone else. I didn't realize it was the girl from the coffee shop. She's cute. Kind of young for you, but cute," she says.

Ugh, Blake. Fuck *you*, Blake. Why would he say anything? I love him like a brother, but he wasn't always the most reliable character. He likes to talk more than he likes to think.

"It's not like that. We're close. Don't get me wrong. I'm not her type." I rub my hand at the back of my neck and stare at the floor.

"You are everybody's type, Xander." The words roll off her tongue like the hiss of a snake.

Not knowing what to say or do, I just stare at her for a moment. She truly is a beautiful woman—a body with curves in all the right places and dark brown hair that falls thick over her neck and shoulders. Emerald green, piercing eyes that are as dangerous as quicksand. Once your gaze falls into them, it's almost impossible to get back out.

But I have to. I have to break free from her and all her traps.

"What do you want, Mariah? I had a good night, a good show. I'm kind of on a roll here, and you show up. In your voicemail you told me not to contact you. You told me not to come looking for you." My shoulders rise and fall with every unsteady breath I take.

"I was hoping you would anyway," she whines. "You are stubborn, Xander. It's one of your more charming qualities." She steps forward and runs a finger down my chest as she speaks, her lips only inches from my throat. "I thought you would disregard what I said and come anyway."

"You thought wrong. I don't want you here, Mariah." My comment cuts deep. I can see in her eyes that it hurt her to hear the words.

Stepping aside, I try to walk past, to leave her as injured as she left me, but she grabs my wrist.

"Will you please just try to talk to me?" she pleads. She digs her nails into the veins at my inner wrist. Tearing my hand from her grasp, I stare into her eyes for what is hopefully the final time.

"We don't have anything to talk about—or at least I don't. In fact, not only do I have nothing left to say going forward, but you can also forget anything I ever said in the past. Since it was all based on a lie, you might as well forget I ever had any feelings for you at all." My heart rate rises as I say the words.

Leaving her backstage, I walk away from the area with my hands shoved deep in my pockets. My boots hit the wooden floor in heavy, fast-paced steps. The back of my neck is hot with tension.

Tonight is just not my fucking night.

Chapter Seven

Prophecies is a small bar down the street from The Rock Room, with an open dance floor and a DJ who always managed to keep people on it. It has this comfortable atmosphere with good music, great drinks and a reasonable crowd. It isn't exactly a club, so to speak, as in 'the young kids with their fake IDs wouldn't be caught dead here', but the staff always treated us well and we've always had a great time. I guess we're regulars now.

We stand at the bar, order a round of drinks and Blake hands his credit card to the bartender to start a tab.

I haven't taken a sip of my drink. Instead, I twirl the liquid around the bottom of the glass, trapped inside my own head, looking up only when the door opens.

Hopeful that Natalie and Kelly decided to come.

Fearful that it will be Mariah who walks through that door.

"Xander?" Blake barks, irritated, like he's been talking and I haven't been paying the least bit of attention. *Probably accurate.* "What's gotten into you tonight? It was great show, and the tour is finally coming to an end. Snap out of it, man."

"Sorry," I mumble, more out of obligation than sincerity. I try to spit out some bullshit excuse for what I'm thinking about, but Blake punches me in the arm.

"Xander!" he says. "She showed."

My heart pounds, his words switch my mood from despondent to elated but only for a moment. Kelly walks in alone, waving at us as she heads to the bar.

"Hey," she says in a whisper.

"Hi," I respond, but before I can ask about Natalie, Blake cuts in, offering to buy Kelly a drink. She nods her head and names her drink order through a smile.

"I'm sorry, Xander. She's really set in her ways," she says, taking a seat at the bar and resting her face in her hand.

"It was just an invitation for drinks. It's not a big deal," I say, now chugging the drink I have been avoiding.

"I know. But I know you, and I can tell you really wanted to get to know her."

"Here you go," Blake says, reaching directly in between me and Kelly, placing her drink on the bar top.

"Blake," Kelly says, "why don't you go snag us that high top over there in the corner and I'll come join you for a drink in just a minute." She bats her eyelashes and his eyes light up. Blake, unsurprisingly, does exactly what he's told.

"You know, I guess I just don't get it," I say to her, sliding my empty glass toward the bartender. "Has she ever dated someone…uh…*not* Deaf?"

"It's important to her, Xander. It's not a preference thing. It's not liking blondes more than brunettes or having her bar set too high," Kelly explains. "Natalie was born Deaf. As she got older, her parents put her in speech therapy and did, essentially, the very minimal things they could do to help her—but they gave up on her. They wanted her to speak so badly. They wanted her to speak and understand their language, but they never even tried to learn or understand hers."

"Her parents don't sign?" I ask, trying to follow along.

"No. Not at all," Kelly says. "They refused to learn. It's why she grew up with me. She was lost in her own home. She never had anyone to talk to or ask for help or navigate problems with. But my parents, they were committed to ensuring she had family who she could turn to—even if it meant learning a new language."

"That's...wow," I say. The bartender slides a freshly poured drink into my hand.

"Anyway, she's had enough bending over backward, trying to accommodate her hearing family, her hearing friends. She just wants to meet someone who understands her—both her language and her culture—more than we ever will as hearing people."

"So...why doesn't she just get one of those hearing aids or implants or something?" I ask.

"That, right there is *exactly* why she doesn't date hearing guys," Kelly says, shaking her head. "It's complicated and I could explain it to you, Xander, but I don't think it would kill you to do a bit of research before you try to talk to her again."

I raise my eyebrows and part my lips.

"You think I should try to talk to her again?" I ask, surprised.

"No," she laughs, "but you're going to. You wouldn't be you if you didn't."

"That was before you gave me a full lecture on all the reasons why my chances suck."

"I know, I know," she says, her voice set in a quiet surrender, "but I know you. There's a good guy in there somewhere beneath your stubborn exterior. I think she wants to meet you too, but your recent antics and her experience with trying to break down the language barrier in the past are both holding her back."

I nod, taking in the words Kelly speaks.

"I'm going to go," Kelly says, sliding off her barstool. "You have a great night. It's so great to see you."

"You were never going to go sit with Blake, were you?" I ask, tossing my head the direction of the table he's sitting at.

"Not even for a second," she says with a wink, waltzing out of Prophecies.

I've known Kelly more than half my life — and I realize now that I don't really know her at all. We all came from the same tiny, hardly recognized town just north of Boston. We walked the same hallways at the same schools. When asked where we are from, we say Boston, more out of necessity than habit. No one has ever heard of our tiny town, which requires us to explain its whereabouts, so we cut to the chase and name the closest major city. In the end, the answer matters very little. As for the band members, people tend to care more about where we are going than where we came from.

Kelly and I grew up taking the same classes in the same run-down schools. She helped get us on stage at The Rock Room when we were an unheard-of band from that unheard-of town, and all this time, I never really knew her at all. I never knew about her life outside The Rock Room. I never knew she was bilingual — or why. But I do know one thing, the single motif that continues to come full circle in every aspect of my life.

I still have a hell of a lot to learn.

* * * *

The Rock Room hosts occasional acoustic sets for solo artists and lesser-known bands trying to make their way into the big leagues. The night is well underway by the time I enter. I stand at the back, listening to the music, acting as if I have no ulterior motive other than listening to aspiring artists.

Natalie's eyes find mine, but I don't move from my spot — no wave, no head nod. I just keep to myself. She raises an eyebrow at me, then waves a slow, questioning motion. I wave back this time. A half-smile crosses her lips. She turns away and lifts a whiskey bottle above the bar.

She was paying attention the other night. I shrug, as if she twisted my arm and this wasn't all part of the plan in the first place as I walk toward the bar. She fills the glass halfway and slides it toward me.

"Xander," Kelly says, finally noticing my presence. The venue isn't crowded, and the music from the acoustic guitar is hushed. Calm. Perfect.

Natalie leans into the bar nearest me, watching the acts on stage.

I take the napkin and a marker from the bar and write *So do you come here often?*

She reads the message and laughs a short, loud sound, crumples the napkin and lobs it my direction. She shakes her head, still laughing lightly.

She places her hand on the bar top near me, returning her attention to the singer on stage.

He sings about taking chances and never missing out on what's in front of us. Even though she can't hear his message, I can, and I take his advice.

I place my hand on hers, briefly, a gentle touch of the fingertips to gain her attention.

She turns to me. Her different eye colors find the solid deep brown of mine.

I take a chance.

I point my index fingers toward her, touching the tips of my remaining fingers toward her. A sign I researched and practiced, hoping this time, asking her out in her language, she might say yes.

And she does. She bites her bottom lip, still considering her options, but eventually nods an enthusiastic yes and writes her number on my forearm before turning to serve a customer at the bar.

"So, dessert, huh?" Kelly asks, having seen my attempt.

"Dessert? I didn't…" I ramble.

"This is the sign for dessert," Kelly says, repeating the motion I signed to Natalie. "*This,*" she says, adjusting her hands so her index fingers point up, "is the sign for date."

I wipe my forehead with my palm. *This is going to be harder than I thought.*

Well into the night I stare at the arm with her number written on it and debate whether I should message her or not. Is it too soon to text her? Is it too late at night? Or, too early in the morning, I suppose.

I can't recall when I've had to fight this type of battle. Before Mariah, I'd never asked for any woman's number. I had no use for them. If someone gave me their number, I lost it. When someone did end up in my room, it was a 'tonight without a tomorrow' deal.

I hardly recognize this version of myself — the guy who checks more than once to see if a woman has written to him, getting hung up on one girl. It's just not me. I'm not one to spend time thinking about someone I hardly know. In high school, I was in a short-lived relationship but then the band had the opportunity to go on tour. The relationship ended somewhere between prom and when the tour began.

For the most part, touring and being part of the band over the last eleven years was exactly what I thought it was going to be — playing music, crashing or throwing parties and a few too many one-night stands. I know the reality is that I let that phase live on much too long. I knew it was time to grow up and stop, quite literally, screwing around. Then I met Mariah.

Mariah was the first person I was truly and honestly committed to for the first time since my music career had begun. It felt right, having something stable. But in time, I realized that what I had with Mariah wasn't stability. It was settling.

Mariah was gorgeous and successful, sure, but I wasn't in it because I loved her. I was in it because she answered the phone when I called, met me at various places along the tour and made me feel like there was someone waiting for me when I got off the stage every night — even if it was just via technology. But I realized in time that it wasn't Mariah I wanted. It was just someone to trust and talk to. When the trust disappeared, the talking went with it, and the relationship fell apart piece by piece until there was nothing left but two successful people who didn't know anything better than each other.

So now, I sit here, toying with the idea of giving it a few hours before I message Natalie. I don't want to give her the wrong impression — but I don't want to wait any longer, either.

What the hell. I type and send a short, simple message.

Hey, it's Xander.

I click send and reread the words. I'm unsure I said enough — but more would have been too much.

Three floating dots appear on the screen, but then disappear and no text follows. They appear again, but they dissipate, and I still don't receive a reply. *Too much, too soon, Xander,* I say to myself. I place my phone next to me and put my hands under my head.

A few moments later my phone buzzes. I open it too quickly to a short message from Natalie.

Well it's about damn time. The message reads with a winking smiley for emphasis.

Natalie and I message back and forth endlessly. Texting makes everything seem so easy. She's witty and bright and sarcastic and has mastered a well-timed joke. She keeps the conversation going in such a seamless way that I never bother to close out of the screen and check the time, but the sun peeking through my windows is a good indicator that we've kept each other company until daybreak.

Tired yet? I type to her.

Surprisingly, no, she writes back.

It has only been a handful of hours since I had seen her, and I find myself not wanting to wait to see her again.

Do you want to get a coffee? I type quickly into the text box.

Chance's? she types, and I type back a yes.

See you in 30, she adds.

* * * *

"Are you here because you're buying me a coffee?" Jana jokes. "I told you Mariah would get in touch with you."

"Disagree," I say. "You said by the end of the show, and the show was *technically* already over by the time she showed up."

"*Touché.*" She laughs and pulls a cup from the stack to her right.

"Make it two?" I ask. "Natalie is meeting me here."

"Natalie? The cute bartender Natalie?" she says as she raises an eyebrow and retrieves a second cup. As the milk steams for the lattes, she leans into the counter and continues talking to me. "She served Nellie and I our drinks at the show the other night. So, what do I need to know about her?" Her voice that straddles the line between curious friend and defensive sister.

"She's smart, funny, kind…beautiful…" I start. Jana searches my eyes, probably wondering if I'll keep talking or if she will have to ask the real question she wants an answer to.

"Is it weird?" she asks. "I mean, I'm not trying to be an awful person. But it is it odd that she doesn't talk? How do you know if you're into someone who can't respond?"

"She responds," I say, much too quickly, a defensiveness in my voice. "She signs and she writes things down. She texts. She makes eye contact. She speaks through body language and gestures. Communication takes a little bit of work, but the way I see it, isn't the case whether two people speak the same language or not?"

"Aww, somebody's smitten," Jana teases. "So, what happened with Mariah then?"

"Nothing. I don't want to talk about her. I don't want to talk *to* her. I need her out of my life. I have better things to focus on," I say as the jingle from the bells on the door rings through the shop.

I can't stop the smile that grows across my face as Natalie enters Chance's in a warm, fall outfit. She wears black leggings and a red flannel button-up shirt. Her hair is knotted into a long braid over her shoulder. She waves as she enters, and I return the motion.

"Have fun," Jana says in a sing-song tone.

I put the two coffees on a nearby table and Natalie walks over to me. She reaches up on her tiptoes to hug me and I wrap my arms around her in response. Her hair smells like strawberries, which I never had been a fan of, but they may now just have become my favorite fruit.

We sit at the table and sip our coffees. She doesn't look the least bit tired, which is surprising, all things considered.

She reaches into her purse and pulls out her phone. She punches in a message. My phone vibrates in my pocket.

Good morning, she writes.

How'd you sleep? I joke.

She smiles over the edge of the phone and taps in a response. Her fingernails click against the screen as she types.

I didn't. Some guy was keeping me up all night.

She smiles as my phone pings with her response.

Must have been a hell of a conversation, I reply.

It was just okay, she responds and laughs out loud as I read it.

We send and receive messages through the screens in front of us, but with the added benefit of being able to see each other's reactions and hear the laughter and scoffs and gasps when one of us rolls out a lighthearted jab at the other.

Our conversation leads to signs and their meaning. I tell her I would like to learn, and she wants to teach me. She pulls a menu from the holder at the edge of the table. She points to the word 'coffee' and raises her eyebrows at me. I nod, assuring her I understand what word we're starting with. She puts her hands into fists and places one on top of the other. Her bottom hand stays still, while her top hand moves in a cranking motion. I attempt the motion but must be doing something incorrectly because she shakes her head no, places her hands on mine, tightens my fists a bit and corrects the sign.

Her hands are warm and her fingertips are soft against the back of my hand. She removes her hands from mine, though I wish she hadn't. I try the sign again and she nods enthusiastically as I sign 'coffee' correctly.

She moves on and points to other words and food items on the menu. I do my best to sign out the words as she does, but we spend most of the time laughing at my failed attempts.

Her fingertip runs the length of the menu, stopping at the word 'dessert'. She raises an eyebrow and one corner of her lip.

I get a napkin from the holder on the table and wipe my lips. "Right, I do still owe you that," I say out loud. She laughs and shakes her head, then opens her cell phone screen once more.

Maybe later this week. I'm going out for drinks with Kelly tomorrow night. You should come. Bring a friend.

A chuckle escapes my lips as I read the text. Blake will be thrilled. Kelly, not so much.

Jana comes by to see if we need anything and takes both empty cups out of our way. We stand up from the table and walk outside, the cool fall air nipping at my bare arms.

Natalie signs away as if I know what she's saying, but she mouths *See you tomorrow?*, slowly and clearly.

"Looking forward to it," I say out loud, and she reads my lips as they move. Wrapping my arms around her, I pull her in for an embrace I don't want to move from. As we part, I give her an innocent goodbye kiss, placing my lips lightly at the intersection of her cheek bone and ear.

She places her hand at my neck and runs her thumb at my jaw where my beard has grown in. Her perfect, two-toned eyes stare into mine, but I hesitate, and she breaks the embrace.

I want to kiss her—to *really* kiss her, but before I make my decision, she's taking a step backward and waving a final goodbye to me before heading the direction opposite the way I will be going.

.

Chapter Eight

When I reach my apartment door, I fish for my key in my pocket, but I realize the door is cracked open. Did I leave in such a rush that I didn't close it tightly? No, I locked it. I know I locked it. I scratch my head and think back to leaving my place, wrestling with myself internally over whether I locked the damn door or not. I step closer to it and hear sounds beyond it.

There is someone in my apartment.

I can't make out the sounds. It sounds like some whistling and scattered voices. I crack open the door, and from where I'm standing, I can see the back of a head of blond, messy hair and leather high top sneakers on my coffee table.

"How the *hell* did you get in here, Blake?" I let out the breath that I didn't even realize I had been holding. I had thought someone had broken into my apartment, but no. It was just Blake being Blake.

He extends one hand straight in the air, holding one loose, silver key.

"Where did you get that?" I ask as I walk up behind him, snatching the key from him.

"Mariah gave it to me. Well, she told me to give it to you, but you weren't here," he says, still staring at the football pregame on the screen.

"Oh right, speaking of that…" I hit Blake in the side of the head with the back of my hand—half kidding, half not kidding at all.

"Hey!" he says as he rubs his head, "What the fuck was *that* for?"

"Why are you telling Mariah I'm interested in somebody else? In fact, why are you talking to her at *all*?" I ask, raising my voice into a frustrated yell.

"I was just trying to help you! She asked where you were, and I told her not to bother. Said you'd moved on and she should to. That's it, man. I didn't mean to piss you off."

"Oh." I rub my palm at the back of my neck. "I guess… I didn't really think of it like that."

"So, did you sleep with her?" Blake jumps over the back of the couch and heads toward the refrigerator.

"Mariah?" I ask. My voice raises an octave in confusion.

"No, the Deaf chick," he responds. My jaw clenches and my eyes narrow.

"Don't call her that. She's so much more than that," I say through gritted teeth.

Blake has been there through good times and bad with me. He's been the closest thing to a brother I have ever had, and I wouldn't be where I am without him, but he wasn't always playing with a full deck. He has said some of the most ignorant things sometimes, never thinking before he speaks.

"Okay, okay, I'm sorry. Just don't hit me again," he says, rubbing the side of his head once more.

He cracks open a beer and chugs more than half the bottle before taking another breath.

"It's like…ten a.m.," I say.

"It's noon somewhere," he responds, opening the door again and tossing me a bottle.

* * * *

Prophecies is more crowded than I would have thought. Kelly and Natalie are seated at the bar, very few seats available around them. We approach, and Natalie turns on her barstool toward me, reaching her arms forward for a hug.

"Blake," Kelly says, proceeding to swallow every last drop of her drink.

"Kelly," he responds, trying and failing to hold back a goofy grin.

Natalie looks at me from under long, dark lashes and I'm as speechless as I have ever been. I stand about a foot from her, gawking at every inch of her and having no idea what to say or do next.

The awkwardness has nothing to do with our language differences and everything to do with the captivating allure she possesses that I can't explain and can't get used to.

A two-person high top by the windows becomes available and I extend my palm, face up, suggesting we migrate to that spot. She nods and follows me to the table, where I pull her chair out for her, then take the remaining seat. Kelly stays behind at the bar with Blake, but her gaze wanders our direction.

Natalie sips her drink and I contemplate what to say or do or try. I want to know everything about her.

As if she can read my mind, she pulls a pencil and an orange keno slip from the container on the table.

In large, bubbly handwriting, she writes, *Where is your favorite place to travel?* Then she slides the paper across the table to me.

This is a question that I have to think about for a moment as no obvious answer comes to mind. With a half-smile, I write *Boston, MA* on the paper and she scrunches her eyebrows. She either thinks I'm kidding or can't read my impossible chicken scratch.

There's no place like home, I write and wink when she looks up.

She laughs and writes *I hate that movie* under my messy handwriting, to which I respond, *Willy Wonka and the Chocolate Factory is worse.*

We continue this for a bit, back and forth about favorite movies, colors, books and food and somehow an hour has ticked by and I have smiled more and enjoyed tiny, handwritten notes more than I have enjoyed anything in recent memory.

She has a sense of humor that comes through in what her eyes say and her smile does, and she's so easy to be around that it's effortless to think of what to write next.

After a while of the written Q and A, Natalie holds up one finger and excuses herself from the table. As she walks away, she stops to talk to Kelly. The way their hands move is like a rehearsed dance. They speak to each other through sign language so smoothly and effectively, without hesitation. Their eyes, facial expressions and the way they lean into each other or away from each other accents their language perfectly.

The sign language I do know is sparse, if existent at all, and I'm mesmerized by the fluidity of the hand motions, though I feel like an onlooker to a game of charades that both players are exceptionally good at. Natalie continues her walk past the bar toward the back of the building and Kelly joins me at the high top.

She eyes the penciled words over the orange numbers of the keno papers and smiles at me.

"You've lasted longer than I thought you would," she says. "It can be a really challenging adjustment. A lot of people get frustrated trying to figure out what someone who doesn't speak is saying."

"So...she doesn't speak at all then?" I ask. The thought has been running across my mind all night, but I wasn't sure who or how to ask.

"She can, actually. It's uncomfortable for her. She doesn't like the way it sounds or feels to her. She mouths every word as she signs, so if you're any good at reading lips, it's a start. Sometimes she whispers as she signs, barely there, but if you listen for it, you can hear it, and she probably doesn't realize she's making sounds at all. She's so used to ASL, and my parents and I have adjusted so well that she hasn't needed oral communication.

"Honestly, there are times Natalie isn't even in the room and my dad and I communicate in signs because sometimes it just flows more naturally. Or my mother and I will be talking and we realize we're simultaneously talking and signing for no reason," Kelly explains, glancing over her shoulder occasionally. "She laughs. She sobs. She gasps. I mean, she's not completely silent. Her reactions and the sounds associated with them exist. She just usually doesn't go out of her way to speak vocally."

And just like that, all in a few sentences, I feel like I have a clearer understanding of Natalie.

"Anyway, I think she was just using the restroom. She will be back in a minute," Kelly says.

Natalie stops at the bar and holds up two fingers, then points to me then at herself. The bartender pours the same drinks we had previously ordered, and she picks them up from the bar, bringing them to our high top.

"Thank you," I say out loud, but decide to take a chance on a bit of the only sign language I have mastered. Bringing a flat hand up near my lips, I then direct the motion toward her, similar to the motion used to blow a kiss. That's how 'thank you' is signed, I think. At least, I *hope* it is that and I didn't just sign something inappropriate or embarrassing.

She smiles widely and nods her head enthusiastically. She gives me a thumbs-up and looks at me with bright eyes that say she's appreciative of my attempt.

I'm surprised at how much time has passed when Blake approaches our table. "Are you guys just about ready? We're going to head out."

Natalie's eyes meet mine, trying to read an answer in them. I want to say no. I'm not ready to leave. I want to continue to learn about her — and learn *from* her. Kelly approaches and signs to Natalie. She nods and stands up from her bar stool.

So, I guess that answers the question for me.

"Yeah, we can head out," I say begrudgingly.

As we head toward the exit, Natalie turns back to the table for a moment.

The crisp night falls cold around me as I stand a few paces back from the group, wondering what Natalie is doing. She joins us outside and slides her jacket on then walks toward me and hands me the keno slips with all our notes on them.

She waves goodbye as she turns and walks quickly to catch up with Kelly.

My mouth grows into a smile as I reread some of our written conversation. Once I've reached the end of our too-short conversation, I flip the last slip over to a new message.

"Dinner Thursday. I'll cook. You're in charge of dessert."

Back home in bed and as awake as I have ever been, I lie there with no intention of falling asleep. The image of Natalie's two different colored eyes and the way she speaks with them sits heavy on my mind, making it difficult to think of anything else.

Chapter Nine

The remainder of the week, as it so often does, consists of interviews, guest appearances, band meetings and photo shoots. Somehow, the times we are home are often busier than the times we are touring. Cooper keeps us occupied and scheduled, but he also keeps us very successful, so I guess my complaints are limited. Through all of it, though, I could only think of one thing.

Thursday.

There were days this week that felt longer than any other day — days that felt like the clock wasn't moving at all — but eventually the minute and second hands came full circle enough times to turn one day into the next, and the next and finally, it was Thursday again.

In front of the windows, I pace the length of the living room a few times then stop to examine the floor, wondering if I had left a track in it where I've shuffled my feet along this same path, back and forth, time and time again. Writing song lyrics, making big decisions, getting lost in my own thoughts... It was all done right here, pacing this same path.

Something about repetitively walking this short route at the full-length windows, looking out over the city lights and being able to see for miles and miles made me feel less stuck in my own head.

After a while of pacing, I sit down and turn on the TV to a station that plays top songs, shows music videos and counts down the top charts to the number one hits of the week. Two men sit behind a desk in what looks like a radio station booth, talking about an upcoming release of an album from one of our biggest rival bands. I click the volume up two notches to hear what they have to say, or what they expect, but there is knock at the door before they reveal anything of value. I'm more interested in the person on the other side of the door than anything the TV DJs have to offer.

Natalie stands on the other side when I open it. She's holding two large paper bags full of food, which I take from her. She waltzes into the apartment wearing ripped jeans with canvas sneakers and a gray, fitted T-shirt. Her carefree, casual appearance is striking. She wears very little makeup and allows her hair to fall in natural curls, but her minimal maintenance look is one of the things I find most appealing about her. She seems comfortable and confident in her own skin without burying it in artificial color.

She starts unloading the grocery bags on the counter, pulling out vegetables, meat, seasonings and ingredients I had never heard of and wasn't going to attempt to pronounce. Lastly, she places a slightly outdated tablet on the counter. I stand behind her, wondering if she needs any help, though when it comes to cooking, I'm about as useful as a straw hat in a snowstorm. She turns and looks up at me, then takes both my hands in hers. Walking backward, she leads me to the chair at the island and has me sit.

She returns to the other side of the counter and pulls a bottle of red wine from one of the bags, then points to the cabinets in a manner that suggests asking where the glasses are kept. Honestly, I'm not sure I even own wineglasses, but I point to the cabinet where the barware is located. She opens the cabinet and, to my surprise, locates two stemmed glasses. The multi-function bottle opener is in the same cabinet, and she takes that as well. After rinsing the glasses off, she opens the bottle of wine. As she pours each glass, I realize I have never *actually* had wine before. Not even a sip. I'll try anything once, and it *is* alcohol, so how bad can it be?

We both lift our glasses and she taps her glass against the rim of mine, the *clink* the edges of the glasses produce echoes through the kitchen. She takes a sip but watches me over the glass.

I take the first sip and try to be courteous, but my face contorts as my tongue rejects the taste. I swallow hard and cough, like a preteen taking the first swig of something strong from his father's liquor cabinet.

She swallows her sip and giggles.

It's so…*dry*. How can something liquid possibly be that…*non-quenching*? Red wine has no business calling itself a liquid — or an alcohol, for that matter.

She returns to the cabinet and pulls out a short crystal glass. She places it in front of me and grabs the whiskey bottle from the counter, pours the golden liquid into the glass then combines the remainder of my red wine into her glass. She lifts her glass and we 'cheers' a second time. Only this time, I'm much happier with the sip that follows.

Natalie investigates my kitchen, opening every cabinet and drawer while making herself right at home. She prepares our meal in a mesmerizing, effortless way that makes it seem like I'm watching a professional cooking show instead of sitting in my own kitchen. I don't know what we're having, but I am enjoying watching her make it. She seems happy and comfortable on that side of the counter, chopping vegetables and seasoning meat while making her way around the kitchen like she's been here hundreds of times.

She leans into the counter and stares at me, her lips parted into a gentle smile, her eyes glistening with a contagious happiness.

"What are you making?" I ask, her eyes trained on the movement of my lips. She points to the tablet, and I run a finger across the screen. It springs to life, showing the recipe for an incredible-zlooking roast.

I slide my finger across the screen to view the whole recipe, but accidentally open a screen that previews recently viewed pages. The page loads to her last search.

Xander Varro.

Multiple tabs are open, stories and articles from all different parts of my career and life—more bad than good—fill the screen. She cranes her neck to see what I am looking at and I make no effort to hide what I have found.

Her lips turn down at the corners. A hint of red flushes her cheeks as her eyes dart back and forth from me to the screen.

She swallows hard and wipes her hands clean with a dishtowel, her eyes focused on my mouth, awaiting whatever it is I'm going to say next. I clear my throat.

"If you're looking for reasons to not be with me, I promise you *will* find them," I say, and her forehead creases. "Kelly said you were skeptical of me because of how I'm portrayed in the media. So, don't buy into it. Don't go out of your way to read these things. I'll tell you anything you want to know."

"The truth?" she mouths, accompanied by the signs for the question.

I bite my bottom lip. There are so many parts of my past I'd like to omit, but if it's honesty she wants, that's what she will get.

"More of truth than the media will give you," I reason, and it's enough for her.

She takes the device, clicks the X in the corner, and all the media fables disappear. If only it were that easy in life, deleting your reputation as easily as someone erases a browser history.

She places the meat in the oven and sets the timer then washes and dries her hands before making her way back toward me. She takes her wineglass in one hand, and my hand in the other. I stand up and lead her on a short tour of the apartment. Our footsteps echo down the hall as we view the guest room, my bedroom and the main bathroom. We return to the living room and I walk her to the windows which are, of course, my favorite aspect of the apartment.

We stand at the floor-to-ceiling glass, looking out over the illuminated city. She takes a sip from her wineglass and leans in closer to me. Her fingertips skid over my low back and she settles her hand around my waist. I wrap my arm around her shoulders and pull her close. We stand there for a few moments — enjoying the view and each other — as I run my hand up and down her ufpper arm. She hooks her fingers into my belt loop.

She looks up at me with her perfect, two-toned eyes. I'm drowning in them with no sense of which way is up and no intention of trying to find it. She bites at her bottom lip, and I talk myself out of kissing her.

I want to. *Damn*, do I want to. But I don't know if it's what she wants. We just met, and I am trying really hard to work at this 'gentleman' thing — to not move too fast for her.

I pull her in so she's facing me. She wraps her other arm around me and holds the wineglass at my low back. Moving my hands, I rest my palms at her shoulders, then lift one hand to move a loose curl away from her face, tucking it behind her ear. She leans her cheek into my hand, and I run my thumb across her cheekbone.

Her eyes light up at my touch and my usual, impatient self takes over. I can't wait any longer. I lean forward and place my lips on hers. It's a light, slow kiss. I try to pull away, to ensure that it was okay with her, but she doesn't allow it. She pulls me in and kisses me with an alluring force and passion. Her kiss says this is okay more than any words could. Her tongue glides against my own, and suddenly I find myself craving the red wine taste I didn't think I'd enjoyed — but I had been wrong.

She pulls away long enough to place her glass on the table but turns back to me and puts her hands on my shoulders. I kiss her again — then her hands are in my hair and my thumbs are tucked into the waist of her jeans at her low back.

Her hips rest at my thighs and she pushes against me so I'm walking backward until my back is pressed against the cold windows.

Somewhere in a distant mind, I think about this window breaking loose and we both fall to the ground below. It's a hard descent, but it's a perfect parallel for the way I'm falling for her—fast, unexpected, thrilling.

As I kiss along her jawline and her ear, she lets out an audible breath. I step forward and lift her at her waist. She wraps her legs around me and I hold her body weight—not that her small frame offers much of it—and walk to the couch.

I bring her body down gently until she's seated, and I'm kneeling on the hard wood floor in front of her. She has her hands on either side of my face and tilts my head back. She places her lips against mine and kisses me lightly once…twice…and a third time. Her lips linger on the last one, and I can feel her mouth form into a smile against mine.

I plan to take things slow, to get a good, solid sense of what she does and doesn't want. She gathers a handful of the hem of my shirt in her hands, like she wants it off, but hesitates, trying to figure me out too. I wrap my fingers around her wrists and together we pull it over my head. She explores the landscape of my chest and abdomen and the tattoos that cover them. She kisses near my collarbone and pulls away, gazing into my eyes.

We are two grown adults and yet, somehow, I can't stop wondering if this is okay—or if I'm going to mess this up by taking too many steps too quickly.

I place both hands at her hips and slide my thumbs under the hem of her shirt, but I wait for some kind of indication or permission before I go any farther. She nods, and I slowly pull the fabric up, revealing her hips, then abdomen, and —

The oven starts beeping.

I pull away, jumping at the sound that reminds me there is a world outside the one I was momentarily lost in. I look toward the kitchen and she follows my gaze. Three LED zeroes flash on the oven screen, indicating the end of the timer. Losing myself in her also meant losing track of time, forgetting there was anything going on in the background.

My shoulders and chest rise and fall in a sigh, and I shake my head. My mouth forms a half grin. Natalie leans forward and kisses my forehead before standing up and heading toward the kitchen to check on the food.

I wish she would just let it burn.

When I'm near her, I'm not the unwound, self-destructive guy I am with everyone else but more importantly, I don't want to be. She takes me, a man who knows how to run, and teaches me how to walk. She slows me down, shows me how to look at the world from different angles — and she doesn't even know she's doing it.

As she reaches into the oven, the mouthwatering scent leaves it and fills the apartment. I take a seat at the island again, looking at her with a sideways expression as she punctures the roast with a meat thermometer. I don't think I have even *seen* a meat thermometer before, never mind knowing I owned one.

Everything is perfect — timed to the minute, so the sides and meat are ready at the exact same moment. She looks up to give me an indication that dinner is ready to be served, but the TV screen catches her attention. I look back to see what she's looking at, and find I'm staring at...*me.*

To this day, it is still strange to see myself on TV.

Blake started this band. This whole charade was his idea, but somehow, the lead singer nearly always gets all the facetime on screen and in interviews when it comes to the media. The spotlight doesn't fall on him nearly a fraction of how often it should. But there's my face, blown up in dozens of images floating across the TV screen with my voice playing behind them.

I look back at Natalie with a new emotion, one I hardly recognize. *Panic, maybe?* I rub my finger and thumb hard across my brow line. I know I should do something. Shut the TV off. Interfere. Tell her my side, but I don't have the chance.

The story begins to unfold before I have the chance to inform her myself. I hold my breath, because I have no idea what to expect, but the way she tenses up only leaves me with the option to do the same.

Two men in black shirts sit in front of microphones and talk between themselves for a moment, and Natalie's eyes shift from them, to me and back again. The screen changes from the radio station-type atmosphere, to a concert venue much like The Rock Room. A poorly recorded cell phone video takes over the screen where I wear a threatening expression as I approach another man, then hit him with an unexpected punch. They play the video again in slow motion and display sections of the video as still frames plastered across the screen.

There are more than a few questions running through her mind. I can see that. I look back at the TV with white knuckles clenched tight around the arms of the chair I'm sitting in.

One of the show hosts comments the "only thing worse than Varro's temper is the band's current rating on the charts," which has apparently dropped since my outburst. I never wanted this to impact the band the way it has. I never wanted any of this to impact *me* the way it has. The room feels a mile long as I head to where the remote sits, but I make the walk, pick up the remote in my unsteady hand and click the TV to a dead black.

A cold sweat breaks across my brow. I'm shaken, embarrassed and silent, all at the same time. Turning around and looking at Natalie is an option, because her voice is so eminent in her eyes and I expect hers will be filled with disappointment.

There is a fine to pay for my actions. I know this. I just don't want that asking price to include losing a girl I could really care about. She barely knows me, and I didn't plan on introducing her to that particular side of me anytime soon.

Or ever.

With silent footsteps, she walks across the tile floor, places her hands on my arms from behind me, and I turn to face her. Her eyes don't reflect disappointment but sympathy. She bites at her bottom lip, then signs a few things I don't recognize. She walks back to the counter when I shrug my shoulders, not guessing what she's trying to say. Using a pen and an old newspaper from the pile of mail on the counter, she writes in the corner of the faded paper.

What happened?

The situation is too many words to fit on the page, so I write back.

I had a bad night, but it's in the past. It doesn't matter now.

She looks at me with wide, inquisitive eyes, like she wants to ask a lifetime's worth of questions but chooses only one.

Will it stay in the past? she writes, and I hesitate, because I don't know the answer to the question. But I want it to— I want the pain and confusion and vulnerable version of me to stay as far away from her as possible, so I nod my head yes, even if it is just wishful thinking.

Still dismayed over the clip shown on TV, I stare at the tile floor, but Natalie places her fingers gently under my chin and lifts my face so my eyes meet hers then places her lips against mine with a kiss worth a thousand words.

The notion comes with the message that everything will be okay, and she's going to be the one to make sure of it. For weeks, I have been holding on to a single thread. That one fiber is all I have control of, but she kisses me and I let go of it. I loosen my grip on everything I had left, on the past version of me I was so vigorously holding on to and I drift into her completely. No parachute, no safety net—just a free-fall into her and whatever else waits for me.

Chapter Ten

Dinner is mouthwatering. I was full about halfway through the meal but I can't stop shoveling the delectable food into my mouth. I don't want to let a single morsel go to waste. I think back but can't recall the last home-cooked meal I had. I'm sure it paled in comparison to this.

We write messages back and forth to each other in the margins of the unread newspaper in between bites. It turns out Natalie is about halfway through a Culinary Arts program here in the city, which isn't surprising, given the deliciousness and detail of the meal in front of me.

What would you be if you weren't a singer? she writes, and I think long and hard about the answer. My teeth press into my bottom lip while I drum the pen against the wooden tabletop.

Finally, I lean forward and press the tip of the pen to the newspaper.

A teacher, I write. Her eyes widen at first then narrow as she cocks her head as if she thinks I'm joking.

Music? she pens, then turns the paper toward me again.

I don't know. But I think I could get through to some kids. I sucked in school, though, I write, and she puts a hand to her chest and laughs.

She bites at the end of the pen then flips the paper to a new page. Across the top of the page, she pens, *I'd really love to hear your music someday.*

As I read the words, she signs them, and the more she offers these lyrical hand symbols, the more I start to think I know what they mean. Of course, it's not going to be a skill I learn overnight, but some of the motions are obvious and understandable, which makes communicating easier.

The sign for music is this smooth, elegant series with a flat palm on one hand and a sweeping motion with the other, and all in a matter of seconds, I have figured out my favorite sign.

She nods encouragingly as I repeat the sign for music.

She pushes her chair back from the table and begins picking up the dishes.

"No, no, absolutely not," I say out loud, and take them out of her hands. She rolls her eyes as I walk to the sink with the dinner plates. She follows closely behind with more dishes and I just shake my head. It didn't take me long to assess that she's extremely stubborn, and there is almost no changing her mind once she's made it. In many ways, it's my favorite thing I've learned about her. She knows what she wants, and nothing gets in her way.

She turns on the water and starts washing the dishes. I take the towel from beside the sink and snap it her direction, lightly catching her leg at the upper part of the back of her thigh. She turns toward me with her jaw dropped wide and one eyebrow raised. She runs her hands under the faucet then flicks the water toward me, splashing my face and hair. I use my T-shirt to wipe my eyes and when she doesn't expect it, I lunge forward and reach for the sprayer at the sink.

She lets out a high-pitched, girly squeal and turns away from me, though I had no real intention of spraying her—or maybe I did. She turns toward me, laughing so hard she forgets to breathe, and I set the nozzle back in its place at the base of the sink.

She reaches her hand out, calling a truce. Wrapping her hand in mine, I pull her into me and put my free hand at the back of her neck. I run my thumb across her hairline, and she stares up into my eyes. I kiss her, softly and slowly, and when she pulls away, she rests her forehead against mine and we lock eyes on each other.

How could it be that we have only known each other for a handful of days? She fits so perfectly in my arms and in my life in a matter of only a short amount of time. I can't imagine going forward without her being a part of it all.

I have always believed love at first sight was an ideal reserved for the books and movies and the 'when you know, you know' concept was just a validation among my friends who were moving much too fast. But maybe all the fairy tales and fables had the potential to be true, after all. Maybe we all have a once upon a time and a happily ever after, and mine is standing just inches from me, completely unaware of how strong my feelings for her are becoming.

Perhaps, that's why it's called *falling*. We don't do it on purpose, and we don't have any control over it.

I part from her, remembering our dessert sits untouched in the refrigerator. I pull out a vibrantly decorated cake. Her eyebrow bends into a curious arch. Her eyes find the message that reads 'Happy Birthday, Martha' and her expression changes from confused to amused. She points to the cake and shrugs her shoulders. "Who is Martha?" she signs and mouths in unison.

"The hell if I know," I say, handing her a fork and diving in without cutting the birthday cake Martha is surely missing.

We both overfill on birthday cake, then Natalie walks toward the living room, stopping in front of the shelves that hold my expansive DVD collection. She pulls a DVD out from the shelf and holds it up, seeking approval. I nod and take it from her to put it in the disc player, without even checking which title she has chosen. If it's what she wants to watch, we will watch it. If it's on the shelf, I've probably seen it more than once, and I planned on being too distracted by her to care what's on the television anyway.

The spot on the couch closest to where she sits is inviting, and I accept, pressing play on the remote as I crash into the couch in the free space beside her. I would be lying if I said I didn't question how this works. A movie without sound doesn't seem very entertaining to me, but this is obviously something she's accustomed to.

She settles in close to my chest, and I wrap one arm around her shoulder. As the movie begins, she takes the remote from the arm of the chair and turns the subtitles on.

Of course! I think to myself, frustrated that I didn't think of doing that for her before she had to do it for herself.

Reaching an arm to the side, I pull the chain on the table lamp, leaving us in a darkened area only lit by the picture on the screen.

My head falls forward and I jolt myself awake. Natalie breathes in deep, even breaths against my chest. The DVD on the screen is stuck on the main menu, repeating a series of clips from the movie. My cell phone clock reads four-eleven a.m. and I don't remember seeing even one minute of the movie. We must have fallen asleep early on, which is to be expected, thanks to our frequent late-night texting.

Natalie starts to awaken as I adjust my position. She looks at me with a confused, groggy expression and points to her wrist. I show her the clock on my phone and her eyes widen with surprise. She yawns and rubs the tired from her eyes.

I open the notepad feature of my phone and type a quick message.

You should go back to sleep. You can go lay down in my bed. It's more comfortable. I'll take the guest room.

The corner of her lip upturns and she rolls her eyes. She takes my hands and leads me into my room.

She slips off her jeans and climbs into bed next to me. Nothing happens, and for the first time, maybe the first time ever, I don't need it to. Having her in my arms is enough for me, because the sound of her heartbeat and the look in her eyes draws me in more than anything physical can.

I've played the one-night-stand game. I have rushed into things and let myself lose control, and I already know I don't want that with her. I don't know nearly enough about Natalie as a person, but I want to. I want to learn everything I can about what she keeps inside — and not just what she keeps underneath her clothing. I don't want her to think that's all I am interested in, because maybe with other women that was the case. But this time is different. *She's* different. I want her to know and I want her to understand that I see her as so much more than a body.

Closing my eyes and inhaling deeply, I take in the strawberry scent her hair holds and fall into a deep sleep, knowing the dreams I find in my head won't be as nearly as spectacular as the one I hold in my arms.

* * * *

The sun beats hard against the windows just a few hours later. Natalie's back is against my chest and my arm is draped over her abdomen. Her skin produces heat against my bare upper body. Her long, dark hair is a mess of curls sprawled in every direction across the pillow.

My phone pings and I reach for it, slowly and uncoordinatedly, trying not to disturb her. Through narrowed, groggy eyes I read a group email that includes all the members of the band, originated by Cooper.

Below you will find information for the upcoming make-up show in New York.

I lock my screen without responding or opening the attachment and slide my phone across the bedside table. I want to be frustrated with Cooper, but the only person I can be frustrated with is myself. I did this. My moment of weakness, my very public display of emotion, my inability to choke down my feelings and suffer quietly through a two-hour show got us here.

I slide my body away from Natalie's slowly and smoothly, hoping not to disturb her. I find my jeans on the floor, reach into the pockets and retrieve an almost-empty pack of Marlboro Lights. I slide on whatever clothes I can find and leave the apartment, closing the door quietly behind me.

I make my way down the hall and step outside the main doors of the apartment. The usually busy city streets are still vacant and hushed. I tip my head back and expose my face to the sun's rays, unsure how many more sunny days we will get before the New England season switches over from fall to winter. The sky is a crystal clear, cloudless blue and a light, fall breeze sweeps across my face and through my hair.

Stories above me, Natalie steps out onto my balcony. She puts her head in one hand, resting her elbow on the balcony railing. She runs her free hand through her hair. The sun reflects against her black hair, illuminating it to an almost blue color. She notices me staring at her and smiles downward, holding up one finger, then disappears back into the apartment.

I'm still looking upward, waiting for her return, but she doesn't reemerge onto the balcony. Instead, a few moments later, she pushes open the main door and joins me outside, holding two cups of freshly brewed coffee.

I take one cup from her, using the same hand that holds a lit cigarette, and set the other at her low back, pulling her in close to press my lips into her hairline.

I run the lit portion of the cigarette across the cement wall we lean against. I know she disapproves. The commercials and warnings and doctor's advice have reached me time and time again. I've heard it all, the consequences of being a smoker. I just never gave a damn. But the way her nose scrunches up, the way she pulls back from my kiss just slightly quicker than she usually does? It makes me rethink my vices.

Most of me is trying to change — for her, for the band, for myself. Many of my downfalls, they are manageable.

But not all of them are within my control.

One moment, we're alone, enjoying each other's half-awake appearances and stealing kisses from the other. There is me, and there is her.

And there is a photographer.

I place both my hands at her shoulders and turn her in the direction of the main door saying "Just go inside" as I give her a gentle push toward the door, but she's not looking at me, not reading my lips, and she pauses and turns her head, looking directly into the lens of the camera. He continues to zero in on us, his finger moving incessantly against the shutter button.

We abandon our coffee cups and my cigarette pack on the cement ledge near the door and rush inside. My heart is racing as I think about what those photographs show. A girl with unbrushed hair and an ensemble composed of half of last night's clothes and half oversized clothes that belong to me. My life has been exposed enough for me to know that the articles will scrutinize her, calling her normal and boring before they have the chance to learn that she is anything but.

My heart clenches. This is the part I was afraid of. Life under the microscope is not one everyone craves. Now she has been exposed to it well before I ever intended her to be.

* * * *

We sit across from each other on the couch sipping a second — and much-needed — cup of coffee. I pull my phone from my pocket to show her the email about Consistently Inconsistent heading back to New York.

She nods through a sip of steaming hot coffee.

In the same textbox, without pressing send, I type, *Come with me?*

She doesn't jump at the opportunity, but instead, places her coffee on the living room table and takes my phone from me.

All Things Black and White plays that weekend, and I'm bartending, she types, but I can sense it isn't the whole truth.

Call out, I write with a smile on my face. *No one listens to their music anyway.*

She starts to laugh but swallows it back, then shakes her head no. Her eyes soften, like maybe she *wants* to go but is finding reasons not to.

For me, these last few days are an intermission to the perpetual show that is my life, and eventually, I will have to get back on that stage. The indecision in her face says she thinks this is just a pitstop of my million-mile-per-hour lifestyle.

And maybe it is.

I'll fly you there if you want to come, I offer, and she thinks about it for a moment, but ultimately shakes her head in a drawn-out, final *no.* I read her expression, and I can tell by the distant look in her eyes that it's not because of work or any other scheduling conflict. She tears her gaze away from mine, preventing me from further analyzing her expression.

I gently place my fingers at her chin and lift her face to mine. My mouth turns down at the corners as my gaze flickers to her hands and back again. I'm waiting for her to explain, but she doesn't.

She turns away from me and shuffles to the kitchen, where her phone sits on the counter.

Fiddling with my coffee cup, I wait for a long, typed-out rejection and wonder what the hell just happened. Last night, things were light, easy-going. One night's sleep later and something's different.

She ties her hair into a loose bun at the top of her head with the elastic she always keeps around her wrist. My coffee splashes over the cup as I place it on the living room table before I stand and walk up behind her. My hands rest at her shoulders, then I run my fingertips down her arms. I can feel the rise and fall of her back at my chest.

Still facing away from me, she types in a text message, sending the explanation to my phone.

I'm enjoying this, Xander. A lot. I'm having fun, but that's all this is going to be. Just fun. Nothing more.

I part my lips and my shoulders fall in confusion, defeat.

She turns to my phone again and punches in one long answer.

You can't honestly think is going to work long-term. Judging by the overall emptiness of the apartment, I can tell you are gone more than you are here. Communication for us is challenging in person. How do you expect it to be when you leave again?

Natalie's expression is drenched with sympathy and worry and confusion when I look up from my screen.

The clip of me she saw on TV last night plays fresh in my mind. A clip that seems like a lifetime ago, a completely different version of me ago, but wasn't. It was recently, and still being dwelled on by the media and Internet. I can't get away from it, and in turn, she wouldn't be able to either.

Lowering my eyebrows, I point to the television, asking if this change of heart is because of what she saw, but she shakes her head no and types.

You just got out of a relationship. From what I understand, a serious one. I won't be your rebound girl.

I take her hand in mine and bring it to my lips, kissing every knuckle individually. "You wouldn't be," I say, and I mean it. I have no control over the timing of when she came into my life.

She leans her forehead into my chest for a moment then types another message.

Do we have to complicate things? Can we just see how things go?

The nod I give is a silent lie, but her mind is set, and I fear trying to change it will have the opposite outcome than I hope for. Instead, I swallow my feelings back and hope in time hers change.

Natalie leaves my apartment after too many goodbyes. Neither one of us really wanted to part, but Blake and I committed to an interview with a local radio station.

I shower and get ready for the day, pulling on a long-sleeved, tight-fitting shirt, jeans and a Red Sox baseball cap. I make my usual walk to Chance's on the corner. Jana waves at me through the window and pulls a cup from the stack to start my order before I even open the door. The bells on the door echo through the cafe, announcing my arrival.

"Just one today?" she asks with a smirk.

"Yeah, just one. Blake's on his way but he's on his own." I slide a bill across the counter. "How's Nellie?"

"Amazing. She can't stop talking about you."

"Me?" I ask.

"Well, Blake, actually. But I didn't want to hurt your feelings. You were the one who got us in, after all." She chuckles. "Speak of the devil..." she says, nodding toward the window.

Blake is walking toward the shop with a tall, thin, large-chested brunette. She's wearing a tight-fitting red dress that is much too formal for ten a.m. on a Monday. Blake has her high-heeled shoes dangling from his fingertips. He stops and faces her. She leans in for a long, aggressive kiss.

I look at Jana and she covers her mouth with her hand. It's almost impossible to look away, but at the same time, it's uncomfortable to watch. She's practically undressing him right there on the cobblestone pathway. He finally breaks free of her grasp and hands her shoes back to her. She holds up a thumb and finger to her ear in a 'call me'-type fashion as Blake enters the coffee shop.

"Good morning, you fabulous, gorgeous, perfect specimen," Blake says in a sing-song tone as he jumps up to sit on a tabletop and puts his feet on the chair.

"Good morning," I say through a sip of coffee.

"Not you," he adds pointedly. "The lady, of course."

"What do you want, Blake?" Jana says with an eye roll.

"Coffee, black. None of the complicated, girly crap you serve this guy. Please and thank you."

Jana pours the coffee and I turn a seat from the table Blake sits on and adjust so I am facing him.

"Who's the girl?" I ask.

"No idea," he responds in a casual tone. Typical Blake. New girl every night and doesn't even bother figuring out their names or inviting them for coffee.

It's easy to forget that he and I are the same age. Every time we step off that stage, I feel a little bit older, while somehow, the music has been a fountain of youth for him. He has kept his young, exuberant livelihood while I tinker with the idea of settling down, growing up. I love the music. I love the fans. I can't imagine my life without either, but I'm interested in seeing what else life has to offer in addition to the concerts and shows and travel.

"Are you ready?" Blake asks, pulling me out of my head and into the coffee shop. "We're already late for that interview," he adds.

He pushes himself off the table and I stand, following him to the door. We wave a goodbye to Jana and walk down the street toward the radio station headquarters, jaywalking and weaving in and out of the Boston traffic.

Chapter Eleven

We enter the radio station offices and check in with a young secretary at the front desk.

"Oh, uh, g-good mor... Good m-morning," she stammers. She stands up to greet us and knocks an open bottle of water over the desk. She corrects the bottle's position and wipes her hands on her skirt. She keeps apologizing, making it abundantly clear that she is a fan of ours who didn't anticipate being quite so starstruck.

"I mean, bands and celebrities come in here all the time, and I'm usually cool about it," she continues as she walks us down the hallway. We stop at the end of the hall and she continues to apologize.

"You're doing great," Blake says. He puts his hand on her shoulder, and the color leaves her face. It's all she can do to not pass out from excitement.

She leaves us alone and I peer through the glass in the door. The radio show host is talking, so I'm assuming he's on the air. Knocking or announcing our arrival seems intrusive if he's mid-show, so I hold off until I know he's ready for us. He fingers a few buttons on the soundboard in front of him and removes his headphones from his ears. He waves us in, and I push open the door.

"Good morning, good morning! I'm Donny Davers." He speaks through a heavy Boston accent that makes Davers sound more like Da*vahs* and extends a large hand toward us. "Of course, I know who you both are. Everybody does. I'm honored to have you here."

"Thanks for having us," I respond.

"Sure thing. Let's get started. I know you both have busy lives to get back to."

He gestures to two seats across from his and we take them. He wastes no time at all getting us set up in front of microphones, though I suppose we were late to begin with.

He plays a few commercials and jingles then starts talking to his listeners.

Being a radio host lacks appeal to me. I feed off the energy of the crowd in front of me. The better the crowd, the better I play. I'm usually hesitant to play during sound check and I'm substantially better in a show, because the energy from the crowd fuels me. Being a radio host means doing your job for fans and listeners you can't see. You can't take in their reactions. You can't get a cue from their emotions. I would have a significantly challenging time doing that.

"Well, ladies and gentlemen, do I have a treat for you. Sitting directly across from me are two of the four, previously *five*, members of the hit band Consistently Inconsistent, Xander Varro and Blake Mathews," Donny starts. The keys in front of him light up with calls the moment he says our names.

Blake and I both offer some variation of "hello" and "happy to be here" as Donny jumps right into his list of questions.

"Well, we all know the name of the band is Consistently Inconsistent. That's not news. But where does a name like that come from? There has to be a story there," Donny says, rubbing his palms together and leaning across the desk. I can smell coffee on his breath as he speaks.

Blake and I look at each other, playing a mental game of rocks, papers, scissors to determine who will answer the question. We've been asked this question countless times and have managed to leave it unanswered with every intention of keeping it that way.

The meaning behind our name has become something of an enigma for the band. We live our lives very publicly. People know things about us. The public is invited in to almost every aspect of our lives, except this. It's like a secret only we know. The kicker is, the story isn't even all that great, but it's become like a game to us to try to dodge the question.

"It's just a name," Blake finally says. "No big reveal behind it."

"Okay, okay," Donny says. "Well, you've just completed a cross country, seven-month tour. How's it feel to be home?" he asks.

"We're not quite done yet, actually," Blake jumps in. "We have one more show in New York this Saturday."

"Oh, *right,*" Donny says, "the big make-up show. Xander, how do you feel about returning to the scene of the crime?" He waves his bushy eyebrows up and down and lets out a fake laugh as he asks the question. "Last time you *attempted* to play a show in New York, it ended in fisticuffs. Are you sure you're ready to face that crowd again?"

An uncomfortable lump forms in my throat — a mix of all the things I wish I could say on the air. Rude comments, smart-ass remarks and expletives flood my thoughts all at once, but I, uncharacteristically, take the high road.

"Well, Donny, it's a new day. A new week. A new weekend. That night was in the past, am I right? I gave an apology, and we have an awesome show planned for Saturday."

Now, suddenly I'm glad I can't see the listeners, and they can't see me. But Donny can. He can read the body language I give off. My answer has a false cheerfulness to it that hides my disdain for the question, but my narrowed eyes and my tense shoulders don't hide the underlying message that he should drop the conversation.

"Glad to hear it," Donny says into the microphone. "Can you give us any insight to any plans for the show? Should we expect anything special or different?"

"We have always been about the music and not the gimmicks," Blake says. "We pride ourselves on being a talented group of guys who offer a show that consists of real instrumentals and authentic voices. So, you should expect that, because it's what we're known for and what we will continue to do. No smoke and mirrors, just the music."

"Well said, well said." Donny steers the conversation. "Do you think the recent unexpected departure of Julian Young has affected you negatively at all? He was truly a fan favorite and added so much to the music. What changes will you make for the next album to accommodate for such a massive talent loss?"

Blake and I look at each other for a moment, having another lengthy conversation using only our eyes. Neither of us knows how to answer that.

"I don't recall seeing or hearing any complaints after any shows this tour, do you, Blake?" I ask in an over-dramatic, sarcastic manner.

"No, not at all, Xander," Blake replies, matching my tone. "Look... We made some changes. Bands have changes all the time. We had to adapt to a diverse set-up and some of the songs play a little differently, but we did it. It was, overall, a fantastic tour and the fans really seemed to enjoy it. So, whether we stay four guys or five guys or thirty-six guys, we just play our music and put on the best show we have in us," Blake says with bite I didn't even know his usually relaxed self was capable of.

"All right, all right," Donny adds, holding his chubby-fingered hands up as if he is surrendering. "Let's play a track from the latest album by Consistently Inconsistent. I'm Donny Davers, and I'll be with you right after this." He jabs a few buttons with a thick finger and returns his attention to us. "Okay, so after the commercial break—"

"No, Donny, I think we're done here," Blake interrupts.

"But, I—" he insists.

Blake pushes his chair back and removes his headset, tossing it onto Donny's desk.

"You asked us to come here to talk about the music, but you failed to do that. You talked about the drama plenty but didn't ask us anything about what our future plans are, when our next tour will start, what our upcoming compilation album will consist of," Blake rattles off. "Everyone is already talking about what's happening off stage or outside the sound booth. You had the chance to talk about the music and the future and you wasted it talking about the negatives and the past. Xander can stay, but I have nothing left to say."

I remove my headset and leave it on the seat, not bothering to look back as I follow Blake down the hall. He's walking quickly ahead and uses his full body weight to throw open the doors at the front of the building.

I catch the door as it swings back and push it open again. Blake is a good distance away already as he powerwalks away from the radio station doors.

"Blake!" I yell after him, taking my steps into a light jog to catch up with him. "You okay?" I ask as I reach him.

"I'm just tired." He runs his hands through his blond hair and stares at the sky, squinting against the light of the sun.

"Maybe you should *sleep* instead of having sleepovers with random women every night," I joke, but he glares at me.

"That's not what I meant. I'm tired of people constantly asking us about the bullshit. Everyone's always bringing up the drama and the issues. There's so much more. There's so much good, but the media wants to bring everything down. We are just as good of a band, if not better, without Julian's issues holding us down." I'm not sure if he's trying to convince me or himself, but he makes a valiant effort either way.

We are still managing just fine, still selling out crowds and still selling music without Julian, but things aren't the same.

"Maybe it's time to find a replacement," I say, even though I know it's not what he wants to hear.

He raises his brows and parts his lips. He has something to say, but he just hasn't chosen the words.

"Is Julian replaceable, though?" Blake finally manages the words everyone has been thinking. "He's a better musician than both of us combined. You know it, and I do too."

I press my lips into a hard line and nod my head. He's one hundred percent correct. Julian was a hell of an artist. That's the thing, though. We're talking about a throwback version of a man who doesn't exist anymore and hasn't in a long time. I'm not sure Julian has even picked up an instrument since he picked up his drug habit. He put one addiction down for another, and he chose wrong.

"So, we stay with four then," I say. "We choose here and now that we are going forward with four people and we vow to make the best possible record. Starting soon... Starting this week if we have to. We put our heads together and come up with some new stuff that sends Consistently Inconsistent in a new direction."

"We stay with four," Blake repeats and nods in agreement, then extends a hand toward me. I take his palm in a hard, firm handshake.

Julian and Blake were close. We all were, but they had a specific bond, especially on stage. Their tastes and styles complemented each other perfectly. I would like to believe that deep down, Blake knows the best thing to do for ourselves and our music is too move forward without him, but I know a fraction of Blake's mind is still holding on to the idea that Julian would join us on stage again, and things would go back to how they used to be—but they won't.

They can't.

We left the Consistently Inconsistent of old in the rear view of that tour bus when we left seven months ago — and that included leaving Julian behind too.

* * * *

"Has anybody seen Xander?" I hear Cooper say through a frustrated exhale as I enter the room.

"Never mind, then," he adds. "Varro, I know how much money you make. I know you can afford a damn alarm clock. Let's try to make a real attempt at being on time every once in a while, okay?"

"You got it, Coop," I respond, placing my guitar case down at my feet. The guys give a round of waves and nods and I sit on a stool at one side of the studio. I am the last to arrive to our meeting — this comes as a surprise to exactly no one — where the band is getting together to go over some newer, unreleased music and ideas for a compilation album with some other local well-known musicians for a charity that Cooper had volunteered us for.

"Anyway, as I was saying. The set list for New York should include *Without a Doubt* and *Delayed Reactions*," Cooper says.

"You really want us to try *Delayed Reactions* again? Blake says with unmasked concern. I don't have to look up to know all eyes are on me.

"Xander," Cooper says as he clears his throat, "can you successfully make it through your own song on stage in New York?" His voice is pointed and sarcastic.

Ready to have the whole event put behind me, I nod in agreement. When that particular song broke me down that night on stage, I was sixty percent drunk and forty percent emotional, which made for a bad combination. I had just been hit with a truck load of information I didn't expect, and that song made the whole situation solidified and real. But the truth was, all our best songs came from defeat and heartbreak and the emotions that coincided.

A huge part of our music was born in moments of trial and despair and *that's* what makes them great. I wasn't going to cut out an emotional, makes-you-think song just because the lyrics didn't apply to me anymore. They apply to somebody somewhere, and if I'm not singing it for me, I'll sing it for them. That's why we make this music, so people can relate to it and need it and grow with it.

"Yeah, I think it's a good idea." It's the most convincing line I can muster.

"Well, that's settled then," Cooper says, wiping one palm against the other.

My phone vibrates in my pocket. Cooper is talking, and I should be listening, but I can't because Natalie's name is on the screen and now that's where all of my already-short attention span is.

Cooper is still addressing the band. My mind goes in and out of the conversation, picking up select words as he speaks.

I type in a message and hit send, hiding my phone down by my side like a student trying not to get caught texting under the desk by a teacher.

"Got all that, Xander?" Cooper says. I shove my phone in the pocket of my jeans.

"Yup. Sounds great," I say without a clue of what I'm agreeing too. I smile a foreign but genuine smile — the direct result of the texts she sent — but the looks on the faces of my bandmates say I shouldn't be smiling at all.

The band is staring at me and Blake is shaking his head no so hard he makes *me* dizzy. He was trying to cover my ass, but I missed the signal.

Cooper crosses his arms and taps his foot. At this moment, he couldn't look any more like my father. Then again, disappointment was the only expression my father ever wore when it came to me, so maybe that's why this is so familiar.

"Let's take a walk." Cooper says, already headed out of the room. Theo accompanies the exit with an ominous 'dun dun dunnnn' on his keyboard, I raise him a middle finger and walk out of the door.

Cooper is leaning against the wall in the hallway. He hands me a stack of papers and I eye them quickly, flipping through each page. They are the numbers from the shows, the tour and overall averages of ticket sales, merchandise sales and other important numbers.

"These aren't bad numbers," I say, but it's more of a question.

"They're not bad, but they're our worst to date. That means in this tour we went from above average to even more average — and what comes next?"

I scratch at my chin where the stubble has grown. My razor has been neglected since well before the New York show, but the look is growing on me — figuratively and literally.

"We need to start recording again, Xander, and soon. We need some fresh, new tracks and give the fans something to care about again. They're growing tired of Consistently Inconsistent's current set list and the same songs that play repeatedly on their apps or whatever the hell they're listening on."

"Blake and I just had that conversation this morning," I say. "We agree. We need to make some changes."

"Good. That's your circus in there. You're the ringleader. So, go in and tell them. After the New York show this weekend, we get together and brainstorm some fresh, innovative ideas. We don't leave until we're finished, and we're not finished until we have something that resembles the start of a new album," he says like a drill sergeant training a new recruit.

My head drops as he speaks. We just got off a lengthy tour. We're supposed have some variation of time off, and now Cooper is going to lock us behind closed doors until we force music from our tired fingers. I was looking forward to getting to know who I can be without the music for a bit and getting to know Natalie in the meantime.

I dug my fingernails into the palms of my hands as I clench my fists. I'm frustrated, but I do understand it. I release my grip and wipe my hands on the front of my jeans.

"Okay, let's go talk to the guys," I say, and we get back to the studio where Blake, Theo and Dom are making sounds that will, hopefully, eventually make a recordable song.

As expected, the guys were just as disgruntled about the extra work we were about to face as I was. The music has to come first, and we all know and understand that.

When we've hit slumps in the past, we've taken a road trip to nowhere. We pack up the tour bus, *again*, get on it, drive around and play music on our instrument of choice and jot down lyrical ideas as they came to us. Our second album, which is still our best-selling album to date, was created this way, so we return to the practice every once in a while, when it was necessary.

Blake and I walk the city streets back the direction of our apartments.

"Whelp, here's to hoping this isn't a massive waste of time," he says.

"That can be our album title," I say through a laugh. "Here's to hoping this isn't a massive waste of time." I expand my fingers and move my hands in a dramatic, arched motion.

We both laugh harder than necessary at the comment and continue our walk.

Blake throws a few lines of a new song idea at me and we bounce critiques back and forth at each other, trying to make a four-minute tune out of a three-second sentence.

Cooper believes in us and wants to see us succeed, more so than we already have, and we wouldn't have gotten this far without him. But there are times that I think he believes we just come up with lyrics on demand, and that's not the case. We write a word or two that becomes a sentence then that sentence becomes a verse and those words prompt a chorus and maybe a bridge and music has to be added. *Then* it's a song.

If we're lucky, that song is tied in with a handful of others and becomes an album. This isn't always the case though. Between the four of us — previously five of us — over time we've probably had more tried-and-failed songs than successful ones. We have dozens of notebooks that hold ideas and lyrics and songs that never made the cut. We brainstorm the entire walk back to my apartment, and truly only come up with one idea worth holding on to, but it's one more than we started with.

Chapter Twelve

The elevator to my apartment is vacant and waiting at the ground floor when I arrive. My shoulder rests against the elevator wall as it rises through the building. The doors part at my floor and I step forward, pulling my keys from my pocket. Natalie is leaning against the doorframe with her hands in her pockets, staring out of the window at the end of the hallway. She's facing away from me and I don't want to startle her. I make my way toward her, tapping my knuckles against the wall as I walk down the hallway, though I'm sure I am over-thinking it. Her intuition and sharpened senses leave her more perceptive than I could ever hope to be.

As she leans into the doorframe of my apartment, she places her hand flat against the painted drywall, feeling the Morse-code-like message I send her. She turns her head slightly over her shoulder. Before she turns completely, my arms are around her waist and my nose is in her hair.

I kiss behind her ear, down her neck, and she dips her head backward into my chest, exposing her neck to my mouth and touch. The lips and mouths we are blessed with are made to communicate in more ways than one, and I have said more in these simple kisses than all the words I could ever hope to say combined.

I place my hands at her hips and turn her so she's facing me. She presses her lips at the area where my facial hair meets my Adam's apple and I tilt my head back in anticipation. My gaze falls downward again. I lean my forehead against hers then place my lips on hers and our tongues meet. I don't bother to part from her as I try to unlock the door while still keeping her against me.

We enter the apartment, still wrapped around each other. I slide both my hands down her back, stopping where her thighs begin and hold her tight to me, lifting her off the floor and setting her on the counter. She leans into my chest and drapes her arms over my shoulders. When we part, I lean my head in close to her chest, letting her heartbeat speak to me.

She passes her hands through my hair. I step backward and move my fingers up to my hair where her hands just were. Taking a lock of hair in one hand, I use my fingers like scissors as if to cut it. She shakes her head in rejection, then reaches for a marker about arm's distance away and writes *Don't you dare* on a paper towel, holding it under her eyes so I can read it.

A thought crosses my mind. The corners of my mouth break the plane and gradually turn up into a mischievous smile.

I hold up one finger and leave the kitchen. She spins herself around and sits cross-legged on the cool granite countertop. Her mouth opens in protest when I return holding two black helmets.

She presses her hands over her eyes and shakes her head back and forth. I wrap my hands around her wrists, removing them from her eyes, laughing and nodding a dramatic yes.

She takes the paper towel in her hands again and writes a new message.

I have never been on a motorcycle.

"There's a first time for everything," I say out loud, and she backs away, laughing and pushing herself backward farther onto the counter. I grab her thighs, pulling her back toward me and she lets out a combination of a laugh and a screech.

I wrap one arm around her back, the other under her legs, and carry her out of the door.

We're both laughing so hard that we can barely breathe, and we lack grace — as I attempt to carry her over the threshold and close the door behind us and she kicks the wall, hard, and accidentally drops one of the helmets. A neighbor down the hall peeks out of the door and glares at us as we pass, which only makes us laugh harder as we head toward the parking garage.

My motorcycle sits in its usual spot. Its pristine, sparkling silver body glistens like it has never seen the light of day. The seating is a royal blue leather that matches the color of the rims in the tires. My face lights up like I'm reconnecting with an old friend who I haven't seen in decades.

She takes a deep breath, puts the helmet on and gets onto the bike behind me.

She's terrified.

Her heart beats against my back and I can hear every one of the breaths she takes, despite the thickness of the helmets. I've worn skinny jeans that don't hug me as tight as she does now. She presses her thighs against me and her forearms clench at my rib bones as if she's practicing the Heimlich maneuver. She holds on as tightly as she is capable of, and we haven't even left the apartment parking garage.

A small voice inside me tells me I should be a good guy and not force her on a ride she doesn't want to take, but the roar of the motorcycle echoing through the concrete walls and emptiness of the garage drowns out that voice. She's going to love it. I just know it. The bike purrs as I back out from the spot and drive the city streets at a reasonable, non-frightening speed.

The farther we get from the city, the more her grip loosens. She's learning to love it, and learning to trust me, all at the same time.

There is one area I love to ride through, outside the city just a short drive away from the city lights. She tightens her grip slightly as we enter a tunnel. We go from the dark sky overhead to a tunnel that's so well-lit it could trick you into thinking it was mid-day. The brick patterns in the walls blur together as we pass through, and the world goes dark again as we come out the other side. Little by little, I pick up speed, hoping she's starting to enjoy the ride.

She keeps her grip at my waist but leans her body backward, parting from mine. It is almost as if she were trying to look at the sky as we flew underneath it, letting the ends of her hair flow with the wind. A fraction of me wishes she wouldn't do that, and the rest of me never wants her to stop. I can tell in the way her weight has shifted behind me that she's let go of her fears and was enjoying the ride, which is, in the end, all I really wanted.

We cruise around the open, vacant roads with no real destination. Occasionally I stop to give her a thumbs-up and she returns the signal. She flips the mask of the helmet and her mouth is smiling widely, but her eyes are smiling even more so.

It is getting late, and the way the clouds move over the moon, I worry the weather will not cooperate with us for long.

We drive the same roads we took here, but in the opposite direction. We're still a good distance from the tunnel when I feel a raindrop at my wrists and neck, and another, followed by a handful more. The sky above us opens and the rain starts pouring down. It's enough to ensure a less-than-dry ride home, but not enough to obscure my vision or render the ride unsafe.

The rain seeps through my clothes, but I continue the drive, taking the corners slow. Natalie has shifted so she's against me tighter than at any other point of the ride. Her helmet is jammed in between my shoulder blades as she holds tight. The rain continues to fall, but we're given a few moments break from the weather under the shelter of the tunnel. The light and warmth are short-lived though, and we exit the other side and the moisture hits us all over again.

As I pull into the uncovered guest parking spaces at Natalie's apartment, I kill the engine and take a deep breath. How mad is she going to be at me for not only taking her on a motorcycle ride she was against, but doing it in inclement weather, leaving her hair and clothes soaked through?

She swings one leg over the seat of the motorcycle and stands in the parking lot in the pouring rain. I get off the bike and turn to face her. My hair falls wet around my face as I slide off my helmet, then she does the same, placing the helmet on the seat of the bike.

Her saturated hair falls the length of her back and her clothes cling tightly to her skin. She leans her head back and puts her arms out by her side. The cold raindrops fall on her face and chest and she welcomes them. Closing the distance between us, I take a few steps forward, and she brings her gaze to mine.

She reaches both hands up and places them on either side of my face. Her palms are wet and cold and send a shiver down my spine. She beams this toothy grin and lets out a laughter-like sound before standing on her toes and pressing her lips against mine. We stand in the parking lot in the increasingly unforgiving rain and cold and darkness, but all we feel is each other.

We take the stairs to her apartment and she heads to the linen closet and returns with towels. She uses her fingers to shake droplets from her hair, then wraps a towel around the ends, squeezing the water into the terrycloth fabric. I wipe down my arms and hair and the back of my neck, but my clothes are soaked and I can't imagine Natalie has anything my size lying around.

Her fingers are cold in mine as she takes my hand and leads me to the laundry room. She takes handfuls of the hem of my shirt in her hands. The fabric is slick and stubborn, sticking as she slides it over my body, revealing my chest, abdomen and all the artwork permanently inked across them. She tosses the saturated fabric into the dryer. She raises an eyebrow and bites her fingernails as I unbutton my jeans. The denim material clings to me and resists removal, but I succeed, stepping out of one pant leg then the other. I twist them into a ball and toss them in the dryer.

I twirl one finger in the air in slow, dramatic fashion. She rolls her eyes and turns around — though I truthfully wouldn't have cared either way. I lob the black cotton material into the drum of the dryer, and before she can turn around, I wrap my arms around her, hugging her from behind.

She slides her hands backward, her fingers at my thighs where she finds the material of the towel wrapped around my waist.

I pull her shirt up over her head, the same way she did for me, and throw it into the machine. I slide my fingers into the hooks at the back of her bra and I unclip it. I wrap a towel around her upper body, and as she turns to face me, I turn away from her, looking the other direction to allow her to remove the rest of her clothing.

Wrapped in towels, we sit on the floor of Natalie's laundry room, leaning against the washing machine and I listen to the hum that the dryer makes. She holds up one finger and leaves the room. She returns with a blue dry-erase marker and some paper towels. She lies down on the linoleum floor and rests her head in my lap.

She opens the marker and draws a large Tic Tac Toe board on the front of the dryer, then hands me the marker. I draw a large X in one corner and she draws an O. We go back and forth in this style until we have filled the squares and there is no winner. We play a few rounds, then move on to hangman.

After a few outcomes of Natalie kicking my stick-figure ass, she writes *Tonight was terrifying, yet breathtaking. Thank you.*

I nod an acknowledgment and she wipes the words away. She picks up the marker and pens, *What are you afraid of?*

No immediate answer comes to mind. I'm certainly not fearless, but nothing truly interesting surfaces. There were many years that performing terrified me so to the point of illness, but I got used to that. I'm not the biggest fan of tight spaces. It wouldn't bother me if I never saw another snake again. There was a time, recently in fact, that I would have said becoming a father is something I fear immensely.

I didn't have the greatest role model in that area. My father hasn't been a part of my life for some time. If I had a dollar for every time he'd told me I was wasting my time, that I had no real talent, or that I would never make it in the music world, I'd never have to play another show. He had zero faith in me or my abilities. I made it despite him—maybe even to spite him.

My mother, on the other hand, has always supported my decision to stick with music. She was more than enough parent for me. We didn't need my father. He didn't want to remain faithful or supportive to us, so we got by without him. I fear being a father because my own father can barely call himself one, but my mother was so incredible that I know I learned from the best. Either way, those fears were years away, and not something I have to worry about currently or burden Natalie with.

There is one thing, though, that I have never really told anyone. I take the marker from her and I start to write.

I've always wanted to play piano or the keyboard at a show, but I've never done it live. Too nervous. She reads the words and wipes them away, replacing them with her thoughts.

Do it! Trade. One motorcycle ride for one piano song.

I'll think about it, I write under her statement, and the buzzer from the dryer sounds.

Chapter Thirteen

Prophecies had started hosting karaoke night a few months back, a ploy to get more people in the door on Tuesdays—and I'd completely forgotten about it.

Natalie sits across from me, sipping red wine and watching each person take the stage. She laughs at the antics, those who get really into their song and dance across the stage. I watch her watch them, her expression changing every so often.

She holds up one finger, her mouth forms the words "one second," and she walks off to the karaoke host, then runs through the song list like a flip book. The host hands her a piece of paper and she jots down her song choice. She gives him a thumbs up and skips back to our table.

"What'd you sign up for?" I ask, and she shrugs her shoulders. *Ahhh, it's a secret.*

"So, how does this work?" I ask. "Signing a song? Now *that's* badass." I take a sip of my whiskey and she smiles through her sip of wine.

"All right, ladies and gentlemen," the karaoke host announces. "We have a treat for you! Prophecies' karaoke has a celebrity in the house!"

The sip of whiskey I take travels the wrong way as I swallow, my throat and nose burn.

"Not a chance," I say to her through a harsh cough.

She nods enthusiastically and stands up, tugging my hand hard, pulling me toward the stage.

Everyone is cheering, clapping and yelling my name. Natalie encourages them, waving her hands and twirling her wrist, motivating them to keep it up, ensuring I won't turn back now.

"All right, all right," I say. "One song." I jump up onto the stage and take the microphone. "What did she choose?" I ask the DJ.

"Hope you like nineties boy bands, my friend," he says through a toothy grin. I shake my head at her, but I'm smiling too.

She bounces up and down on her tiptoes. Her hair falls around her face, framing her elaborate smile.

And I do it. I sing the song she chose. I dance the worst moves I can produce, because I know it will make her laugh — and she does. I can't hear it over the music, but her eyes light up and she throws her head back and I can picture the sound.

The song ends and people cheer and clap me on the shoulder as I make my way back to her. She wraps her arms around my neck, still laughing, and I kiss her, her smile against mine.

When we're back at the table she signs *You were amazing!* patting the air, and I read the words as they cross her lips.

"I don't know about that," I say. "Can I be honest?"

I wonder how much I should keep to myself and how much I should share. She nods. "I almost changed the location of our date tonight when I realized it was karaoke night. I wasn't sure how you'd feel about it... You know...because of the music or whatever."

She taps the pen on the table for a second and writes, *I love music. Really, really loud music. This is actually perfect. I can't hear it, but I can feel it.*

And in this second, reading the words she wrote and seeing the smile that crosses her face, I know I am in love with her.

Her smile grows and her cheeks go pink like she's reading my mind — or maybe the same thought is crossing hers, but only for an instant. She's removed from the moment by her ringing cell phone as it dances on the tabletop, a light flashing along with the vibration.

Her expression hardens, her smile falls flat. Both eyes darken as she peers up at me over the top of her phone. The atmosphere shifts and my stomach drops. That look is all too familiar, worn by the many people I've pissed off or disappointed. My mind starts working, trying to think of what I could have possibly done now, before she has to tell me.

She slides her phone across the table and I hesitate to pick it up. Her screen is open to an article stamped with the photo of us from outside my apartment. Her in my oversized T-shirt, her legs mostly bare and her head tilted back in a laugh. She's not laughing now.

She reaches across the table, swiping across to screencaps someone has sent her of the comments left under the article and picture.

She's probably only in it for the money.

Won't last long. Xander and Mariah belong together.

Xander will get bored and dump her in no time.
He can do better.

"I told you to ignore this stuff." It's the first thought that comes to my crowded mind. She rolls her eyes.

"How am I supposed to do that?" She mouths as she signs. She signs faster than usual, leaning toward me as she talks, her eyes just as expressive as her hands, so that even if I had no idea what she was saying, her body language gets the message across.

"I do." I shrug my shoulders, but they feel heavier than normal.

Our conversation was limited, both as I paid our tab and now, while we wait on the sidewalk for the car I've ordered to take her home.

I take out my phone and type in a message.

It isn't always like this.

You can't even step outside your apartment for fifteen minutes without cameras in your face and in your business, she types back. *And just for the record, it isn't about the money. I don't care that you're a celebrity or whatever. Honestly, I wish you weren't.*

I think back on the comments under the photo.

I know that. I've never thought that, I send.

I have worked hard for everything I have ever had. I've never had anything handed to me, I've never wanted anything handed to me. She slides her phone into her pocket.

Turning toward her, I place one hand at her back, pulling her close to me.

"Come to New York with me." She still hasn't answered my last proposition regarding this, but I know my chances are getting slimmer.

She furrows her forehead and purses her lips.

"I'll show you. It's not as bad as it seems. Our worlds don't have to be so different."

She looks at me, her eyes downcast and unsure. Her tight-pressed lips stay ironed flat.

A little bit of time is all I need to prove to her that one of two things will happen. *One, it won't be as bad as she thinks, or two, she will get used to it.*

But the car pulls to the curb, and she kisses me — a kiss that's barely there, as light as a breath of air but holds the weight of goodbye and goodnight. I would open the door for her, but my hands are full, holding my own heart, offering it to her.

She backs away, her fingertips trailing down my arms until she parts, still withholding her answer behind her enchanting eyes and ambiguous smile.

I wave to the car, and she leans forward, breathing on the glass, leaving a fog through which she drags her finger spelling out one simple word.

Maybe.

* * * *

For Natalie, the week consisted of culinary classes during the day and work at night. My schedule was inundated with band rehearsals and prep for the New York show.

Our schedules were completely opposite, and the free nights I did have, she was usually bartending. I have tried to visit her at The Rock Room, but this presents many challenges. Me hanging out at the bar of a music venue tends to be a small show in and of itself. The buzz and crowds that flocked around me the moment I step foot into The Rock Room caused Natalie noticeable distress, so I made myself scarce.

She's still not convinced I can keep her out of the spotlight. I can tell she enjoys spending time with me behind closed doors — when we're at my apartment, or hers, in a place where we can forget the rest of the world exists. But when it comes to the public, the never-ending stares and people approaching at various moments asking for photographs and autographs makes her hate going out — or even taking the chance.

I was hoping to see her before we left for New York, but we get on the bus any minute. I hoped since Natalie was supposed to have the day off that she would come see us off, but she had plans with Kelly and their family. I look around the parking lot, hoping she'll make it after all, but the only cars in sight are the ones hired by Cooper and the rest of the band. I type a short message.

We're getting on the bus.

She doesn't reply. At the center of the bus, I take a seat and turn up the volume on my headphones until the sound drowns out the voice inside my head that keeps telling me she's not coming.

"Back on board far sooner than expected," Blake says as he jumps into the leather chair next to me on the tour bus.

I nod my head and remove one headphone bud from the ear closest to him.

"You ready to be back in New York?" he asks with concern.

"Do I have a choice?" I ask, my eyes still fixed out of the window, hanging on to an inkling of hope that Natalie might show. "I was really hoping she would come," I say, talking to myself, but out loud.

"I was hoping she would bring Kelly," Blake adds, taking the last sip of an energy drink and crushing the can in his hand.

"You don't ever get tired of getting rejected by Kelly? I mean, she's been saying no since like seventh grade," I say through a laugh.

"All in good time, my friend. She will eventually come around then regret the years she politely declined," he says. "Anyway, man, I hope you two figure this out. Natalie seems to have brought you to a really good place." He claps a hand against my shoulder and pushes himself out of the chair. He heads toward the back of the tour bus.

My phone vibrates in my pocket. The screen has Natalie's picture with a box that reads one new video message.

Returning my other headphone back to my ear, I turn up the volume and press play.

She's sitting on her bed in a tank top and shorts with her hair flowing over both shoulders. She waves to the camera then leans forward and clicks a few buttons. Music plays through the speakers—my music. The guitar solo that plays at first is Blake, but then I accompany him, then can hear Dominic on the drums and Theo keys a few notes on the piano. She stares into the camera and where the lyrics usually start, there is nothing. My lips part instinctively to lip sync the lyrics—but it's purely instrumental.

As the music plays, she signs what I imagine are the words to the song. Some of the signs I recognize but learn some new ones as I match them up to the words of my own song. It's so beautiful, the way her hands do this impeccable dance. I've sung this piece thousands of times, but I've never seen it done this intricately. I'm completely taken by the video and the girl in it, and I watch it over and over again.

Making it had to be a challenge. Since she can't physically hear the music, I wonder how she has figured out exactly when and where to sign each word.

That was beautiful. You are beautiful. How did you do it? I type.

A magician never reveals their methods, she responds. *Just joking... I found this while I was on the Internet and I figured I'd try my hand at it, no pun intended.*

She sends a link to a karaoke-type video with the instrumental background and the lyrics flowing across the screen, lighting up in yellow where each word is intended to be sung.

I think you might actually do it better than I do, I type in and hit send. A few moments later, my phone buzzes with a response.

I thought about what you said. Silence and sound can complement each other. Our worlds don't have to be so different. I don't want them to be.

Three dots float across the screen as she continues to type, then... *I'll see you tomorrow.*

The sigh of relief I exhale echoes through the otherwise-silent bus.

* * * *

The airport is alive with rushed travelers, drop-offs and pickups as well as security screaming into the windows of people who are parked when they should be moving along.

Natalie steps through the airport doors, bag in hand, ready to start our New York weekend together, and it is like seeing her for the first time all over again. I have to do a double take, because I can't believe she flew out here. I was worried she would change her mind.

The driver of the hired car takes her bag and I pull her into me, kissing her forehead before we climb into the back of the car. We sit close together in the back seat where our hello kiss lasts the entire duration of the ride.

We reach our destination and enter the hotel. The elevator we step into is a transparent glass box that looks out over the city as it rises higher and higher until it brings us to the top floor of the sky-rise hotel. Natalie's eyes are wide as she looks out and takes in the cityscape. The elevator stops and the doors open, but she's so captivated by the mile-long view the elevator has to offer that she doesn't step off it. I lean against the door, buying her a few more moments of the staggering vista. She turns to me with wide eyes and an even wider smile, and we make our way to the suite.

The hotel room is a bright white with floor-to-ceiling windows, much like the ones in my apartment. One wall of the suite has wine bottles that lay horizontally on a ladder-type shelf, spanning the distance of the wall. The bed is an oversized king with dozens of pillows and a deep purple decorative fabric over the end. The view from the window fits the city so perfectly that it appears artificial or painted into the background. Her eyes continue to grow brighter as she looks around the suite. She takes the pen and hotel stationery from the bedside desk.

This is all way too much, she jots down quickly. It isn't nearly enough, but she seems pleased, and her happiness and comfort are the only thing that matters this weekend. Well, that is always priority, but this weekend in particular.

She has made it abundantly clear that she fears the life I live—the shows, the parties, the cameras and the lack of privacy. She doesn't want any part of it, but she's willing to try, for me, so I'm going to show her there is nothing to worry about. I only have forty-eight hours to accomplish that.

Though I'm tempted to stay in this room, with her, I have to head to the venue for sound check. I inform her that I will be sending a car to pick her up in the lobby before the show. She plans on taking a nap, since she was up early for her flight and getting ready for the show, so my absence works out. My lips linger on hers too long as I kiss her goodbye and close the door behind me, wishing I had nowhere to be but beside her in the elaborate hotel bedding.

* * * *

For the first time—literally, this has to be the first time in eleven years—I arrive before Cooper or any other member of the band.

I pull up a stool to Theo's keyboard and punch a few keys with my fingertips. The sound echoes through the unoccupied area. I love the sound of the keyboard, the way it feels beneath my fingertips, and how my shoulders and muscles react to the unfamiliar motions. For most of my life I have been a singer and a guitar player, but I truly wish I had started on the piano or keyboard sooner than I had.

For the most part, I tend to be musically inclined. It didn't take me long to make sounds that resemble music on the keyboard since I started practicing over the last half-dozen months, but somehow, I still feared anyone knowing I was trying something new.

Assessing my small audience, I look around the venue. There are some staff members and stage crew, but nobody I know or have to impress, so I play the song I've been working on.

The notes follow one after another with no interruptions or missed keys, like I have been doing this for years. The beat is slow at first, but then grows louder and builds into this explosion of large, booming notes, then recedes again to a twinkling quiet and fades out altogether.

There is a slow, dramatic clap that rings through the empty venue, following the completion of the last note.

"You should try that live sometime," a deep, familiar male voice says. I turn ever so slightly as he speaks. Out of the corner of my eye, I see a large, purple-and-black-inked tiger tattoo that spans the length of the calf of the person the voice belongs to.

"What are you doing here, Julian?" I ask. It is not a malicious, sarcastic question, but it certainly isn't excitement in my tone. I was genuinely surprised to see him in New York, so the question was warranted. What *is* he doing here?

"I was in New York meeting up with a friend. Then I heard you guys would be here. Can we talk?" he asks. The voice he uses doesn't belong to him. I remember very clearly who Julian was before the drugs and the problems. He was a crowd pleaser with a 'zero fucks given' attitude and a booming, captivating voice that demanded the attention of everyone who could hear it.

Julian Young, unlike the rest of us, was no stranger to the spotlight before he became part of the band. He spent our younger years having his name more recognized as one of the best young football players to come out of Massachusetts than as a musician, but it wasn't that way for long. He is shorter than me but noticeably thicker. He managed to keep his athletic build over the years, despite the poor eating and exercise habits that plagued us while we were on the road. He used to be the kind of guy who carried a football everywhere he went for no apparent reason at all and wore high school football T-shirts daily, even years after we walked the stage at graduation. He did, eventually, realize his future was in music rather than football and gave the band his full attention before going off the rails completely and walking away without either.

There was a reason he was a fan favorite. He was noticeable and carefree and now, well… Now he stands in front of me with his head down, making him appear eight inches tall with a voice that's quiet and fades out faster than the song I just played. I nod, then sit at the edge of the stage. He takes a seat next to me but doesn't speak at first, like he's rehearsing what he's about to say in his head before saying the words out loud.

"I don't know who I am anymore, man. Without the music, I mean. I don't know how to go forward without it. I hit rock bottom, and maybe that's not such a bad thing," Julian says, without stopping for breaths. "Cooper once told me the farther down the ladder you go, the farther apart the rungs get, until eventually you're standing at the bottom, looking up — and there are no rungs at all. He was right. And now I'm at the bottom with nothing to reach for, no place to put my foot or pull myself up to get back on top where I was." His voice catches as he tries to explain the way he feels without the music — without us.

Julian speaks, and I listen and yet, I have nothing to say. Music and lyrics are where all my problems, advice, solutions and words into music usually end up and I am terrible at comforting people. Self-destruction and making things exponentially worse than they need to be are my most frequently traveled roads. I am the very last person on this earth I would seek help from, and here he is asking.

"I need to know something, Xander." His usually steady, musically trained vocal chords tremble as he speaks. "I need to know if I should be finding every single way I can to get on with my life and leave music behind, or if you think there is a chance I can get back on that stage with you and the guys again."

His eyes are wide and pleading. His shoulders sink as he says the words out loud, because he knows the reality is that he will never again be part of Consistently Inconsistent. His hands shake, and I can't help but wonder if he is in withdrawal. Or how long he's been clean for – or if he's clean at all.

I run my fingers through the roots of my hair and take a handful of it. This isn't something I should even be talking to him about. Blake and Cooper and the guys and I had already pretty much set in stone our going forward as a four-man group.

"Julian, I don't know, man. You know how challenging it was for you to be on tour with us. This isn't a good lifestyle for you anymore. There are far too many triggers and opportunities to screw up and… Maybe it's time to think about going a different direction. For your own sake," I say, looking anywhere but at him. I can't look at him. Not like this. If someone told me tomorrow that my music career was over, the breath would be stolen from my chest and the light in my eyes would dim. And I, much like Julian, would become a shell of the person I once was.

He nods a few times, slowly and exaggerated. Without another word, without looking back, he pushes himself off the stage and walks across the main floor and out of the venue doors.

Chapter Fourteen

The lights beam down from above me as I lie down at the edge of the stage. That conversation was painful. Somewhere under the layers of poor choices and bad decisions there is a good guy in Julian, but there are too many layers to get past at this point to find who he used to be.

"Xander?" Cooper calls from somewhere backstage. The wood of the stage shifts beneath me as he approaches. His head blocks out the light above me as he leans forward and looks at me.

"Please, please, for the love of all things holy, *please* tell me you are not drunk, high, inebriated, impaired or another other variation of 'under the influence' that would render you unable to perform tonight." His forehead is sweating, and his words come out faster than the Kentucky Derby horses when the gates open.

"I haven't been this sober since middle school," I reply.

He places his hand against his chest and takes a deep breath. "You're killing me, Varro. Seriously, I think I just had a heart attack. I saw you lying there and I figured, *great*, he's plastered, as if things couldn't get any worse." He taps his foot against the stage. I push myself up into a sitting position and the room spins momentarily as my equilibrium adapts to my upright position and my eyes adjust to the dimmer lighting.

"What's going on, Coop?" I ask. He's stressed beyond measure but hasn't told me why.

"Come on backstage. We'll all talk there."

Blake and Dominic sit behind the curtains as Cooper and I enter the room. Cooper gestures for me to sit in one of the chairs and I do so. His lips are pressed into a hard, unreadable line.

"You guys know that Theo was raised by his grandmother. She's the only family he has — and vice versa. Well, she's in the hospital back home. The doctors are thinking a heart attack, but whatever it was, she's not doing well. Theo hopped on a flight a little bit ago, and he obviously won't be back for the show."

Blake, Dom and I exchange worried looks. Of course, we feel for Theo and his grandmother and that is our first concern, but we all have the same second thought. How in the *hell* are we supposed to play this *particular* show — of all shows — with only three musicians? And it's not like we can cancel it. This is a make-up show as it is.

"So, what do we do?" Blake asks.

I drop my head in my hands and my hair falls around my fingers.

"We let Julian play the show," I say. The eyes on me feel like lasers against my skin. "He's here. He's in New York."

"Sober?" Cooper asks.

"He's here?" Blake chimes in with a hint of excitement.

"Yes. I saw him earlier. I don't know if he's sober. He wants to play. He said he misses the music. I told him I didn't think it was a good idea for him to be a part of the music scene right now, but I don't know. It is our last show for a while. It could be a good test..." I suggest, trying to convince myself this is a good idea just as much, if not more than, I was trying to convince Cooper.

"I'll get him on the phone," Cooper says, and leaves us behind. We take the stage for sound check and do our best with what we have to work with.

Sound check usually isn't the best music we've ever played anyway, but with only three of us, we sounded hollow and light. I couldn't even get into the groove of our songs without the keyboard or occasional guitar riffs Theo provides. He plays both instruments. Having him absent is a huge loss.

I consider doing it myself, but my keyboard skills just aren't there yet. There is only one other musician who could switch back and forth between instruments as seamlessly as Theo does, and with any luck, he will be walking through those doors any moment.

The idea of having Julian back on stage with us leaves me equal parts nervous and excited. No one has heard or seen him play in more than seven months, and even before that, he was missing sound checks and practices.

Personally, I am apprehensive about his ability to play a flawless show. On the other hand, there is something energizing about the possibility of having him back. He was part of the original band. That, and he was a fan favorite from the beginning. Many people were rooting against us, expecting us to fail after his departure, but we held it together. The New York crowd would certainly be in for a treat if they got to see him re-emerge to the music scene.

Blake plays me into a number we usually don't rehearse, but I go with it anyway. Dominic keeps pace on his drums and Blake plays his part perfectly. I strum a segment of the song that I haven't played in years, but I hope my fingers remember it in case I have to play tonight.

We continue with the song, and near Theo's usual masterpiece, where he wears his guitar over his shoulder and switches from his keyboard to his guitar mid-song, pumps out an inexplicably glorious guitar solo then returns his focus to his keyboard.

I am unsure what we will do to fill that void, but I continue with the vocals, and just when I think everything is about to fall flat and empty, Theo's guitar solo rips through the empty venue. It almost sounds so perfect, so unblemished and exact, that I assume it's prerecorded — set in at the exact second we needed it. I turn around in confusion, but it's not Theo's solo at all.

Julian executes the melodic passage perfectly, like he had never put the guitar down at all, but even more than that, he finishes the solo and turns into the keyboard, picking up the keystrokes that belong to the song as well.

We finish and I return the mic to its holder. Blake places his guitar on its stand and Dom, Blake and I just stare at Julian in disbelief.

"What?" he asks as casually ever. That one word, that one slightly sarcastic, overly relaxed word, was a portal leading to the version of Julian we used to know. The music still lives in him.

But does the personality?

Can we possibly make it back to where we used to be?

The stage crew is rearranging the stage, setting up for a local New York band that will open for us. We stand backstage, going over set lists and seeing if anything needs to be substituted for an older song Julian may have more practice with, but he seems to be keeping up just fine. He plays and practices so perfectly that it was as if he'd never missed this tour.

The excitement in every move Blake makes is tangible. He is happy to have Julian back. In fact, Blake seemed uncharacteristically down for a good portion of the tour, and I assumed it was because of Julian's absence. Having Julian backstage with us sparks a flame in Blake that I haven't seen in months.

I stand in the wings of the stage by myself and check my phone to see if I have any messages from Natalie. Nothing yet, but she should be arriving any moment. I pace back and forth at the stage exit, running through my songs, lyrics and most importantly, what I was going to say to address this crowd — the crowd I walked out on only a few weeks ago.

Julian approaches and stands a few feet away from me, rocking on his heels in a way that makes me feel uneasy, like he's trying not to get too close.

"Hey, man," he says, "I just wanted to say thanks for all this. I know it must not of have been easy for you to invite me back after everything I've put the band through. I know I wasn't there for you all last time, but things are changing. I'm changing."

"Julian." I take a deep breath and let it out. I place my hand at the back of my neck and try to figure out what to say next. "This... This is just for tonight. I really appreciate your willingness to step up. I do. But I meant what I said earlier. You need to work on you and, well, recording a new album, releasing new tour dates, getting back on that bus... It's not a good fit for you right now."

Pain sets in behind Julian's piercing eyes.

I place one hand in a firm grip on his shoulder. "For what it's worth, I'm incredibly happy to have you back for tonight. We have missed you up there. But, let's just take it one step at a time. Day by day, okay?"

"Day by day," he repeats.

Blake is yelling to us from the center area behind the stage and signaling for us to join him, Cooper and Dom.

We walk over toward them and Blake has multiple shot glasses set out, filled with clear liquor.

He hands out the drinks first to Cooper and Dom, then one to me, then extends one to Julian.

I don't miss the twitch of Julian's hand as if he is considering taking the drink, but his eyes meet mine and he thinks better of it.

"I'm good. I'll pass, thanks."

Blake shrugs his shoulders and downs Julian's drink but saves his other one for the pre-show toast to our final show of what turned out to be a great tour, despite some losses.

My phone buzzes in my hand with a text from Natalie stating she's outside. I down the drink without waiting for the others to join, place my glass on a table and excuse myself from the group.

Cooper hollers, "Make it quick," as I walk out. He's kept me on a short leash all day, as if I'll bolt if given the opportunity. I have no intention of going anywhere—not tonight. I'm lightyears away from the agony I felt the last time I stood on this stage. The happiness I have in me now completely eclipses the negativity that existed during that last New York show.

Natalie is waiting just a few steps away from the main doors when I find her. She looks... *Wow*. If a picture is worth a thousand words, her presence in front of me now is worth millions — and still, none of them would be enough. She wears a whisper of makeup, enough to accent her features but not cover or take away from them, a low-cut body suit and high waisted jeans that show off each perfect curve of her body and heels that give her a few more inches than she is used to.

Previously, I believed that it was not possible for her to be any more beautiful than the ways I've seen her before, and yet, somehow, I never get used to how striking she is. Whether we've been apart for days or I close my eyes for only seconds, she's even more stunning every time I see her again.

She waves to me and her mouth turns up at the corners. She doesn't have to tell me what she's thinking, because I already know. I can sense her indecision from here. She's happy to see me, but she's nervous about what tonight will bring. There will be more interviews and cameras and media around tonight than usual, waiting for me to misstep. Since this is the redo of a show where I walked off the stage and started a fight with a fan, the media presence and buzz tonight is louder than any other show on the tour — maybe ever.

In a deep part of my mind, one I keep trying to turn off, I keep thinking something will go wrong — and I would imagine she probably is thinking it too. All I can do is cross my fingers and hope that's not the case.

She walks toward me and wraps her arms around me. I brush her cheek with my lips take her hand to lead her inside the venue and get her settled in wherever she wants to watch the show from. We step inside the main doors and Natalie stops without warning, staring ahead at something — or *someone*.

Mariah stands in the center of the main entrance wearing leggings with black tie-up boots and an olive-green loose-fitting top — a change from her usual slim fit, skin-tight ensembles. She poses and the cameras of the media flash so quickly and so repetitively that their lights mock the strobe lights we use in the show.

My grip on Natalie's hand tightens, but hers loosens, allowing me to physically feel her slipping from me, questioning me and, in turn, questioning herself.

This night was just as strange for me as it was for her. There are skeletons in my closet, but I didn't expect them to make appearances at my fucking shows. Julian...now Mariah... My father has been unaccounted for nearly half my life, so he's probably sitting front row wearing a T-shirt with my face on it.

Mariah smiles and waves, dismissing the cameras, even though I know she loves every minute of it.

"Xander, just the person I was looking for." She talks to me as if we've been close friends for years and not like she's an ex-girlfriend I had no intention of ever talking to again.

"Hi. I'm Mariah," she says, offering a hand to Natalie.

Natalie wipes her hand on the front of her jeans and places it in Mariah's grasp. Toxicity invades the area the moment their fingers touch, like two opposing chemicals coming together to form a lethal combination.

"Or *not*." Mariah scoffs when Natalie doesn't respond.

Natalie's eyes flicker up to meet mine. I clear my throat.

"Natalie Montoy, Mariah Delani and vice versa," I say, offering an unenthused introduction.

Natalie signs the three-gesture combination I recognize as *'Nice to meet you'*. Mariah's eyes widen, and she purses her lips. It's a look I know all too well — a look I have seen her give hundreds of people — when she sits on her throne and looks down on people she believes are less than her.

She all but dismisses Natalie and looks at me.

"Can we talk?" she asks.

"If I hear that goddamned phrase one more time tonight..." I trail off, thinking out loud about my initial conversation with Julian.

Natalie looks at me with large, worried eyes, but I nod to her and hold up one finger. She places her mouth against my skin at the very corner of my lips — a brush of the lips lost between a kiss on the mouth and a kiss on the cheek. She disregards Mariah as she walks past her and into the main room of the venue, but not before she turns her head over her shoulder one last time, taking a long look at me and Mariah standing together at the main doors before she disappears behind the venue wall.

"Was it not enough for you to ruin my last New York show? You have to attempt to sabotage this one too?" I ask in a breathless, dismissive way.

"I wasn't even at your New York show..." she starts, but she's missing the point. She has no idea what I'm referring to.

"The voicemail. The message you left me confessing all your lies and stories. I got it just before our show the night we were here last."

"I-I d-didn't realize…" she stutters.

"You didn't realize how it would affect me? You didn't think I would care? I wasted a lot of time caring, Mariah. Too much time, in fact. Do you want to hear that you tore me apart? Do you want to hear that you ripped out the floor from underneath me so unexpectedly that it took me weeks to find flat ground again? Because you did. For a little while, I allowed it to ruin me. And that's not just on you. That's on me too, because I let you damage me. But that won't ever happen again. I've moved on. I've found better, and for weeks, Mariah, you haven't crossed my mind…not even once. Let's take it a step farther and not cross paths either."

"Moved on?" she scoffs. "Come on, Xander. How long will this last? A few months? She doesn't exactly scream 'celebrity arm candy', does she? You can't possibly think this is a long-term thing. I can see it, and deep down I know you can. And if she doesn't see it, well, then, she might be blind too."

I clench my fists and the back of my neck grows hot. My chest rises and falls with every deep, angry breath I take. My nostrils flare as I exhale through my nose. Rage courses through my veins now, in this moment, faster and fiercer than it ever has before, and there is absolutely nothing I can do about it.

"You need to go, Mariah. I don't care where. Go to Boston. Go to California. You can go to Hell for all I care, but you can't stay here," I spit through gritted teeth.

Her eyes fill with tears and her lip trembles. She started something she couldn't finish when she chose to speak negatively of Natalie. I try to step around her, but she closes in the gap between us.

"Xander, wait." She presses both her palms against my stomach and stands much too close to me. "I didn't come here to fight, okay? I just want to talk. I want to apologize. I want to start over," she says, and the tears fall harder. She wipes them away with fingertips adorned in long, red painted nails and I don't believe a second of her charade. We've done this more times than I care to admit.

"Why can't you even look at me?" she asks. "Why can't you just try to talk to me?" She tacks on to the end of her already over-dramatic monologue.

"You're really wasting your talents directing, you know," I hiss. She looks up at me, expecting a compliment. "You would be better suited for acting." I walk away and leave her behind, by herself in the foyer.

Stomping through the main doors, I turn the corner and almost straight into Natalie. I place my hands on either side of her face, my fingers lace into the hair at her temples, and I kiss her forehead, the tip of her nose, her cheek then my lips are on hers. I step back to pull away from her but she pulls at my shirt, keeping me close.

The sudden volume increase of voices, footsteps and metal detector beeps indicates the doors have opened, and we're standing in much too public of a place. I wrap my fingers into hers and lead her back. The introductions to the staff and crew are quick. The band joins us. Dom waves. Blake takes her hand, leans forward and kisses the back of her hand dramatically. She laughs, and Blake is lucky I'm in a forgiving mood.

Joking or not, I can be a jealous man. Add it to my list of flaws.

But, then again, perhaps the playing field has been leveled. She did have to leave me alone with Mariah today. I can't imagine that was easy, and yet, just like every situation she encounters, Natalie handled it with patience and grace.

I pull her into the wings of the stage. I want her to myself as much as I can before having to leave her for my performance. I could kiss her forever, but she pulls away.

"What did Mariah want?" she signs. I take a deep breath and shake my head.

"Don't worry about her," I say. "She won't be causing any more trouble."

"I hope not."

The lights over the stage darken, and the crowd screams a ferocious roar. I ask Natalie where she wants to be for the show and she responds, "Anywhere where I can see you" — her eyes flirting with mine as her lips and hands move. I find a spot for Natalie, close to the back of the stage where the subwoofers and speakers are — the closest she can be to feeling the music, but still in a wing so she can see the show. Our opener takes the stage, the lights bright and moving. The vibrations from the speakers and instruments travel over the stage and through the soles of my shoes into my feet. Her eyes widen, her mouth morphs to an excited smile.

I lean in and kiss her — a long, slow kiss accompanied by blue and purple flashing lights that dance across our faces as we share this moment. We watch from the wing, my chest at her back and my arms around her waist. The lead singer takes a bow at the front of the stage. The lights go down and they exit the stage. Crew members in primarily black outfits take the stage and adjust the set-up.

Most of the lights are down and the area is dark, except for the slight illumination of my phone as I type a new message. I wrap my arms around her again, holding her so my chin rests on her head but she can read my phone in my hands in front of her.

I'll see you after the show, the message reads. She nods, slowly. Her hair tickles my throat.

Break a leg, she types, then turns to look at me. I break into a childlike smile I can't control. I don't recognize the happiness she brings me because I never allowed myself to have it before.

But I do now.

Booming music plays us in, and we take the stage. The stage remains dark for a long while, and the crowd is getting antsy. They can see us up there, though the lights aren't on yet. They are yelling and screaming, but we make them wait it out. We're still surrounded by almost total darkness and I take the microphone in my hands.

"Hello, New York," I say in a long, drawn-out style. The crowd erupts. They're ready for the music.

"We meet again," I say in dramatic fashion. Sometimes drawing out the introduction is amusing. The crowd unhinges with excitement and impatience that begs us to get to the show.

"You there, guys?" I say, addressing the band.

"Yeah, we're here. Hello, New York," Blake says, "and go Yankees...or whatever." The crowd laughs. Blake couldn't care less about baseball. That's about all the effort each city gets from him.

"*Psssttt*... New York," I say in a whisper that echoes through the microphone. "I have a secret. Make some noise if you want to know it too."

The crowd hollers and yells a simultaneous response through the darkened venue, but it's mediocre at best.

"I guess they don't really want to know, guys." I say to the band. "New York! Make some noise if you want to know the secret."

And this time, they take the bait. They yell and scream and cheer and only when their vocal chords can no longer take the strain do they fade out.

"All right, all right, jeez, you don't have to yell at us," I joke, getting a laugh from the crowd.

"Here with us tonight," I yell, enunciating every syllable, "a special appearance for this crowd... I give you...the one, the only...Mr. Julian Young!"

My voice thunders through the microphone, drowned out by the love and applause the crowd emits as the spotlight turns on above Julian, proving his presence, and he strikes a few loud, impressive guitar chords.

As expected, the crowd falls in love with the musical style of Julian Young all over again, and it's a tease, for us and them, because it's an experiment with a shelf life.

He still has it. I had doubted his ability to captivate a crowd at a height I know he's capable of after being off stage for so long, but I'd underestimated him. The music lives in him and he lays it all out on stage, not leaving one ounce of talent untapped or any morsel of potential behind. He pours everything he is and was into the music, and the crowd drinks it in.

We play a few fast-paced, well-known songs to get the crowd on their feet and kick off the night. About mid-show, as we usually do, Blake and I sit in stools at the front of the stage with the lights dimmed in a soft blue glow around us. We play a few slow-burning, soft acoustic numbers. As I play, I look around and find Natalie has made her way to the side of the crowd. She stares at me, and I at her, playing each chord and singing each note as if there is not one other person in the world, never mind the room.

We regroup as a full band to finish off the night with more of our number one hits — the kinds of songs where I stop singing, completely cut out the words, turn the microphone to the crowd and let them finish the lyrics because I know they know them.

My eyes shift to the set list taped to the ground — *Delayed Reactions* is up next. Blake strums the opening chords and Dom keeps time on the drums. The song sounds slightly hollow without Theo, and Julian doesn't know this one, but somehow, it works. In some ways, less is more, and this was beginning to sound like a stripped or acoustic version.

The words didn't have the impact on me tonight the way they did last time I took this stage. They almost had no impact at all, for I know when I leave this venue tonight, I'm leaving with a person who doesn't care about the celebrity or the status or the fame. A person who stands by me despite all of my shortcomings, and makes me feel like my life is whole, versus the way I felt the last time I stood there.

We finish out the show and return for an encore. At the finish of the remaining songs, Blake yells into his microphone, "Julian Young, ladies and gentlemen."

The crowd gives him a final, seemingly endless cheer and we exit the stage.

Amazing! Natalie signs, her hands patting the air above her head, then she kisses me lightly.

Her lips leave mine, but her eyes are still on them, watching them move as I speak.

"We have a quick interview and a meet-and-greet, but it won't take long," I promise her. "I'm taking you to a restaurant just a few blocks down the road. Do you want to go get a drink and I'll meet you there?"

She nods. I order her a car and send the restaurant information to her phone. I watch as she exits the stage and heads for the doors.

There is a TV playing backstage and I turn to it, just in time to see Mariah, outside the venue with cameras pointed at her from every angle. I hear the reporters asking her questions and click the volume up on the TV.

"So, you're here, in New York for the show. Does this mean you and Xander Varro are planning on rekindling an old flame?" The reporter questions.

You've got to be fucking kidding me right now. My hands shake and my forehead sweats with the fear that she will say yes, starting a world of drama I don't need.

"Oh, no, no," she says.

Thank God.

"Actually, Xander is seeing someone new," she says, and from where I'm standing, I can see Natalie press open the metal bar to the exit door, and I melt into the floorboards, knowing exactly what's about to happen. I yell her name, a word that echoes through the backstage area and everything seemingly falls into slow motion. She steps directly into a spotlight she has never wanted, a spotlight I promised her I'd keep her out of and there is absolutely nothing I can do to prevent it.

"In fact, that's her right now! Ms. Natalie Montoy!" Mariah's voice rings through the TV.

It's only a matter of seconds before the cameras are in her face and the lights are flashing wildly. Media outlets of all different types are inches from her. She looks around with large eyes and a worried expression and she has nowhere to go, no way to escape the bodies that surround her. There are reporters screaming questions at her that she can't answer. She tries to block her face and step through the media huddle. I know exactly how panicked she feels in that moment, because I feel it too but for a whole different reason.

In the pit of my chest I know that I just let her walk into the one thing she was trying to avoid, but more than that, I knew this was over. This was the one part of me she didn't want, and now that she has it, I know I have already lost her.

The door practically flies off the hinges as I slam my body weight into it and run to the crowd around her. I push my way through, throwing an elbow to anyone in my path and finally reach her. I wrap my arms around her to shield her, to protect her, from the media that flocks — but I just make it worse. Coming out here is like throwing gasoline on a fire. I couldn't put it out. My presence only fed the flames.

Reporters asked us about our relationship, if it was serious, how long we had been together. Someone must have picked up on the fact that she is Deaf — or Mariah told them — because now, they are asking about that too, and she's trembling. Maybe it's nerves but probably anger. When it comes to the media, nothing is sacred, no information is too personal. I can hear every breath she takes. The apprehension is audible.

And I hate it.

I hate that Mariah did this to her.

I hate that *I* did this to her.

The days that Natalie and I shared were ones where I wasted time worried that I wouldn't be enough for her, when what I should have been worried about was me and my baggage being too much. I'd pushed because I'd wanted her and because she made my life easier and better, but I didn't do the same for her.

I was naive to think this wouldn't happen. I knew I couldn't keep her hidden from the world forever. No matter how much I'd hoped I could keep my personal life separate from the music life, I know now that they are one in the same. Hanging out in the wings for long was never a viable option. Eventually, people were going to put it together that she was the person taking up all my free time. Whether Mariah said it or someone else did, it was inevitable. The world wants to know everything about me, and they usually got what they wanted.

I wrap one arm tightly around her and pull her away from the cameras and the people behind them.

We're just far enough away to turn a corner and I place flat palms against the sides of her neck, using my thumbs to nudge her chin upward so she's looking at me. She tears her gaze away from mine.

I move my hands up and down her arms and hips and looking her over as if she has been physically harmed, checking for signs of damage. Though I know everything she's feeling about me, about us, about the media… It's internal, and nothing I can say in this moment will mend it. She leans her head back, pressing her hands against her forehead, and when she brings her eyes and arms back down again, she places her hands on mine and pulls free of my grasp.

She pushes my hands away, tucks her hair behind her ears. Her eyes tell an entire story. She wants some space. She needs some time. I'm not what she wants or needs right now.

She walks past me, down the New York City streets without looking back, leaving me behind her — leaving it all behind her.

Chapter Fifteen

The forty-five seconds it takes me to choose between giving her space or following Natalie as she walks away is forty-five seconds too long. She's been swallowed in the crowds and maze of side streets.

Our hotel *is* within walking distance, just a farther distance than I usually care to attempt. Weaving in and out of bodies and New York traffic, I make my way toward the hotel, smoking consecutive cigarettes, more for stress relief than actual need. My stomach knots as I hope she is there when I get there. I don't need her to talk to me, but I do need her safe.

I'll give her space and time if that is what she wants, but my number one concern is now, and always will be, her well-being. The negative feelings and worst-case scenarios playing in my head over and over again can't be stopped. She doesn't know this city. She doesn't know these streets. If she isn't at that hotel when I get there, I have no clue what I plan to do. At a speed I consider a run, I dash through the elegant lobby and punch the button on the elevator too many times. I'm so close but so far away.

"Come on," I say out loud, beating the button into the wall as if this will make the elevator work faster. My foot taps against the tile until I decide I've waited too long. My footsteps echo as I turn around and run to the stairs, scaling them multiple steps at a time until I happen to meet the elevators open doors about halfway up my route. I jump on and hit the button for the top floor. My breaths come out in deep, fast heaves, accompanied by a dry cough.

Running is not something that is part of my daily, or yearly, activities. The searing in my lungs is an emphatic reminder of how badly I need to quit smoking.

The doors open and I walk down the hallway, my pace picking up speed with each step. With a deep breath, I slide the keycard into the reader. The door opens and she's standing in the middle of the room, facing the TV. I bend forward at the waist, pressing the heels of my hands into my thighs and let out the breath I had taken prior to opening the door. Seeing her here was relieving, among other things.

She doesn't even turn my direction as I approach her. She's staring at the television as her face appears across the screen.

Short clips of the scenario outside the concert venue play, but there's more than that. Her social media profile pictures, her name, other tidbits of information all under the headline, "Who is Xander Varro's New Love Interest?"

The thick wall of dark hair that runs over the shoulder closest to me, shields her expression, but the rigidness of her body tells me she's mortified and angry — and probably a whole slew of other negative emotions.

I have no sense of how much time has passed when she finally turns to me. Her makeup has run down her face, leaving the area under her eyes and her cheeks smudged black. She closes her eyes tightly and bites into her bottom lip.

She holds one hand out, acknowledging the story on television. I know she is shocked this story is already out there, but the media? They work fast. I had grown used to it over the years.

She collapses into a sitting position on to the bed behind her. She picks up her phone and stares at the screen, taking her time choosing her words. She types in a sentence, and hands it to me so I can read the words she has written.

You said it wouldn't be like this.

I deflate as I read the words. I did. I did say that. She was, quite literally, thrown to the lions today. My music is my greatest success and my biggest downfall, rolled into one barely wrapped package.

No matter how much I wanted to see it work between us, I know now that opposites might attract but that doesn't mean they should always find each other. Maybe she was right. Perhaps our lives just couldn't overlap in a reasonable or realistic way.

Her phone rings. Kelly's name flashes on the screen. She swipes to open the video call and Kelly immediately starts signing and asking "What happened?", "Are you okay?," "Where is Xander?" and a series of other third-degree inquiries before Natalie has the chance to respond or I can interject. Natalie moves to the hotel desk and props her phone up, freeing her hands to answer all Kelly's questions.

She, of course, wants to talk to me. Natalie hesitates, but eventually hands me the phone.

Kelly's dismayed expression fills the screen. Her narrowed eyes and tight lips are loud enough to tell me she's not actually interested in letting me speak but plans to give me a piece of her mind.

"You said it was over with Mariah, Xander. You said this wouldn't be an issue," she scolds me.

"I know that. I didn't know she was going to be there. I didn't expect any of this to be a big deal," I defend myself, but she talks over me.

"You know, Natalie wants to come home. Tonight," she says. My heart shatters.

"Can you just… Can you just convince her to stay?" I plead. "Please? I will stay somewhere else. She can have the whole room to herself. I will get her on a plane tomorrow. Just tell her to stay." My voice cracks under the pressure.

Kelly stares at me with dagger eyes, weighing her options, but I can sense she's half out the door, ready to come pick up Natalie herself.

"Okay. Give her the phone," Kelly says. For the second time in a matter of minutes, I am indescribably relieved, because if anyone can get through to Natalie, its Kelly.

Kelly and Natalie continue their soundless conversation, and even though I have no clue what is going on, I feel like I am eavesdropping where I am not welcomed.

Natalie nods her head yes, and waves to Kelly before clicking the red 'end call' button.

She turns to me in the desk chair and leans her head against her hand. I toss my thumb over my shoulder toward the door. My very best attempt at '*Okay then, I'll be going now,'* but she stands up and shakes her head in a long, exaggerated no.

She steps forward and turns down the sheets on the side closest to her, then the side closest to me. She pats her hand against the mattress, inviting me into it.

She walks toward her belongings, pulls her shirt over her head and replaces it with a loose, worn T-shirt, then slides off her jeans and heads to the bathroom.

When she returns, her makeup is cleared from her face, but I can't tell if the redness left behind is from cleansing her makeup or residual from the crying. The latter pains me in a way I can't find the words to explain.

She lies down in the bed and is facing away from me but cuddles in close so her shoulder blades are against my chest. Her hair cascades over both of our pillows and the back of her thighs press against the front of mine. She reaches backward and takes my forearm, draping it over her hips, and I'm happy to oblige.

I hold her close, because I think it is exactly what she needs to settle her after an overwhelming night that went from perfect to broken in no time at all.

I'm not naive enough to think lying this close to each other changes anything. I can sense the difference between being this close to her now and any other time I was lucky enough to do so. She got a spoonful of what living life as Xander Varro's girlfriend would be like, and she didn't like the taste.

So now, she clings to me like I'm the life raft keeping her above water. She's plenty strong enough to tread the waves on her own, but it is always easier to have someone else keep you afloat.

She takes deep, even breaths, her back rising and falling against my chest. I keep one arm draped over her abdomen. We're lying in the coziest bed I've ever been in and yet comfort is lightyears away.

I keep my eyes open as long as I can, trying to keep sleep away. If I sleep now, morning will only come faster, and I know once we get home, this experiment is closed. My attempt to fend off morning is ineffective. My eyes grow heavy, and I drift off to dreamless sleep.

Chapter Sixteen

It was the absence of her bags from the hotel room floor that tipped me off that she had left sometime in the middle of the night. At first, I thought — *hoped* — that she'd gone for a walk to clear her head or find food or caffeine, but everything was gone. Suitcase, toothbrush — everything. The only evidence she had ever even here at all is the note she'd left behind. I sit at the edge of the bed holding the complimentary stationary that feels too heavy in my unsteady hands.

This is all too much.

This is the second time I've read this same note, only now she's not talking about the lavishness of the hotel. This time, the sentence isn't being used in the positive light it once was.

My messy, untamed morning hair falls around my face. Not wanting to believe my eyes, I turn to take a second — or fifth — look at the spot on the bed she was lying in as if the outcome will be different, though I know it won't be.

She left.

She was in my arms one minute, and the next she was gone. The emptiness I feel looking at that spot, and being in this hotel, knowing I'm going home to a town I'll share with her but not to a life I'll share with her, wraps me in a fatigue I can't quite comprehend.

I've fallen in love—real, shakes you at your core kind of love—exactly two times in my life. Once with music and once with her, and I know now that I can't have both.

I take a long, hot shower, hoping it will completely deluge the last twelve hours from my system, but the hot water helps very little, if at all. The bag in my hand holds only the few belongings I brought along. Not bothering to look around the room for anything I may have left behind, I head to the hotel parking lot to get back on the tour bus I originally didn't intend on taking home.

"I thought you were flying home with Natalie later tonight," Blake says as I take the steps onto the bus.

"Do you see her here with me?" I raise my arms up and look around. My words are sarcastic and pointed. Blake was probably either too drunk or too involved with one or more women after the show to have paid any attention to what was happening outside his hotel room walls last night.

My steps fall heavy-footed as I walk to the back of the tour bus. The wall in front of me is home to the old newspaper articles and magazine clips that feature any one of us, usually depicting something we probably shouldn't be doing and most definitely shouldn't be proud of. Staring back at me are the articles Blake had clipped after my last New York show.

And here I thought things couldn't get any worse for me in New York, yet I continue to surprise even myself.

I think about destroying the board. Every article. Ripping the pages between my fingers, their damaged bits falling throughout the bus like confetti. Taking the cork board in my shaking hands and breaking it, throwing the remaining pieces against the walls of this tour bus that seems to get smaller every time I get on it.

But I don't.

Instead, I leave it to mock me another day. The leather chair creaks as I collapse into it and slide my headphone buds into my ears, then cover my eyes with my dark-lensed sunglasses. I acknowledge an overwhelming sense of déjà vu as I stare at the ceiling and the tour bus pulls away from the parking lot.

* * * *

My phone rings as I enter my apartment. My heart skips two beats and I hope that the message will be from Natalie, but it's not. Jana's name and number appear across the screen. It was wishful thinking on my part, willing the text to be from Natalie when I already knew it would be from Jana. I had messaged her and told her to come by as we were returning to the city.

I'm in the lobby. Be up in a minute.

Jana comes in with pizza and beer. She puts everything on the counter and cracks open two bottles. As she hands me one, she gives me this sympathetic look and wraps herself into me, giving me a warm, supportive hug I didn't even know I needed.

"So, she just left? Have you heard from her?" Jana says through a mouthful of pizza after I give her my side of the story, not skipping any details.

"When I woke up, she was gone," I close the story. "I kind of anticipated it, though. I'm used to the quiet with her, you know? But that was a whole new kind of silence."

"I don't know. She had to have known hanging out with you was going to bring her into the spotlight eventually, right?"

"It doesn't for you," I say, and I think she sees my point. It wasn't about being hidden away from the cameras and the crowds forever. It was about the way she was completely thrown into it, at a time she didn't expect, by a person who shouldn't have been in the picture—and having to deal with it completely on her own. I wasn't even beside her to help her. I wasn't there to defend her in a way she can't always do for herself.

"I think she's overreacting," Jana adds.

"She's not," I say around the lip of the beer bottle.

I keep telling myself that I don't want to talk about Natalie anymore, but I can't stop. Somehow, each time Jana and I change the subject, I segue back around to Natalie, and we start all over.

I have tried to hold off on texting her, tried to avoid being the one to message first, but I can't. Knowing she's okay is more important than my pride.

Are you okay? I type.

My heart skips a beat as my phone buzzes only a moment later. I'm almost scared to look, knowing it won't feel great if it is not her name that appears on the screen.

But it is.

Yes.

It is direct and to the point. I struggle with what to write next, if anything. I type and delete, type and delete. I've written songs in less time than it takes me to type out my next message.

I never got a chance to apologize. I'd like to do that. Can I see you?

The dots appearing and disappearing on the screen tell me she is fighting the same internal battle I am. Eventually, she picks her words, and they aren't what I was hoping for.

You are not the one who needs to be sorry. Thank you for everything. Take care, Xander.

* * * *

Blake orders another round at the bar. I'm unsure how many drinks we've had. Then again, I didn't care enough to start counting.

"Thanks," I say as I take the glass from him.

"I didn't buy that one," he says. "She did." He points across the bar to a striking blonde-haired beauty who sends a flirty wave across the bar.

I nod, lift the glass cheers-style and down the liquid but don't make any attempt at starting a conversation with her.

"Take it easy, Xander," Blake says.

"I have a mother, thank you." I slide the glass across the bar toward the bartender clumsily. It shakes and rattles on the bar top.

"Yeah, and I'm sure she'd be super-thrilled to see her only son drunk for the *third* consecutive straight day," Blake says.

He's just looking out for me. I just wish he wouldn't. I've been drinking longer than I've been recording professional music, and apart from one lapse in judgment at the very beginning of the fame-and-fortune-paved roads, I've gotten in trouble very few times while under the influence of alcohol.

"Have it your way then," he says, and orders another round.

Apparently, he is going for the 'if you can't beat 'em, join 'em' approach. For a bit longer, he doesn't even try to talk me out of my decision to keep drinking anymore, but when I signal for another, Blake shakes his head to the bartender, effectively cutting me off. He picks up his hat and places it backward on his head, nodding to the girls across the way.

"What are you doing?" I ask him. At least, I think the words come out coherently.

"*We*," he says dramatically, "are getting out of here...with them." He winks at the blonde's slightly less blonde friend as they approach.

"No, I can't," I say.

"You can, actually. You're single. You can do whatever you want. Or do whatever *I* want, which is get out of here with the twin girls who have bought us drinks all night."

I don't answer. I don't even look at him. The bar stool teeters for a moment as I push myself off it and stumble out of the bar onto the city sidewalk.

Blake runs out of the door behind me. He gets so close to me that I can smell the liquor on his breath. Or maybe that's my own. I'm not sure anymore.

"You need to move on, man," he says. "It's been weeks since Natalie left you in that hotel room. Get over it. Find a new girl."

"I don't want a new girl, Blake. You can't just pick random girls at the bar for me and hope I forget. She's not the one I want," I say, loud enough that the blonde hears me, which was not really my intention.

I turn to walk away from him, unsure of where I'm going, but I know I can't stay here.

"At least this one can talk to you." His piercing, harsh words echo through the dark city street.

"What'd you say?" I say through a clenched jaw, taking large steps toward him.

"C'mon, man. Be serious. How much can you even know about a girl who can't talk?"

Without a second thought—or even a first one—I place both my hands flat against his chest, shoving him backward. He stumbles into the patio tables but regains his footing. He steps close to me with an angry, twisted expression.

"I'm going to give you ten seconds, Varro," he says in a challenging tone. "In that time frame, you can either apologize or throw a real punch. Choose wisely."

I don't want to fight Blake. What was I thinking when I laid my hands on him like that? I had hardly ever thrown a punch in my lifetime and here I am, resorting to physical violence for the second time in a matter of months, this time with my brother, my best friend, my band mate on the receiving end.

In an obvious forfeit, I raise both hands, turn on my heel and walk away, afraid of what my next bad decision in a series of many will be.

* * * *

The next morning—which is actually afternoon—I wake up with my sunglasses and shoes on, with not even one clue of how I got here—*and* my phone is gone.

Just another productive evening in the life of Xander Varro.

From where I sit on the couch, I can see a bottle of whiskey on the counter. Much to my surprise, it's full. My head pounds and my limbs feel heavy as I stumble there. There is one sticky note adhered to the bottle, but I'm seeing double and can hardly read the words. I close one eye and hold the note at arm's length.

Can't have a hangover if you never stop drinking.
Blake.

Oh, *Blake.*

Remembering my behavior toward him, I press my hands into my temples and close my eyes tight. Apparently, he's not too torn up about what I did.

I fall into the couch in the living room and feel an object sticking uncomfortably into my thigh. I reach for it and lean sideways to retrieve it.

My phone.

Well, it used to be a phone. The screen is shattered but it still lights up and the touchscreen still works. I click the home button and have multiple messages.

One from my mother—a missed call. *I keep meaning to call her.*

The others are from numbers I don't recognize, which happens more often than I wish it would, and a few from Blake.

You good? his last text reads.

Thanks for the bottle. You always have to be the hero, huh? I write.

Blake knows me well enough to know that poking fun his direction is my way of apologizing and accepting I was wrong.

I considered hitting you with it, but you were already knocked out when I got there.

I wouldn't have blamed you. I deserve it. I hit send.

Not a big deal, man. It happens. Move on and write about it in the next album.

This amuses me. How many songs I can think of that were written about a fellow band member leaving, coming back or having some kind of fallout or altercation? There are a lot of them. Many songs people would think are break-up songs about lovers are actually about people coming and going from bands.

As if I might have missed something from Natalie in my less-than-sober hours—or worse, sent her something I wish I hadn't—I scroll through my texts. On one hand, I'm relieved to see I didn't send anything to her, but on the other, I'm disappointed to see she hasn't reached out to me either. I know that one of these days I'm going to have to stop looking and hoping. Blake was right about one thing. It has been weeks, and I haven't seen or heard from her. Perhaps it is time to move forward, whatever direction that may be.

The clock ticks on, and, with each passing second, I tell myself to get up and do something, but don't actually make myself do it.

After a lot of mental pep talking, I finally get up, grab a water bottle from the refrigerator and pull on a clean T-shirt. With any luck, I will be able to walk to Chance's on the Corner for a coffee and maybe a bagel—if I could stomach it.

I take small sips of water and use the wall in the hallway of my apartment to balance myself the whole way to the elevator, and when it lurches, my stomach does too. I don't remember ever being hungover like this before. Hangovers of this severity remind my body that it is not twenty-one anymore, while also making me swear off alcohol. For all of about ten hours, of course, but I think about it, and from what I understand, it's the thought that counts.

The doors open and I step outside, inhaling the Boston city air then immediately vomit in the bushes outside my apartment. *Great.* I rinse my mouth with the remainder of the water bottle and spit it into the same landscaping before continuing on to the coffee shop

"Jeez. You look like shit," Jana says, not withholding any opinion as I collapse into a chair at the nearest table.

Arguing with her is not an option. I don't have the energy. The second hand on the wall ticks in a loud, maddening way that sounds on the exact opposite beat in which my head throbs. *Tick. Throb. Tick. Throb. Tick.*

Jana brings me my usual order, but as soon as I smell it, I can feel the color leave my face and my stomach does a backflip. I place my hand over my nose and mouth, and Jana doesn't miss the gesture. She takes it away immediately and returns with a tall, iced glass of ginger ale.

"Sip," she says.

I take one small sip and let the bubbles dissipate on my tongue before forcing myself to swallow.

"What is going on with you?" she asks. I can't tell if she's worried or angry. The latter would be par for the course. It seems like almost everyone I know is aboard the Xander Varro disappointment train.

"Nothing," I lie, taking a second sip of the ginger ale.

She just stares at me, not buying what I'm selling.

"I know you have enough people in your corner telling you what to do, but you have to stop acting like this. You have too much going for you to throw it away over some girl. Or, did you forget you already tried that once this year? With a different girl, I might add."

"What's your point?" I ask. "But tell me your point...quieter." I hold a finger to my lips.

"My point is," she says, making no effort to quiet her voice. In fact, she may be raising the volume just to spite me. "There will be other girls. I know you don't want to hear it, but there will be. But there is no second chance at this career. It took a lot of work for you to get to where you are and you're about one drink away from destroying it—not just for yourself, but for your band mates and Cooper too."

She has a point. It's not like I haven't thought that myself dozens of times, but hearing it from someone else, especially someone who's not involved in the band, makes it vastly more real.

"I'm the last person who should be giving relationship advice, but seriously, Xander. You need to take care of *you*."

"Wait... Are things not going well with Nellie?" I ask, perceptive to the comment she made about relationships.

"No. We haven't been together for a while," she responds in a saddened voice with downcast eyes.

Realizing how little I ask about Jana in all the time we spend together has an oddly sobering effect. I never ask about her life. She makes me coffee and plays therapist to me every day that I'm home, and I realize, at this moment, for as close as we have become, I don't truly know anything important about her but she knows everything about me.

"I'm sorry to hear that. I know you really liked her. What happened?"

"Med school, mostly. The job I want, the career I'm shooting for, it's time-consuming. I spend a lot of time at classes and labs and shadowing hospital staff. My time not spent at school is spent here, so I can pay for school, and when I'm not doing either of those things, my nose is in a book studying. I guess I'm not as much fun as I used to be. But everything I'm working toward, this career, it matters to me. She was either going to support it and take it with all the bad sides, or she wasn't, and she chose the latter," she explains.

I realize as she speaks that Jana and I are in the exact same boat, paddling like our lives depend on it to reach our destination, and the damn thing has a hole in it.

A customer comes in and waits at the counter.

She puts her hand on my forearm. "I'll see you tomorrow, okay? Not drunk, preferably," she says as she walks toward the counter.

"Jana?" I ask as she walks away. She looks at me, waiting for me to finish my question. "Has she been in here at all? Natalie, I mean. Have you seen her?"

Her eyes fill with sympathy as she shakes her head in a regretful no.

Chapter Seventeen

"All right, all right," Cooper says, sliding plain black coffees across the table to each one of the band members. "How are you all feeling? Glad to be back? You had a few weeks off. Let's get down to business."

The band offers a few grunts of agreement, but nothing substantially overwhelming, and he continues.

"We were invited to play a holiday concert with a whole lineup of other bands as a kickoff to the new ocean-front venue appropriately called CommOcean. *Get it*? Great. Yes, it's outside. Yes, it will be winter. Half of Boston jumps into that water New Year's Day for charity, so a bundled-up concert in December can't be that bad, right?"

He waits for our response, but no one offers one, which frustrates him. I'm unsure why. He should be used to this. We perform. We like things loud and lit up. The business side was very underwhelming to us. Tell us where to be and when to be there, and we will put on a show.

"What do you think? I'll only say yes with a majority vote here. We typically leave on tour by February or March, but a *new* album is certainly helpful when launching a tour, *hint hint*." He exaggerates the words, not holding back his disdain about our lack of recording studio time in our off days.

The band votes and decides to play the show. It's something different and certainly could be fun. Hell, if we get our shit together in the next few weeks, we may even have a few new songs to debut at that show.

I haven't pitched anything to the guys or Cooper yet, but I did have a few ideas jotted down. They're coming around and starting to look like real songs. My songs are ten percent lyrics and ninety percent emotion. Heaven knows that lately I have had more than enough to write about.

We go over everything from paperwork to schedules to recording time to T-shirt and merchandise sales and Cooper finally lets us go.

My phone rings in my pocket. I have one text from Jana that reads *Natalie just came into the coffee shop.*

The heads-up is much appreciated, but what was I supposed to do? Show up there? Make her talk to me? She's had the option to talk to me for weeks, and she hasn't. I want to see her, but I left the ball in her court and she deflated it.

But this could be a chance to start over.

I could see her and find out what comes of it. Will she be happy to see me? Will she tell me off for good? We left things in such an up-in-the-air manner, maybe seeing each other would either offer some closure or propel us into a new beginning—and there was only one way to find out.

I push my feet as quickly as they will move, bounding toward the shop, and pull the door open, sounding the bells on the door handle.

She's sitting in the exact same spot she was sitting in the very first time I was fortunate enough to see her. She faces away from me and her unruly curls fall down her back. She stares out of the same window she did that very first day. It all seems like a long time ago instead of just a matter of weeks, and here we are, with the perfect setup to start over. To try again. *Take two.*

I take one small step forward and my breath and heart rate quicken.

What do I say? What will she do?

I wipe my sweating palms on the front of my jeans, and as I do so, a tall man with dirty blond hair and a blinding smile enters from the door at the opposite side of the shop, walks toward Natalie's table and kisses her cheek before he sits down.

Just for a moment, I wait, with some hope that this isn't what I think it is. She signs a series of words, and he responds to them as if he's a mirror image. He executes the signs as seamlessly as she does. Only seconds into looking at this picture I wasn't meant to see, I know he is the better fit for her, and my breath is lost somewhere between an inhale and an exhale.

Up until this second, I had been frozen— paralyzed—in time, stuck between what was and what might be, unsure of my footing, unsure of my next step, unsure of what was in front of me.

And now I know.

It is clearer than ever before, in that moment, that there is no 'what comes next' for us.

I back up slowly into the door and push it open, leaving as quickly as I came.

* * * *

My eyes don't move from the spot they've found on the ceiling. I'm unsure if I ever close my eyes, or fall asleep, or just run through my thoughts so many times there is no material left to run through, but suddenly the sky outside my window is darkening, and I haven't moved once. An entire day, wasted. No effort put in. No progress made. Just minutes that turned into hours of a day spent doing nothing but feeling sorry for myself. And I have zero remorse.

A few hours too late, I push myself off the mattress. At this point I should just stay in bed until tomorrow. Unsurprisingly, I end up at the window of the apartment and stare at my reflection in the glass. It moves when I do. It does what I do. But I don't recognize the person looking back. The reflection in the mirror is foreign. I don't know him, and he doesn't know me.

A pack of cigarettes sits on the coffee table. My gaze travels to the kitchen where there is more liquor than I even know what to do with. My eyes dart back and forth between the two, but I don't know what I want. I can't quite make out if its hunger or thirst or tobacco withdrawal that I'm losing a battle to — but I realize that it's none of the above.

What I'm experiencing is…numbness — and it has taken over completely.

I just want to feel *something*. That's when my eyes settle on my black motorcycle helmet on the hutch at the front door. I ignore the cigarettes and whiskey and grab the helmet — though I considered leaving that behind too.

My steps echo as I make my way through the parking garage and straddle the seat once I reach the bike. The engine roars and reverberates through the cement-walled garage as I kick on the engine. The vibrations of the motorcycle run through my hands and the length of my spine.

The screech of the bike as I peel out of the garage pierces the silence of the city streets as I pull onto them, jolting myself forward as I pick up speed.

The cool air blows by and the roads aren't too crowded. It was just me and the roar of the motorcycle. Taking my bike out for a late-night spin was the perfect distraction, but only for a moment. The idea was to *feel* something, to drive until there was no more road, to throttle forward with no destination at all, to leave everything behind me as I sped forward.

But feeling something, led to feeling everything.

Now I'm flying down the highway, thinking all the way back to Mariah and the pregnancy that never was.

Then, the New York show and the guy I got into a fight with.

Letting Cooper down and not maturing in the way he hoped I would.

I think about Julian, both before and after the drug issues.

Thoughts of Natalie flood my system and overload it, practically shutting everything down. I think about when we met, about when we kissed. I think about the notes we wrote and the signs I learned. Then I think about her, just hours ago, sitting across from a man who's not me, but who is a vastly better fit for her life.

I drop my eyes and look at the speedometer. The orange needle is moving upward, well past an acceptable speed. It is oddly therapeutic the way the orange point ticks past the white notches, so I keep staring, and it keeps moving farther around the circle dial.

I never even saw the yellow signs ahead, a well-documented warning for the sharp curve in the road. I went straight when they warned me to turn left. By the time I had registered that the road was turning and I was not, my reflexes weren't fast enough to correct my direction.

I lie face down on the street, inhaling asphalt and rubber and gasoline with every breath. I'm not moving and I'm not even sure I can. My breaths are painful and labored.

My eyes are heavy. I don't want to close them, but my body doesn't give me a choice. The last thing I see is thick red liquid as my own blood pools around me and the world turns to the deepest, starless black.

I see nothing. I feel nothing.

I hear nothing.

Chapter Eighteen

Natalie

The flowers sit on the bar at The Rock Room — white gardenias, wrapped in a bouquet so extravagant that it takes up a quarter of the bar top. I sit in a stool at the bar, tapping my fingers against the wooden top. The sweet scent of them it so inordinate that it almost masks the beer and liquor smell the place typically boasts.

They look out of place here, their bright white, fragile clusters against the dark, lackluster atmosphere of The Rock Room.

Kelly takes the stool next to me and places an unopened bottle of red wine, two glasses and a bottle opener on the bar top.

"From...Xander?" she asks before picking up the bottle opener and piercing the cork with the spiral portion.

I shake my head no. "Ethan," I spell out, signing each letter.

She raises a perfectly plucked eyebrow my direction then pours the red wine into each glass and hands one to me. We tap the rims of our cups together, the ping of the glass echoing through the venue, and I'm lost in the petals of the flowers again. I imagine picking each pedal off, one by one, and letting them float freely to the floor, getting lost in the memories associated with them.

'There's a guy at the other end of the bar asking for you.' That's all Kelly had signed to me the night I'd met him.

'Me?' I had asked, thinking and signing simultaneously. She smiled and nodded her head. I was more than half expecting Xander to be standing at the bar, but to my surprise, it was not.

This gentleman was tall and tanned with dirty blond hair and kind, hazel eyes—well-dressed, slightly older, perhaps. He smiled when our eyes met for the first time and I couldn't miss the mouth full of perfectly straight, whitened teeth.

Kelly appeared next to me, elbowing me a few times in a sisterly, joking manner.

"He is handsome," I signed.

"And not the lead singer of a band," she signed back. I smiled at her joke, but it was forced. Behind the grin lies a deep emptiness that still exists in the spot Xander used to fill.

Ethan stood in almost the exact spot Xander had the night I was introduced to him at the bar—but that spot is about all the two had in common.

The length and lack of style of Xander's hair is something I had grown extremely fond of, but historically, my taste in men was more of a clean shaven, short-cut type, like the one Ethan sports. But, for some reason, I couldn't resist Xander's rugged charm. I was into every inch of him. Somewhere between the scars above and below his eyebrow that I could only imagine was pierced at one point, his incessant need to wear sunglasses indoors or on shady days and the full sleeve of ink and art that covers one entire arm and parts of his chest, I became enamored with his entire style.

Then again, change is exactly what I needed.

I feel the defeated sigh leave my chest. Kelly places one hand on mine, ending the memory I'm lost in. My eyes find hers, and she places her wine glass on the bar top.

"You never told me what really happened with Xander," she signs. I swallow hard at the mention of his name, and shrug. I don't know what to say. "Truthfully, I thought you'd end up working it out. I could tell on our video call that you were so torn."

Torn.

That's exactly how I felt. I wanted to be with Xander without any of the lifestyle he came with. What I realized in the end was not that it wasn't fair to me to have to adjust, but it wasn't fair to him for me to ask him to miss out on any single moment or part of the lifestyle he had sacrificed so much for.

I lay next to him that night, his breath skating across my ear, his chest rising and falling with each breath. I removed his hand from my waist, ripping off the proverbial bandage. I was only prolonging what was going to happen next.

I hung my legs over the side of the bed and pushed myself to my feet, turning only to watch him for a moment.

I stood there, with only one thought eminent in my mind. He is…everything.

I was ripped into two even halves. Part of me wanted to crawl back into that bed and back into those arms and kiss his lips and tell him that I was over it, that I was in it, all of it, for good. But the other half was screaming at me, telling me I wasn't interested in learning to love the kind of lifestyle I experienced today, and there would never be a time I'm not sharing Xander Varro with the world.

The latter of the two ideas won the internal tug of war, sending the parts of me that are enamored by him into a tumbling heap on the ground.

As I opened the bathroom door, I looked over my shoulder to see if he'd stirred, but he doesn't wake. He's as stubborn in his sleep as he is when he's awake. The light brightened as I flicked the switch, and I slid into the clothes that were nearest the top of my bag and tossed what remained into the duffle. Before leaving, I thought about leaving a note. A laugh escaped my throat when I retrieved the stationary — not in a humorous way, but more of a sarcastic scoff as I read the very last thing I wrote.

With unsure lips I kissed his temple before walking out of the room that was meant to be the setting for an intimate first page of a beautiful script and was then nothing more than a deleted scene.

"There's really nothing to say," I finally sign back to her, the memories of New York and the night I left Xander still sitting fresh in my mind.

Dinner. Tomorrow night. 7:30

That's all the simple, heart-shaped cardstock note says.

That's Ethan though — direct, sweet, to the point.

* * * *

The night I met him I wasn't sure what to expect. I certainly didn't foresee the flowers, extravagant dates and spending this much time with him this fast, but things are easy with Ethan...light, uncomplicated.

I knew it wouldn't hurt to at least say hello to the man attached to that blinding smile. I had nothing to lose. I approached the end of the bar, hiding my nervousness behind a warm smile.

He placed his hand to his chest, then tapped two fingers on each hand together, followed by an unpausing, steady flow of signs that spelled out *Ethan*.

He turned his head ever so slightly and behind his ear, at the back of his head, rests the unmistakable transmitter of a cochlear implant.

We signed back and forth for a few moments — for as long as I could get away with while being on a shift. He asked if he could see me after the show. Taking even myself by surprise, I said yes.

We had late night Chinese food at the local restaurant near the venue. I had almost forgotten what it was like to talk to someone who was fluent in ASL and not have to think about my communication or how to get my point across. I mean, of course I had Kelly and her parents, but I was used to them. It is infrequent at most that I meet someone new who can carry on a long conversation with me without pens or paper or technology.

The conversation flowed so smoothly and easily, and I barely had to think about keeping it going. I was barely thinking at all, until he asked me something that hit me like an oncoming vehicle I never saw coming.

"So, are you with Xander or not?"

Unblinking, I stared ahead and a million questions flooded my thoughts. I raised an eyebrow and cocked my head to the side.

"I've seen you together around the club," he signed, and hesitated before adding, "and I saw the segment of you in New York."

Of course he had.

I didn't answer his question outright, but then I reprocessed what he mentioned. *'I've seen you together around the club'*, he had said, and so, I asked him exactly what I was thinking.

"Do you spend a lot of time around the venue?" I signed. He looked into his drink and then back at me and finally signed a replied.

"I own it."

It was odd, at first, knowing that he owned the club I bartend in, but his wit and charm help me overlook that fact.

He's sweet. He's charming. He understands me.

He explained that he had noticed Kelly and I signing to each other way back when she was training me, but by the time he'd worked up the courage to ask about me, he was informed I was seeing someone else. So, he took a step back for a while but decided enough was enough and he just had to know me. His words, not mine.

The way he communicated was captivating, and whether he was being sincere or extravagant, I melted a bit more every time he signed even the simplest of words to me. He understood me on a level I had stopped looking for long ago.

Though we share a commonality in being hard of hearing, I was born without functioning auditory nerves. I've never known what it is like to hear, and for that reason, speaking has always come to me with tremendous difficulty. Even with years and years of attempts and practice, speaking is something I choose not to engage in. Words feel strange and uncomfortable to me, so I lean on ASL, the only language I've ever truly known.

Ethan, however, lost his hearing after a temporal skull fracture from falling out of a tree fort at a young age. He spoke a full spectrum of the English language. He knew words and he used them. He heard music, and birds, and cheers and laugh and cries — then they were gone.

His parents chose to have him fitted with a device that has restored some of hearing to a certain degree — of course, nothing is ever close to the real thing — but I can't help but wonder which one of us is luckier, or, contrarily, more unlucky. I can't miss something I've never had, but he had full hearing and lost it, allowing him to have heard sounds I only wonder about.

Kelly lets out a contagious yawn, and I do the same. I didn't even realize I was this tired, almost closing my eyes while sitting at the bar top.

Chapter Nineteen

I tuck my hair behind my ears and stick my nose into one of the fully bloomed flowers in the vase that now sit on my kitchen island, then head to my room to get ready for dinner, which I requested to cook.

A little black dress hangs in the closet, and I run one hand down the fabric. This was the dress I had chosen for my dinner in New York with Xander.

Xander Varro. Celebrity lead singer of Consistently Inconsistent. Well-known, award-winning rock star who could have a different girl on his arm any day of the week — and he had chosen me.

When I think about it, it feels like a dream. The details feel foreign, like they'd happened to someone else and I'm watching a recording of it. Even though I'd lived it, even though I'd spent time in his arms, it feels unreal. Unbelievable. Made up.

It feels like a lifetime ago — someone else's lifetime.

I skip past the dress, pushing it and the memories aside, and choose a more casual outfit — a black, loose-fitting shirt and dark jeans.

Dressed and readied, I power on the radio and turn the volume knob until I can feel the vibration of the music in my chest and through the soles of my feet. I dance around my kitchen as I toss herbs and spices into a bowl to begin preparing homemade meatballs and a hearty red sauce. As the days continue to pass, I'm starting to feel rebuilt, like I'm climbing out of a hole I had been stuck in, and I am certain things could not go any better than they are going right now.

I dance — poorly, I might add — shaking my hips and doing an exaggerated twirl when out of the corner of my eye, I realize I am not alone.

Kelly is standing behind me, watching my overdramatic, under-coordinated dance session. She raises an eyebrow and requests an explanation for my whimsical antics.

I tell her that things are right, and easy, and a good fit. I'm happy.

"So, you're completely over Xander then?" she asks. It's still a question I can't answer.

I'm not over him. I'm not sure I ever will be. But I can try. And Ethan is a lengthy leap in the right direction.

Kelly looks around at all the ingredients, then at me. *"Ethan is coming for dinner tonight," I inform her, and her mouth turns to a light smile. "There is a game on TV he wants to see. I'll cook and we'll watch it together."*

She sticks around for the remainder of my recipe prep, and I light the burner under the saucepan.

The kitchen fills with a delicious aroma of garlic and fresh tomato as we sit at the counter, sip a red wine and

Kelly applies a light layer of makeup to my eyes before Ethan is expected to arrive. I was getting used to applying my makeup on my own. I was even getting pretty good at it, I think, but it is nice to have Kelly help every so often. Sitting here with her as she brushed a light gold shadow to my eyelids and a subtle pink blush to highlight my cheekbones, it felt like the days when we were younger and I leaned on my older cousin—more like an older sister—for everything.

Just as I return to the stove to stir the sauce, the lights connected to the doorbell start flashing, and Kelly heads to the door to let him in. They talk for a moment, not signing, but rather using their voices for conversation. I'm still mad at her for not telling me he owned The Rock Room, but she was right, I would have said no and I would've missed out on this amazing man.

His gaze flickers up and meets mine, and his eyes light up. He's happy to see me, and I'm thrilled to see him too.

Kelly offers us a quick goodbye and makes her exit, leaving us alone in the kitchen of my small apartment.

He wraps his arms around me and presses his nose to my hair. I inhale the sweet scent of the cologne he wears, and I feel safe and comfortable here in his arms. He pulls away and kisses my forehead.

Waving his hand in front of his face as if he's redirecting the aromas of the kitchen into his nostrils then brings his fingertips near his lips and back toward me—the signs that translate to "*Smells good.*"

I'm unsure why, but I blush. Cooking is something I truly love. It is a skill of mine that is becoming more perfected every day, but having him here, having his tongue be the next one to taste my recipe, makes the butterflies in my stomach work overtime. I just want him to be impressed.

He sits across from me at the table and we sign a perfectly lovely conversation, getting to know each other more by the second. We sip wine and enjoy each other's company in a way that makes the minutes feel like milliseconds, and suddenly the dinner timer is vibrating furiously, dancing across the island countertop. *"I'll check on dinner,"* I sign to him, and he responds that he's going to turn on the game accompanied by a wink I almost missed.

I excuse myself and test each item I'm cooking. Positive everything is cooked all the way through, I make two plates and walk toward where Ethan is standing with the TV on.

He hasn't changed the channel to the game yet. Instead, something on the news has his attention.

Short, quick clips flash across the screen. Blue and red lights flash on top of an ambulance as it leaves the scene. A crumpled, almost unrecognizable motorcycle is on top of a tow truck.

But not completely unrecognizable.

Not to me. I'd know the silver-and-blue of that motorcycle anywhere.

They are currently just calling him 'the crash victim'. They don't know his name.

But I do.

As the worst possible scenarios flood me, and thoughts I can imagine but can't unsee flash in my restless mind, I drop both plates and they shatter into pieces as they hit the floor.

I can't breathe. Not hyperbolically, not poetically — my lungs *forget* how to work. My eyes stay wide open until dryness takes them over and my instincts force me to blink. My hands are shaking in a way I couldn't hope to control. Ethan runs toward me with worry plastered across his face. He places one hand at my hip and the other at the back of my neck, holding me steady — but only for a moment. He moves his hands off my shaking body and signs to me to ask me if I'm okay, but I don't answer. I'm staring at him blankly, not responding to any of his attempts to get through to me. I'm looking through him, at the news clips that repeatedly show the motorcycle I know belongs to Xander.

Ethan is screaming at me, yelling my name followed by "Are you okay?" And "What's going on?" Even though I can't hear it, I can see it. It's what his lips are saying. It's what his eyes are saying. He's worried about me, beyond measure. I'm frozen to the flooring that tiles this section of my apartment.

I look at Ethan, but only for a second. My eyes fill with hot tears that release and pour down my cheeks. Mostly, because I'm worried about Xander, but partly, because I feel awful for what I'm about to do to Ethan. He's falling for me, and I thought I was falling for him too, but I was wrong.

One hundred percent of my heart belongs to Xander Varro, and at this point, I'm not even sure his is still beating.

Ethan presses his hand to my cheek and wipes a tear away from my face with his thumb. His eyes are downcast and knowing. Somehow, he's expecting what comes next.

I take his hand in both of mine hold it tightly and offer every apology I can muster in one sympathetic look. What he does next makes me feel fractionally better and significantly worse all in the same action.

"*I'll drive,*" he signs, then pulls his keys from his pocket.

My heart beats so hard that it hurts as I climb into his car, unsure of where we're going but knowing it's where I want to be.

He navigates down the roads and gets stuck in one-way-street hells, U-turning through the city streets as I stare at my phone, hoping someone will call or text with further instruction of where he is. I'm hoping for some kind of sign or glimmer of hope that he's going to be okay but my gut says otherwise. I've got a bad feeling about this that I can't explain and I can't shake off. Somewhere at my deepest layer, I question if Xander is still alive.

My phone vibrates in my pocket. I hesitate to look, because I don't know what I will do if it is him, but I shudder to think about how I will feel if it's not—or at least someone on his behalf. My phone buzzes a second time, then a third.

Ethan keeps driving, looking over at me every few moments. I take a deep breath and glance at the messages. They are all from Kelly, confirming what I already knew—the motorcycle accident on the television was Xander. Three little dots appear on the screen, and I wait for her text, still holding the last breath I'd taken. It seems like hours before her next text comes through, but finally, my text box reads one new message.

I don't have a lot of information, but he's in surgery.

The tears I cry drip from my eyes to my phone screen and I'm unsure if they are new or if I have been crying this whole time.

I want to see him. I want to tell him I'm sorry. I want the chance to say I'm in—I am *all* in. Beginning to end. The cameras, the questions, I'll take it all the way, whatever way I can get it, as long as I have him. If he is beside me, I'll take everything else too.

I'm not sure I'll get the opportunity to say any of it at all. Regret strikes through every available nerve. I feel the pain of what I missed out on from the top of my ears to the tips of my toes and I know that the minutes I spent avoiding him were wasted and nobody's fault but my own.

Ethan picks one of the major hospitals and heads that direction. It is a better option than listening to me cry as we drive circles in the city with no destination. The news vans outside the doors tell me I'm in the right place, and Ethan pulls up to the emergency room doors. He exits the car, comes to my side and opens my door for me, hugging me and wiping the tears from under my eyes. He plants a kind, single kiss at my hair line, and drives away as I enter the emergency room.

I approach the reception desk and the woman sitting behind it gives me a stern look as I approach. She asks me a question, but she looks away as she speaks and I've missed what she says as I couldn't read her lips. I take a pen and a sticky note from her desktop and write *Xander Varro* with a large question mark and turn it back to her.

She *laughs*.

I can tell. I can see it in her mouth and read it in her eyes. She probably assumes I'm some fan or reporter trying to get a sneak peak of the celebrity singer at his worst. Perhaps the crews outside have already even tried.

I can feel her eyes on my back as I make my way toward the waiting area. I collapse into one of the only available seats in the crowded room. If I'm being honest with myself, it's because I don't have it in me to leave and have no clue where else I would go.

The night hours pass and I don't leave. I don't sleep. I don't eat. I don't take the blanket that is offered to me by a caring nurse. I just sit and think, and think and sit, and have no idea what comes next.

There's no news. There are no updates. The news has released his name at this point and the media is selfishly eating it up every second they can. They probably saw dollar signs when they found out it was Xander and not just some average person with an unrecognizable name, because seventy-five percent more viewers just tuned into their station once they realized who that bike had belonged too.

Naturally, the first thing they release is his drug and alcohol toxicity screen. Thankfully, these tests were negative, and the Boston Police release a statement stating drugs and alcohol were not a factor in the crash.

My chair and position changes so many times through the night that I must have sat in every available area of the hospital. Giving up and going home crosses my mind but fades when I see a girl with a long strawberry-blonde braid attached to a very familiar face.

Jana.

The chair wobbles on its legs as I jump out of it. Jogging toward her, I close the distance between us and place a hand on her shoulder. She turns toward me and her eyes and mouth open wide in surprise. Obviously she'd not been expecting to see me.

My tears start falling almost immediately. I have so many questions that I want answers to. She wraps her hand around my wrist and leads me to a smaller waiting area in a different part of the hospital and asks the reception desk for a pen and paper.

In messy handwriting, she gives me a quick rundown of the overall situation—a list composed of words that only sounds worse as it goes on. Breaks in both arms. Injuries to one ankle. Road rash that covers a significant part of his body. Surgery to remove his ruptured spleen. Lung collapse. If he hadn't been wearing a helmet, he would probably be dead.

Can I see him? I write. She shakes her head in a no.

Family only, she writes. I raise an eyebrow at her and cock my head, wondering if she's lying to keep me away from him. Perhaps she's just playing the protective-friend role because she knows I hurt him before, and she doesn't think I deserve to see him. She has seen him, and she's not family. I point to her with curiosity in my eyes.

She returns her attention to the paper she previously wrote on.

In his emergency contacts on his phone, he listed me as his sister.

I nod my head and fight back the tears I know are forming. These specific tears are ones of guilt, because I know it should have and could have been me they called. I could have been added to that list. It could be me holding his hand, but it's not because I left him behind when I thought things were hard—and now that they *are* hard, I don't know what I was thinking before.

Jana says she will text me the minute anything changes. A fraction of me believes her but a more convincing part of me thinks she doesn't trust me — and possibly blames me for all this.

I'm running solely on caffeine at this point, because I haven't slept in multiple nights. I toss and turn and check my phone and never get any information I want. Kelly checks in. Even Ethan sends a kind, concerned message, but I don't respond to them. I don't have the energy to commit to anything that's not related to Xander.

Finally, after a length of time there is no existing measurement for, Jana messages me.

He's awake and you can see him. But I'm warning you... The Xander Varro you are about to see is not the same one you left behind in that hotel room all those weeks ago. Prepare yourself. It's a lot to take in.

If she meant for the words to burn as I swallowed them, she heated them to exactly the right temperature. I didn't need the reminder that I left him in New York, but Jana didn't really seem like the type to care what I needed. To give her credit, she fit the sister role for Xander perfectly. She cared about him immensely and protected him like family, and I respected that about her.

Check-in at the hospital was easier than I expected, and I am led to his room by an extra-helpful nurse. My pace is slow, anchored by the weight of the last few days, but I don't want to be away from him even one minute longer. Regardless of the physical and mental turmoil that is guaranteed to follow, I need to see him.

The knob slips in my sweating palm, but I enter the hospital room slowly, and silently. The tears start falling as soon as I see him. I press my hands against my mouth and sob into my palms. He is bruised and injured all over, but truthfully, he doesn't look as bad as I'd expected.

One arm is casted, the other braced. His left leg is casted as well. The areas of skin that aren't covered in a hospital gown are wrapped in layers and layers of gauze, I can only assume, to protect the exposed area where skin once was but is no longer.

There are many visible injuries, though it looks like his arms took most of the impact. I can tell from where I stand that he is struggling to breathe, but I was told to expect that. The nurse had handed me a pamphlet regarding traumatic pneumothorax – or collapsed lung after unexpected injury – as she walked me to the room, and I glanced quickly at the info.

I don't step forward. I don't knock. I just continue to analyze him as he lies there in the hospital bed. I realize that the more I look, the bandaging on his left arm completely covers the area where there was once permanently tattooed art, and I can't help but wonder if the dozens of hours' worth of ink and portraits will still look the same as they did before when those bandages are removed.

Not wanting to disturb him, I step forward and sit on the outermost inch of the bed. He stirs a bit and blinks open his eyes.

His gaze shifts to mine, but his expression is unreadable. And in that hardened glance with silent eyes that offer no readable emotion, I realize that I needed to see him. I wanted to see him. But it never crossed my mind that he might not want to see me.

Chapter Twenty

Xander

The worst headache I have ever had is a tickle compared to the searing pain between my temples now. My mouth is so dry that my tongue sticks behind my teeth, and my throat resists when I try to swallow. I open and close my lids a few times, blinking through hazy eyes. Pain courses through both my arms and my lower half, but I know the pain is a good thing. It means I still have feeling.

The room is a blur. There are two of everything when I finally manage to keep my eyelids spaced apart. I can barely make out the figure of the person sitting on my bed. Between the pain, the fatigue and whatever drugs they were loading me up with, my eyes and brain aren't working as a team quite yet. After a few seconds, the image steadies, and I can see the crystal-clear outline of Natalie sitting at my bedside.

It must be a dream. A hallucination induced by the IV medications flooding my system.

I turn my head slightly — the best I can, anyway — to get a better look at the vision in front of me, to see her face and eyes and overall beauty.

She takes a deep, gasping breath and presses her hand to her mouth. Tears pour from her eyes and I know it's not a dream. It's not my imagination. She's here, in what would be arm's reach if mine were usable. I consider extending my arm to touch her, to feel her body heat against my swollen, damaged hands. The risk of pain would be entirely worth the reward.

She's still crying, and there's not much I can offer her in this moment.

"Hey now, none of that," I say out loud, barely annunciated, my voice cracking and unsteady. I know it's a wasted effort, but I can't write to her. I couldn't sign to her, even if I knew how.

She moves from sitting at the edge of the bed to sitting in the chair next to me. She's balancing on the edge, leaning her face into my shoulder, holding fistfuls of my hospital gown and sobbing into my chest. Ignoring the pain, I turn my head to her, pressing my lips into her hairline. I can smell the strawberry shampoo scent in her hair and hear her labored breaths as she tries to control herself. I want to stay here with her in this moment forever, but I can't. I can't fight the heaviness of my eyelids. My eyes close and I drift off, with only the hope that she will still be there when I wake up.

And she is.

She's sitting in one corner, flipping through the pages of a book. Blake and Cooper stand at the foot of my bed. The bags under Cooper's eyes say he hasn't gotten much, if any sleep.

"*Christ*, Xander," he says, shaking his head as he assesses my casted injuries. He takes a knee on the floor near the top of the hospital bed and places his hand at the side of my head, his palm against my temple, his thumb at my forehead. "You scared me, boy." His shaking vocal chords cause his voice to tremble. I've always looked up to Cooper, but this moment solidifies him as the closest thing I have ever had to a father.

"Hey," Blake chimes in, "I printed you a new article for the tour bus wall of shame." He holds the article in front of me, and my eyes scan the headline. I furrow my forehead and look at him.

"Amputation *possible*?" I say, unsure whether to laugh or be utterly mortified that people will actually read and believe this shit. "Where in the hell would they even come up with an idea like that?"

Blake clears his throat and smiles a mischievous, knowing smile. "An anonymous source," he says, barely able to swallow back a laugh.

"You're an *ass*," I say, accompanied with a loud enough laugh that it causes me to cough, reminding me that my lungs aren't quite where they need to be yet.

"We are going to get out of here. We just wanted to check on you," Cooper says. "Theo and Dom will be in later. You get some rest." He glances at Natalie, who still has her nose in a book. "*Rest,*" he reiterates.

The eight days that I was hospitalized for felt more like months. The doctors and staff have paid special attention to the incision where my spleen once was and monitored my labs and imaging closely. I could be released from the hospital provided I have someone at home with me twenty-four hours a day to assist me with daily activities.

Between Natalie, Jana, Blake and Cooper, that wouldn't be an issue. Their main job, apparently, was going to be keeping me off my injured leg, but I am as stubborn as anything, going a little stir crazy and determined to do everything on my own. This isn't a favorable combination with only one good leg to stand on and a plethora of impressive internal injuries.

Personally, I enjoyed the times where everyone else was off doing other things and Natalie was with me. At the hospital, she didn't want to get to close to me, feared hurting me, and she didn't want to be in the way of any of the physicians. So, she stood back, farther away than I wanted her to be. Being home, out of the hospital, makes her more sure-footed around me, as if being out of the hospital is synonymous to being less fragile.

Here, I relax in bed with my injured leg up on pillows and she cuddles in close on my right side. Even with a braced right wrist, I still manage to wrap my arm around her. For the most part, my injuries are largely left sided. My left leg and arm are both casted, and the skin on that side of my back and upper arm received the worst of the road rash. I have a hefty amount of stitches at my upper left arm, which secure a laceration that caused so much blood loss that I required a transfusion upon admission.

I'm almost asleep when I hear my apartment door open. Jana, Blake, Cooper and the other band members come and go so often these days that my door might as well remain open.

"Hello?" I call, and Natalie sits up, tucking her long hair behind her ears.

It isn't Blake or Jana that steps through my bedroom doorframe.

It's my mother.

Natalie had met her briefly at the hospital but had stepped out to give my mother and me some space. I hadn't seen my mother in a while, and she didn't hold back her feelings about our reunion occurring while I was confined to a hospital bed. But she visited every day during my stay. She and I have caught up, and she has spent a lot of time with Natalie since her arrival the morning after the accident.

She holds her arms open, and Natalie rises to give her a welcoming hug. When she pulls away, she points to the pad of paper and pen on the bedside table. Natalie hands it to her, and she jots a message I can't see.

Natalie starts writing back a lengthy response.

"What did you ask her?" I say, annoyed that I'm not privy to information that is clearly concerning me.

"I asked her how you were doing today," she says, reading over Natalie's shoulder.

"Why didn't you just ask me?"

"Because she will tell me the truth," she says, holding her hand out as Natalie hands over today's progress report. She uses her finger to run down the list Natalie has made, seemingly pleased with most of the responses, but rolls her eyes and looks at me with a narrowed glance over the note pad.

"You have to eat food with these medications," she says.

"I forgot the two dozen different doctor's instructions regarding that," I say, my voice never changing tone or pitch. "Thank God you're here to remind me." I try to adjust my position, but the movement is painful and awkward. Natalie rushes to my side to help, adjusting the pillows around me to help me into a sitting position.

"*Alexander,*" my mother snaps. I know I should be patient with her, but I have very few undamaged nerves left, and she tends to get on them.

"I just haven't found my appetite yet, okay?" I say. "I'll get there."

Natalie steps out of the room. By the sounds of the cabinets opening and the way the water is running, I'd guess she's putting on some coffee for my mother.

"You need a haircut." She eyes my overgrown locks from the foot of the bed.

"I'll get right on that." A yawn interrupts my cynicism.

The smell of the coffee Natalie is brewing fills my room. "I'm going to try to get some rest," I say. "I'm sure Natalie is patiently waiting to inform you how terrible of a patient I have been over a cup of coffee."

"I'll be here when you wake up." She closes the door behind her.

My mother, from what she has seen of Natalie thus far, approves. It's nice to see them bonding as much as they can before my mom heads back to her home in Arizona.

I never realized how much I looked like my mother until this visit. I have the same dark hair and eyes, the same olive skin tone. But more so than that, our personalities are identical — outspoken, stubborn, strong-willed.

My mother hasn't quite gotten the hang of conversing with Natalie, still writing things down and gesturing wildly rather than speaking out loud and letting Natalie follow along, so listening in to what they may be discussing is useless. It's silent on the other side...until it's not.

I hear the TV come to life, voices ringing from the box on the other side of my wall.

The initial reports are weather-related—a male newscaster chatters on, reading a forecast that is better than likely impressively wrong—they usually are—then he introduces sports. The sports anchor says his piece, then indicates a transition to local news.

And they're *still* talking about me.

As if anybody has missed the story, the news reporters recap the accident, describing the sharp corner it happened on, accompanied by, I'm sure, the pictures of my broken-beyond-repair motorcycle.

I can't keep listening. Those images are already imbedded into my thoughts. Pain shoots through my arms and abdomen, a reminder that I shouldn't be getting up. But I do, struggling to make it down the short hallway and into the living room under my own power. I hop on my good leg and balance against the wall with my casted arm.

The stool Natalie sits on rocks and threatens to fall as she pushes herself off it and dashes to me, draping my arm over her shoulder and taking as much of my body weight as she can. I am much taller than she is, and I would guess I'm pretty damn near close to twice her weight, but somehow, she finds the strength needed to keep me upright.

I glare at the TV. My eyes narrow and darken as the pictures of the accident continue to surface on the screen.

"Turn it off," I say to my mother in a voice that doesn't hide my physical or mental exhaustion. "I don't want to see it. I don't want to listen to it. Just turn it *off*."

I'm leaning far more weight on Natalie than I want to, but I can't help it. I greatly overestimated my strength. I can feel the sweat bead over my eyebrows as the color leaves my face and the room spins around me.

"You are supposed to be resting, Alexander," my mother says in a hiss. She approaches us and attempts to help, but before I can protest, she places her hand on my back where the skin is seared with road rash. I gasp in pain and take a step backward that I can't handle. I feel top-heavy suddenly but catch myself against the wall.

I don't want to admit it to them — I don't even want to admit it to myself — but I need to get back to my room and lie down. Holding hardly any of my own weight, leaning on Natalie and my mother as much as they can handle, I make my way back to my bedroom with no intention of attempting to leave it again any time soon.

* * * *

Natalie is running her fingers across the skin of my right arm in light, gentle, repetitive movements when I open my eyes. I could wake up to this, to her, one million and one times over and still never get used to it or tire of it.

Having a brace on one wrist and a fully casted other hand made communication with her very difficult, but Cooper brought us large, touch-screen tablets that made it slightly easier. I punched in words the best I could on the app we used to send messages back and forth.

Is my mother still here? I type in, and she nods in return. *Can you send her in?* She nods again, accompanied by a smile and kisses me before leaving the room. My mother comes in, knocking lightly on the door, even though I was expecting her. Natalie brings a chair in, sets it by my bed and leaves the room, giving me some time alone with my mother.

"Are you feeling okay?" she asks.

"Better every day," I respond through a forced smile. She needs to think I'm okay. She needs to believe I am making progress or she will never leave. It's not that I don't want her here—having her here has been great—but I don't like inconveniencing anyone. I don't want anyone's plans or life to pause on my account. She is missing work and staying in a hotel. She should be at her home, enjoying her space instead of living out of a suitcase and using her vacation time on me.

She's looking at me as if she has something to tell me but is unsure how.

"Your father wants to see you," she says, looking away from me. I can sense the bitter taste the words leave as they roll uncomfortably off her tongue.

"Yeah, well, he can fu—"

"*Alexander*," she scolds, and suddenly I am a child again, being reprimanded by the only parent I ever really had.

"It's just Xander—"

"Not to me," she interrupts. "I never understood that, anyway. Why the change? What's wrong with your full name?"

"It's *his* name, and I refuse to share anything with him. I was never allowed a nickname, you know? People would call me Alex, and he'd correct them. Which was fine, because I hated that shit anyway. But he would say '*You'll be called by the name I chose for you.*'"

I can still picture him saying it in his pretentious voice as he straightened out his tie and looked down on me with dark, disappointed eyes.

"So, when we started getting big and I started being more widely recognized as Xander, I kept the name. I made it to the top, and I made it without him, and I didn't want anything he chose for me."

She looks at me with sympathy in her eyes, but I don't want it. I don't need it—from her or anyone else.

"So, as I was saying," I continue, "he can fuck right off."

This time, a slight grin breaks at the corner of her pursed lips.

"I miss you, Alexander," she says. "Let's see each other again soon, preferably under better conditions."

"I miss you too. We will. I'll do better. I promise," I say, and tears fill her dark brown eyes.

"I am *so* proud of you. I love seeing my son, the young boy who had a big dream, turn into a grown man who's keeping that dream alive. It is exciting to see your face come across on TV and interviews and in the news. I love seeing all that. I do," she says, and I feel a 'but' coming. "*But* I want to see more of the awards and music and honors and less of the punching people and totaling motorcycles. That isn't a phone call I ever want to receive again."

Her voice and tone bring me back to my first of many bad grades, detention slips and other times I trended more on the reckless side. My rebellious side bloomed when my father left us. Both instances were hell on her. She reminded me, now, sitting here, though I was almost thirty years old, so much of the single mother who was doing her best to keep me in line when

I was determined to destroy everything she had created for me.

I like to believe I have come a long way since then, though, I am casted in three places and covered in road burns that say otherwise.

Apparently, I still have some growing up to do.

"About Natalie."

I prepare myself for the worst. Historically, my mother has been openly opinionated when it comes to my relationships.

"She's amazing. Perfect for you. Dare I say it…much, *much* better than Mariah."

I involuntarily smirk the way I always do when I think about Natalie.

"Don't let that one get away." She places emphasis on each word. She reaches out as if she's going to place her hand on mine, but pulls back, realizing there is very little uninjured area for her to touch.

"You don't have to worry about that. I learned that lesson already."

"My flight out is tonight, but you call me if you need anything at all. You promise?"

"I always need you," I say, more for her than myself. Her lips turn to a flattered pout. "But I will be okay. I have a lot of good people in my corner."

"One of the very best." She nods Natalie's direction as she returns to the room with a plate of food.

Chapter Twenty-One

My agitation level grows exponentially with every passing day. Being stuck at home is not my style. In fact, this is probably the longest I have ever spent inside these apartment walls since I've owned it. We're usually touring—or recording or on some kind of adventure. Now, I'm not doing any of those things. I can't even pick up a friggin' guitar—and the walls are starting to close in.

I have no idea how long it has been since my accident—two weeks? Maybe three? I've lost count, leaving me confused and unsure. I do know this, however... I have not taken as many steps—figuratively or literally—as I would have liked to at this point.

I'm staring ahead at some old movie on TV but not really watching it at all. Natalie hands me a sticky note that says *Doctors appointment two p.m.* on it, but I crumble it up and toss it to the floor, shaking my head and returning my gaze to the TV.

The breaths that Natalie takes come out in an uneven sound. She stares at me with frustration in her eyes, her arms crossed.

"*You have to go,*" she signs. "Not *optional.*" And even though I understand very few signs, I get that message loud and clear. But still, I don't respond.

She just doesn't see it from where I'm standing — or *not* standing, which is a huge part of the damn problem. I am feeling unhinged about everything. The TV plays the same movies repeatedly. I want to play guitar and can't. I am sick and tired of depending on everybody for every damn thing and I *want* to leave the apartment and go outside, literally anywhere, but I know it's too much of a nuisance. That, and I refuse to leave the house — doctor's appointment or not — until I get a real shower. My casts make it difficult to do that, so I have relied heavily on Natalie's assistance with wash cloths and soapy water bowls.

Natalie's patience has grown thin. She stomps out of the room. It's impressive how her small frame can shake the whole apartment when she's upset with me. She pushes my wheelchair to the side of my bed. She smiles a false, forced grin and points to the seat, and I raise an eyebrow at her. She points again, and once more, her message is clear.

"*Your ass, that seat. Now,*" she demands, but I don't budge.

She steps forward, puts her arms underneath my legs and physically pulls me to one side of the bed.

"Stop, *stop!*" I finally give in before she hurts herself too. Helping her the best I can, I get from the bed to the wheelchair. She pushes me into the bathroom where, thankfully, I have a very large walk-in shower with a bench built in. She points to the bench, and I understand what she is suggesting, but I don't see it working well. I'm barely stable on dry land. Wet shower tiles offer a whole new level of instability.

This is pointless. It is never going to work. I shake my head and start to wheel myself away. She turns the chair and stands in front of me, facing me, her hands on the arm rests of the chair, her face just inches from mine.

The frustration leaves her eyes. A playful smile grows into her cheeks as she backs away, stepping into the shower. She turns the water on and backs up into the spray, unzipping her sweatshirt and tossing it aside onto the tiled floor. I'm watching her intently, very aware of what she's doing, but still not completely sold. She unclips the button on her jeans and slides them down over her hips, just enough to reveal the pink lacey number she is wearing underneath.

"Oh, now you're just not playing fair," I say, shaking my head, pressing my teeth into my bottom lip.

She reaches her arms toward me, coaxing me, tempting me...and it is working.

I reach out my braced hand to her, ready to make an attempt at joining her. I mean, how am I supposed to say no to that?

She's pleased with herself, and I'm pleased too. She has me motivated to try *something* instead of lying around in this apartment being miserable at best.

Using the forearm of my braced arm to push myself up, I leave all my weight on my right leg. I know keeping myself in a standing position will be a short-lived experiment, but I know a quick shower could do a world of difference for me, physically and mentally.

Natalie gets me into the tiled portion of the walk-in shower, cautiously assessing each move I make. She suggests I sit right away, but I refuse. I do my best to leave my casted side just outside the glass pane that separates the shower from the rest of the bathroom, and I reach over her to adjust the shower head so it's pointing toward my body, soaking her in the process. She gives me a playful scowl, and my lips turn up at the corners. I lean my body weight into the glass wall of the shower, and Natalie helps me remove the plastic brace from my right hand, tossing it to the tiles outside the shower stall.

As the water runs down her hair and face and neck, I lean in and press my lips to hers. The water is falling over me too now, saturating my shirt and shorts. She takes fistfuls of my T-shirt in her hands and peels it over my head, revealing my slow healing, but better than they were road rash areas, arm laceration and splenectomy scar. I move my brace-free hand to the back of her head where her hair meets her neck and I take a handful of her hair. My hand is stiff, pained — but I'm too distracted to care. Gently pulling her head back, I kiss her throat under the warm stream of water. Letting go of her hair, I run my hand down her neck and back. I stop at the clips of her bra, releasing the hooks with almost no effort at all — impressing myself since this is one of my first unbraced motions in days.

I hold her closely, partially for balance, but more so in desire. I need her in more than one way — first, to keep me upright, but second, and by and large the major factor — because I need *her*. Everything about her. Physically, mentally. I need her in my life in every aspect.

My bare chest is against hers. Her hands are in my hair then at my shoulders and running down my back. Her fingers find the elastic waistband of my shorts and boxers, and she pulls them off me, paying special attention to my casted leg that I, for just a moment, had also forgotten about.

I kiss her like I can't get enough of her — and maybe I can't. Without warning, fatigue rushes over me and I stop. My limbs feel heavy, my body telling me it has had enough. I lean my forehead into hers and feel the amount of weight I put on her increase. My face twists to a painful grimace and I shake my head in a slow, frustrated *no* against her forehead. I can't stand anymore. Truthfully, I made it longer than I thought I would.

Steadying me, she helps me into a seated position at the built-in bench. I tip my head back, placing it against the tile wall. My breathing is heavy — partially pained and partially disappointed. She spends the remainder of our time in the shower handing me shampoo and body wash and assisting me when I need her. The water stops as she turns the knob, then she wraps herself in one towel and comes toward me with another.

It is no secret that my mental health is even more fractured than my physical health these days. I feel trapped. Stuck. Helpless. Defeated. And *itchy* under these damn casts. But Natalie has improved my mood tenfold. I can't imagine where I'd be if she hadn't come back to me — and I don't want to.

Taking a shower made me feel like a new man. Taking a shower with her…? Well, it made me forget for how much discomfort I was in for a while.

Losing myself in her and looking at her like that made me forget entirely what was going on with my body and become only interested in every inch of hers.

Her body is indescribable. I am a lyrical person at my core, but not even I have the words to paint a good enough picture to encompass all that she possesses. She is faultless at every inch.

I started the day frustrated at an abundance of things, was distracted by her for a short time and now was frustrated I couldn't participate in more — more of her, more of us, more of what would have come next.

With much effort, I pull on loose-fitting sweatpants, a T-shirt and a baseball cap and sit at the end of my bed, waiting for Natalie to be ready to leave for my appointment.

She brushes through her dark hair and quickly ties it into a long braid over one shoulder. She's looking at me in the reflection of the bathroom mirror and I want to walk up to her, wrap my arms around her from behind, take in her scent and feel her skin against mine. I want to hear her breathe and taste her lips and look into her beautiful, separate-colored eyes but I can't, and suddenly the two dozen feet between us feels like miles.

* * * *

The lobby of the orthopedic doctor's office is crowded. A few people recognize me. Some I would assume have been fans for a while, but others are probably only aware of who I am because the media hasn't shut up about me in weeks. The whispers and the stares and the obvious pictures truly didn't bother me. I think it bothers the receptionist more than it fazes me, because she has one of the nurses take me back sooner than expected.

She first brings us back to a dark room where X-rays are taken to monitor progress, then once those are obtained, brings us to a regular exam room.

She takes my vitals, asks me about my pain on a scale of one to ten, verifies my medications and pharmacies and asks how much alcohol I intake.

Truthfully, for the first time in years, I have to think about when my last drink was.

She leaves the room and Natalie taps her foot nervously. After some time, the doctor finally knocks and enters.

"Ah, Mr. Varro. I'm Dr. David Sawyer. I saw you when you were first admitted to the hospital, but I would imagine that's not something you remember. Anyhow, let's take a look at some pictures here, shall we?"

He pulls up some images on the computer and turns the screen toward me so I can view them too, as if any of the imaging makes sense to me. I'm not even sure what body part I'm looking at.

He points to the screen and explains what he sees on the X-rays.

"This one here, Alexander? This one is of that right hand. This looks great. I'd say we can probably see how you do without the brace, if you're feeling up to it. That was your least worrisome injury in the hospital, but the swelling was initially bad enough that I was concerned for severe sprains, muscle injuries. But this picture? This is beautiful."

That's good news. One body part down, two to go.

"This picture here is of that left leg. Everything seems to be moving into place as we'd like. This is also good news," the doctor continues. "When we see poor healing processes or bones not setting the way we'd like, that's where we get into surgical options and we don't want any unnecessary procedures. I'd like to take another picture of this leg in two weeks and possibly discuss the potential of getting you out of a hard cast and into a walking boot. That would offer you great protection and stability while giving you a little more freedom.

I nod in response. That sounds much easier than my current cast.

"Okay, Xander. Here is where things get a little rocky," Dr. Sawyer says.

He pulls up the final pictures — the one of my left hand, arm and elbow — and points out all the places he is concerned about.

"This arm and hand are not cooperating as I had hoped. They're healing incredibly slow. There is a lot of swelling in that hand that is preventing the bones from sliding back into place as we'd wanted. I have a physical therapist in mind who works with patients both while they are casted and post cast removal. I think it would greatly benefit you to consult with her a few times and see if we can get this swelling down and promote good healing," he explains.

I don't say anything, and Natalie is looking at me with large, worried eyes, waiting for me to give her some indication of how this visit is going.

"I know it is a lot to take in," Dr. Sawyer says, "but make an appointment for two weeks from now and we will reassess. I highly recommend the therapy. The front desk staff can help you get situated with that before you leave, if you'd like to try." He reaches for two pamphlets from a brochure holder on the wall and gives one to me and one to Natalie.

He leaves the room and the nurse returns to help me back into the chair and to push me to the checkout counter. They offer to help me set up a physical therapy consult but I decline, and we leave the office.

Since we are out anyway, Natalie decides we can handle a trip to Chance's on the Corner for some coffees.

Jana pours us our steaming hot lattes. Natalie goes to the counter to pay and her and Jana write back and forth, having a conversation I am not privy too.

It's Jana who returns to the table with Natalie's and my coffees. She is wearing a disgruntled expression, staring at me with anger in her eyes.

"What?" I ask, genuinely curious about what I possibly could have done to upset her. She whips the hat off my head and hits me with it, before lecturing me in a loud voice.

"Are you seriously not going to start physical therapy? Is it stubbornness or stupidity? You need to go to physical therapy, like, *yesterday*," she instructs.

I take a sip of my coffee and stare at her over the cup.

"Physical therapy just seems like a massive waste of time," I say.

"Xander, you are post-surgery. You have a casted arm, a cast on your leg, healing lungs and did a hell of a number on your skin. You have nothing *but* time right now. Go to therapy."

"Why? I'll go when the cast is off. It's stupid to go before."

"I'm going to say this one time, then we never have to talk about it again, but you need to hear it once," Jana says in a stern, concerned tone. "Xander, if you don't do this, if you don't take every opportunity at your very best shot of a hundred percent recovery, there is a chance you will never play guitar the same way again. If that hand heals incorrectly, you may never hold a guitar the way you once did. You may never be the musician your fans know and love because you're busy being the stubborn *jackass* who I know and love. But don't. Don't be like that. Think about how hard you've worked. You need that hand, Xander. You need to go to physical therapy if you want full range of motion back. Guitar. Piano. The friggin' *oboe*. Whatever it is you plan to try going forward, you need to be working on it now or you will lose it all."

A customer enters, and Jana leaves the table.

"You're going to physical therapy," she yells, loudly, echoing through the sitting area of the coffee shop as she returns to her spot behind the counter.

I sip my coffee and stare into Natalie's eyes. She is, at this moment, the only thing keeping me from unraveling all together. Sometimes, when I'm at my lowest, when I think of the pain and injuries, sometimes I think they were entirely worth all the damage, because they brought her back to me, and in this instance, the positive vastly outweighs the negatives.

I didn't waste any time at all ditching the brace that was stabilizing my wrist. At least I had one hand free, and it is my dominant side. I felt the stiffness and soreness set in almost immediately, but one free hand was better than none at all.

As we leave Chance's, Jana holds the door open and Natalie pushes me through it. I hate being toted around everywhere, but crutches weren't even an option with hand injuries on both sides. Even with a brace-free hand, I wasn't anywhere near ready to support my body weight using a crutch.

"I'll see you tomorrow morning, okay?" Jana says as Natalie and I cross the threshold of Chance's. Jana has been coming over during the day after her shifts to help me out while Natalie is in class. I keep telling them that I am fine, but they choose not to hear me — and they say *I'm* stubborn. There was a time Jana wanted Natalie to stay as far away from me as possible, but now that they've bonded, they constantly team up against me. It's brutal.

"Yeah. I'll be there, you know, because I have *literally* no other option," I say.

"Great," Jana says. "You may not be able to play guitar yet, but you are sure getting great at playing that tiny violin."

I take a deep breath in and try not to laugh as she pokes fun at my apparent wallowing.

"See you tomorrow," I say with a wave.

It's slow going, but we finally make it home.

Blake is waiting for us when we arrive at the apartment. He brought a few new release movies and we plan to order Chinese food while Natalie works her shift at The Rock Room. She leaves for the evening and Blake helps himself to the fridge.

"Hand me one of those, will you?" I say as Blake pops the cap off a beer.

"You can't drink while taking those medications, Xander." His tone is pointed.

"Watch me."

He's skeptical and hesitates to do what I ask.

"Fine, I'll do it myself." I lean into the counter and try to push myself into a standing position. I exaggerate the difficulty slightly.

"Okay, okay, jeez," he says, the words rushed together. "Just sit down." And he hands me a cold beer from the refrigerator. I know he doesn't want to, but I'm an adult, capable of making my own decisions, despite what my band of babysitters say.

The constant hovering is the hardest part. I appreciate everything they are all doing for me, but at the same time, I just want it all to stop.

"The band is going to get together next week, play some music and brainstorm, hopefully take a few steps toward some new songs." He sips his drink.

"Okay," I reply, with no meaning behind the word.

"Okay, like you'll be there?"

"Okay, like, I'll see if I'm feeling up to it," I snap at him.

"Come on, man. You have to snap out of this. I know things suck for you right now, but you have got to pull yourself together." He is, apparently, getting just as frustrated with me as I am with him. I take a long drink and avoid eye contact.

"Where is the music that used to pour out of you, even when we didn't ask for it? You used to be a continuous fountain of lyrical genius and lately you haven't even tried. Where are the songs and lyrics and musical combinations these days, Xander?"

"You could check the corner of the road where I left my motorcycle, half my skin and a majority of my dignity, if you'd like. They're probably lying around there somewhere."

I was trying to be purposefully spiteful, but Blake laughs and I join him.

Chapter Twenty-Two

The clock on my phone reads three-fifty-three a.m., just about ten minutes since the last time I looked and twenty-seven minutes since the time I looked before that. This is part of the routine now. Closing my eyes, then opening them, checking the time to see if I have even made it one full hour of sleep before the next time I look — but I hardly ever do.

It's the lack of sleep — and maybe the lack of music too — that makes me feel like I'm fighting a losing battle day in and day out. I sit up and stare toward the window, wanting to get lost in the vastness of the sky and the moon and the few stars fortunate enough to burn bright despite the city lights' attempt to extinguish their reach, but the blinds are closed.

This has been a nightly occurrence since I came home from the hospital weeks ago. The restlessness, the attempt to find things to do to pass the time. I find sleep only occasionally throughout the day and for some stretches of the night, but not nearly enough combined hours to count as a sufficient amount, especially while I'm still healing.

Things are getting better, sure, but I'm uncomfortable—both physically and mentally. The painkillers and muscle relaxers they gave me for my injuries turned down the pain, but they don't turn off this constant stream of thoughts—and that has been the bigger demon.

I sit awake at night, worried about playing the guitar again—or not playing again—wondering if I will fade from the scene in this time off. I won't admit it, but I wonder what happens next. When I heal, things go back to normal and I step back onto that stage and into the spotlight that she is intent on avoiding—will it be enough to scare her off? Will she be gone again? She tells me she's not going anywhere and I want to believe it, but I wouldn't be me if I didn't overthink everything.

The mattress shifts slightly as Natalie joins me at my side of the bed.

Tonight was easily the hardest night yet, mentally. Natalie squints into the light of her phone and types me a message, asking me if I'm okay—trying to figure out how to make things better. She has been asking questions regarding my wellbeing and I ignore her, mostly because I don't have the answers myself. I'm not confident there are any such answers. But she wants a response and I give her one, whether it is what she wants to hear or not.

I'm having a hard time accepting the fact that at the end of all this healing and therapy, I still may not have a career in music. Not the way it was. It might not be a part of my life anymore. Which I'm not okay with, but I am sure you are.

In a bleak moment, I meant the words to hurt as bad as her eyes tell me they did.

But she doesn't back down or shy away. Instead, she suggests that it's possible that physical therapy isn't the only kind of therapy I need.

She might not be wrong. There is something going on with me that I have locked away and lost the key.

She kneels behind me, massaging my neck and shoulders—a gesture I certainly don't deserve but she, once again, puts my feelings before her own and stays in my corner.

My muscles loosen under her fingertips, and eventually I shift until I'm lying down, and she does the same. It's her patience and touch that help me fall in to the sleep I find.

When I awaken, she's gone already, off to a full day of class then work.

Jana should be arriving in the next few hours and she will spend most of the day here. I am far enough into this recovery to be by myself, but they refuse to believe that. Jana is great, but there's no room for joking around with her. She's like a drill sergeant—on me about every little thing and has no time to take any of my usual bullshit.

Her methods are effective, though. She tends to keep me more in line than the rest of them. I think Natalie tiptoes around me, worrying about bruising my ego, and Blake just gives in to whatever I want, but Jana doesn't. I don't know if it's because she is on her way to becoming a medical professional or if it's just that she has a stubbornness that parallels mine, but she's good for this healing process. She has even convinced me to go to physical therapy this afternoon, and as annoyed as I am about it, Natalie is thrilled—the silver lining, I guess.

"Good morning, sunshine." Jana leans against my doorframe.

"It is morning. I'm not so sure what's good about it."
I yawn.

She rolls her eyes and comes into the room.

I pull the sheets back, revealing the new black removable boot that covers my foot and ankle.

"Hey, look at that. Shiny and new. When did that happen?"

"Last night. Just in time for physical therapy today," I say with a hint of sarcasm and overall lack of enthusiasm.

"I brought coffee," she says in a sing-song tone. "Why don't you test that out and walk with me to the living room?"

I accept the challenge and slowly push myself to a standing position. I'm sore and stiff everywhere, but sore and stiff is a huge upgrade from pain and agony. It's odd taking steps in the boot. I haven't held my own weight on both legs in weeks, and the boot was awkward. I take a few steps, lose my balance for only a second, and wave Jana off as she steps forward to help me.

"I've got it. I've got it," I say, but the words lack confidence. By the time I reach the doorframe, I start to get the hang of it. I use the wall for assistance, but for the most part make it to the living room under my own power. It's oddly satisfying. As I fall into the couch, I realize the toll the short walk took on my body and I feel like I could sleep for a week.

We sip coffee, watch YouTube videos and laugh at stupid things we find on the Internet. She stands up after a while and walks around the apartment, picking through items. She finds a shelf full of vinyl records.

"Do these actually work?" She pulls an album from the shelf.

"Seriously?" I ask. "Of course, they work."

"I've never actually heard a track on vinyl before," she says quietly, with a sense of embarrassment about the words.

"I think that's the case for a lot of people," I say with a light laugh. "But as far as quality goes, there's live music, then there's vinyl then there is the rest of it. MP3s and streams have nothing on the sounds of vinyl."

She offers me a hand, and I take it, pulling myself up and hobbling to the record player. She hands me the vinyl record she'd chosen and I lifted the turn arm and position the needle at the outermost groove of the record.

She swings and sways, truly getting enveloped in the wholesome, full sound that the vinyl offers, and I laugh at her as she spins wildly around the mostly empty room. I can't help it. Her ridiculous twirls and carefree steps have a contagious joy to them.

"You're laughing. Good to know there is still a human in there." She comes back toward me, reaches up and knocks on the side of my head with her knuckles.

"I never said thank you, you know." I scratch at the overgrown hair on my chin and jaw.

"For what?" she says, finally coming to a stop.

"Everything. I don't have family here anymore. I don't really have a huge circle of people I trust outside of the band. At the time of my accident, I didn't even have Natalie. But I had you. I'm sure when we first started talking during my coffee runs, you didn't ever expect to be sucked into all this." I wave my finger around the room.

She looks at me, then the floor, then stares out of the window. I can see her reflection as she stares blankly ahead for a moment, but then turns around and speaks in a quiet voice.

"The day I came out to my family was the same day they told me I was no longer a part of it," she says, biting her lip. "I am pretty much on my own here. I worked my ass off to put myself through school. I have goals and ideas and, for the most part, I was reaching for those dreams completely by myself…until you." Her voice shakes, threatening to crack at any second. "I wasn't in contact with anyone who I shared a bloodline with. Then you come along and *chose* me to be your family. When I found out you had listed me as your sister on your emergency contact info? That was pre-planned, Xander. And you didn't even tell me. Cooper told me you have had my name down on all the band paperwork and information he has held onto for *years*. When I saw my name on that paper, you made me part of something."

She pauses for a moment, and as much as I'd never admit it, she has me choked up too. "You are all I have, Xander. And when I got that phone call…" She pauses and swallows down her emotions, the same way I always do. "I'm just really glad you're okay, because if you weren't, I would have brought you back and killed you myself. So start being smarter, you crazy, stubborn jackass of a man. Because maybe it's selfish, but I need you around."

"Come here." I wrap my arms around her shoulders. "You can always count on me. I'm not going anywhere," I promise her.

I have never seen Jana show any kind of real emotion in all the years I have known her, but talking about my accident tossed her over the edge. She tried to keep it together, but finally breaks down, barely able to breathe through the tears she finally allowed. It's been *weeks* since the accident. She has been holding it all together this whole time and she has finally come untied.

Silence surrounds us. The song she'd chosen had stopped playing.

We part and she takes a deep breath.

"You have to go get ready for physical therapy. *Now*." She returns to full boss mode seamlessly, ditching the vulnerable version of herself who I got a chance to meet for no more than five minutes.

"I'm going. I'm going." I use the walls and furniture for balance.

"Should I send for a car?" she calls from the other room.

"Yeah, unless you want to take my motorcycle," I holler back. There are metaphorical crickets for a moment, and she appears at the doorway. "Too soon?" I add through a half-smile.

"You are *so* not funny," she says with a glare and a pointed finger. "Now hurry up!" And she walks away again.

* * * *

Physical therapy is considerably more exhausting than I had initially anticipated. The therapist is a woman about my age with light brown hair and kind eyes. She concentrates mostly on my right hand, since it was now brace-free, and my left leg, which has the walking cast for easy removal. She takes some time to show me some stretches and very minor movement involving my knuckles and fingers to try on my casted hand to promote flexibility and range of motion when the cast comes off.

She hands me packets of paper with information regarding at-home exercises and the importance of doing them.

"What is the overall goal here, Xander?" she asks, with a pen and clipboard in her hand.

"To...heal...properly?" I ask. "Is this a trick question?"

"No." She laughs. "Usually if there is more motivation than just all-around health, if you have a goal we can work toward, physical therapy is much more motivating and interesting. So, I like to ask — What is the end goal?"

"I need to be playing guitar — as good as before — as soon as possible. I know it's a reach, but I'd like to be full speed well in advance to play guitar in our performance at the holiday show at CommOcean. That's what? Six weeks? Is that doable?"

"You will be on your feet for that show, Xander. I can promise you that. We will do our best to get that hand back around the neck of a guitar, okay? It's a great goal."

I nod because I can't speak. She can't tell me with confidence that she thinks I'll be playing guitar again by December because she doesn't think I will be. I can hear it in her voice, I can see it in her eyes and because of that, I can feel it in my chest.

I'm not going to be performing at full capacity, if at all, any time soon.

Though physical therapy exhausted me more than I had anticipated, I decided to join the band for a session today, which is a remarkably huge step in more than one way. Natalie suggested therapy, and truly, this, for me, is one in the same. I keep my fingers tightly crossed that this is what I need to snap out of the perpetual despondency I have found myself in. Even if I'm not holding an instrument yet, I can still sing and write and compose.

Ever since the accident, I have had this restless thought that keeps telling me the music is gone. That it isn't in me anymore, and I haven't been successful in silencing that voice. My hand isn't progressing the way I or the doctors hope for, and I can't explain it, but my breathing has changed. It feels different—like it's forced. There is a heaviness in my chest that makes it feel as if my lungs don't fill the way they need to, which is crucial to a singing career.

I haven't even tried to sing yet—not even one note. But I need to. I need to find myself again.

But today, in this music session with my band mates—my brothers—being in a room I was meant to be in, creating music I was meant to be a part of? Well, it was healing. It was therapeutic. My mood is improved today. I'm even...*inspired*, maybe.

Hours after my time with Cooper and the guys, I'm still sitting at the counter making ideas become magic on the once-blank pages in front of me.

The weight I've been carrying around lessens each time an idea comes together. Natalie sits across the room, reading a book, but glancing up at me over the binding every so often as I write down words that could become the band's next album.

Chapter Twenty-Three

Forty-seven days. It has been forty-seven painful days accompanied by forty-six sleepless nights since my accident. Six and a half weeks.

Natalie sits in the corner of the doctor's office rolling her eyes at me as I pace back and forth, walking boot and all. I'm not concerned about my foot. I've been doing well and making advancements in physical therapy, but if I have any shot at playing for the upcoming holiday show, I need to be holding a guitar as soon as possible to be ready. For that to happen, the doctor needs to tell me today that this cast is coming off and I can start some real therapy on the hand and wrist. That's a lot of pieces that have to fall into place, and the anxiety that comes with waiting is overwhelming. So…I pace.

The doctor comes in, new X-ray images in hand, and I sit on the exam table. Natalie stands and comes to my side, holding my uncasted hand tightly. Her grip cuts off my circulation. I think she's even more nervous than I am.

The doctor places the new images up on the lighted screens and I hold my breath.

He keeps quiet for a moment and my heart beats loudly in my ears.

"Let's get that cast off, shall we?" he says, and I almost have to ask him to repeat himself.

"Off. Like...*off* off? For g-good?" I stutter.

"We will fit you for a soft brace. Wear it when you can. And don't give up on physical therapy. It's important. That hand is not necessarily a hundred percent. You will need to regain some strength and range of motion," he instructs.

"I understand," I say through a beaming, foreign smile.

The saw buzzes against the plaster, cutting through it like scissors through paper. The noise doesn't bother me. It's not all that different from the song of the tattoo gun I have spent countless hours listening to. In fact, it's an inviting noise, because it means I'm only a few minutes of buzzing away from a free hand.

Natalie is bouncing up and down on the balls of her feet, anxiously waiting for the end result.

It feels odd, being able to move my wrist and fingers without obstacle. I wiggle my fingers a bit, though it feels my muscles are protesting.

I stare at my own hand like it's a new extremity. With only mild discomfort, I turn it over and back again, analyzing it as if it's a transplant, testing the fingers to see if my brain will still send a signal to them after almost two months of being barricaded. They bend when I tell them to. They move freely when I suggest it.

And now all I want to do is pick up a damn guitar.

* * * *

Blake asks Natalie and I out to celebrate my newfound freedom. Natalie invites Kelly and Jana and we all meet at a club in the city. Dancing was Kelly's idea — one of her absolute favorite things to do. She immediately convinces Blake to go out on the dance floor with her — though he doesn't put up much of a fight, and I open a tab, ordering a round.

A few people snap pictures of me and Blake as we are noticed in the bar, but they don't stir up too much commotion. Blake loves it. He's taking selfies with people on the dance floor and Kelly is all smiles, laughing at Blake's antics. Though she continuously denies any feelings for Blake, reiterating that it's *never* going to happen, they are damn near perfect for each other.

At the edge of the dance floor, Natalie waits on me and our drink order. I walk up behind her, wrapping my arms around her. She reaches one hand up, placing it underneath my hair at my neck. I'm wearing my brace on my recently uncasted hand, which I considered leaving behind, but I know full speed ahead and skipping steps is not the way to get myself back on track.

I rock and sway, moving Natalie's hips with mine, making her involuntarily dance. She tries to resist but tilts her head back in a laugh and eventually gives in.

I kiss her ear and jaw, then turn her hips so she's facing the bar, where we head to get our finished drink order to deliver to our friends, who are having way too much fun on the dance floor.

Everyone is drinking, dancing and enjoying themselves — especially Natalie, which is so important to me because she has been just as homebound as I have over the last six weeks. I want to stay out on the dance floor with her, watching her dance and joining in too. But I *can't.*

My legs grow weak, not ready for the stamina that goes hand-in-hand with dancing—even standing. I haven't been on my feet much and this is just too many steps too fast.

Natalie looks at me with worried eyes, a look I've grown used to since it seems to be the only one she wears lately. That's why I don't want her to leave the dance floor. She needs this night out.

I assure her that I am fine and throw one thumb over my shoulder, letting her know I am going to find a seat. She nods her head and steps forward to join me, but I place my hands on her arms, turn her around until she's facing Kelly and Jana, and give her an encouraging push toward the dance floor.

Blake comes with me and Kelly and Jana take Natalie's hands and shift her arms back and forth trying to keep her involved and dancing with them rather than worrying about me.

A broad shouldered, brunet man steps in close behind Kelly and places his hands on her hips. She doesn't seem to mind, and dances with him with no questions asked. But Blake...? Well, Blake minds. I can see it in his eyes. He has no hold over Kelly, but I know how he feels about her, and I feel for him.

I look at him as he chugs his drink, but then he stops, dropping his hand quickly to the table, the glass shaking across the wooden tabletop. "Xander," he says, pointing back to the dance floor.

My eyes find Natalie. A tall, muscular guy with blond slicked-back hair stands behind her, chewing on a drink stirrer. Her hands are up, creating space between them—and he's not taking no for an answer.

"Easy, Xander," Blake says. "Don't do anything I wouldn't do."

"The sky is the limit then, eh?" I step off the stool bad foot first, the soreness reminding me I'm not in tip-top shape.

I make my way toward them, Blake flanking closely at my heels.

This guy places one hand at Natalie's wrist, holding her to that spot, and is talking to her, but her expression tells me she has no idea what he is saying. She pulls her arm free and turns away, running straight into me. I keep her close to my chest, my arms around her.

My clenched jaw rests at the top of Natalie's head for a moment, but I part from her and she steps aside toward Blake.

"She doesn't want to dance with you. Take a few steps back." My voice is unchanging and monotonous.

"I didn't hear her object," he says in a haughty, challenging tone that works its way under my skin instantly. I run my fingers down my jawline, across the unshaved stubble, willing myself to keep a clear head.

"I'm not stupid. I know who you are," he says. "Why don't you just head back to your seat at the other side of the bar before I put you back in those casts."

He steps far enough forward that I can smell the liquor on his breath. I feel a hand on mine and lower my eyes to see it belongs to Natalie. She laces two fingers into my hand.

I shake my head and step back from him. He is surprised, but not nearly as surprised as I am. As I wrap my arm around Natalie to lead her off the dance floor and out of the bar, I see Blake reach forward and swat the guy's drink right out of his hand. It crashes to the floor and soaks his shoes and pants. He yells a mix of profanities at Blake over the music, and Blake grabs

Kelly's hand and pulls her along behind him as he leaves the bar. Jana follows close behind.

We all regroup outside, laughing too hard at Blake's dramatic exit.

"Where to now?" Kelly asks over the last of our echoing laughs as they begin to fade.

"I'm feeling like playing a little guitar, singing a few songs. What do you think?" Blake asks. Kelly nods, but it is me he's asking.

I roll my wrists and stretch my fingers at my side.

"I honestly can't think of anything I would rather do," I say, ready to test my physical limits.

Everyone nods and we make our way back to my place.

Blake sits on the back of the couch with his feet on the cushions and one of my guitars in his hands. I pull a chair into the living room and sit in it, holding an acoustic guitar—the very first acoustic guitar I ever played—across my body. It seemed right, commemorative, to pull this particular instrument out and blow the dust off its strings. Since, in a way, I'm brushing the dust off myself too.

The neck and body of the guitar feel heavy and unfamiliar to me. I mock-play a few notes without producing any sound, just to see if I can comfortably reach all six strings. I find myself running through the basics in my head. I can almost hear my guitar instructor from middle school making me play the same notes over and over again until I perfect each chord. I haven't had to think about playing guitar in a long time. I don't think. I just play, and that has always worked for me. But this time, holding this guitar, leaves me feeling like it's the first time all over again—like I have to put a genuine effort into the mechanics of it all.

Blake starts the intro of *Without A Doubt*, a song we have played thousands of times. He plays the same chords repetitively, waiting for me to jump in.

Deep down I know I'm hesitating because this is the real test. This is the moment I'm going to know if I'm going to be rehearsing, guitar and all, with the guys for the holiday show or if I'm just doing vocals. I'm terrified to know the answer.

I close my eyes tightly, press my sore, stiff fingers against the strings and jump into the chords Blake strums.

I feel normal.

I feel like I can keep up.

I just...*feel*.

Natalie beams a brilliant smile as she follows my finger and hand movements up and down the neck of the guitar. She's resting her head in her hand on the arm of the couch and in that very second, the look in her eyes changes from worry to relief.

Chapter Twenty-Four

Getting the go-head to get back into music means more time at rehearsals and meetings and less time being at home with Natalie, which in many ways is a great thing, but in some ways, I miss it.

Now that her constant presence isn't required, I always feel like something isn't there. I was getting used to spending most of our time together. Now, when we are apart, I have time to miss her.

I haven't put my guitar down since the night I first played it after the bar with Blake. Natalie still challenges me to play the piano, because she knows how strong the desire burns inside of me, but I have put that dream on the back burner while I refamiliarize myself with my guitar.

The last seven weeks were challenging, but I can sleep at night knowing we are finally on the other side. Natalie and I are better than ever, despite our collective shortcomings the first time around. My music is starting to come to me as naturally as it had before. I'm coming up with lyric ideas left and right. Blake and I have spent a lot of time with Dom and Theo, trying to fit harmonies and solos and drum sequences behind our newly penned lyrics.

Additionally, I have even picked up a large amount of sign language through my one-on-one time with Natalie. I understand a considerable number of signs now that I didn't recognize before and have even started attempting to use many of them myself, especially since I have been without the casts.

I'm happy our lives are slowing down and returning to normal, but I already miss the closeness that was thrust upon us over the last almost two months.

Natalie made a lengthy and painful recovery more bearable. Even when I didn't deserve it—*especially* when I didn't deserve it. She never stepped away, never second-guessed doing everything in her power to make my life easier—and I owe her a thank you that one million words couldn't measure up to.

I send a message to her phone.

Taking you out tonight. It will be special, I promise.

What's the occasion? she types back.

A thank you for putting up with me and all your support over the last few weeks.

I smile at my phone, rereading the words until the screen goes black, then place it back in my pocket.

* * * *

"Where are you taking her?" Jana asks, not taking her eyes off the video game on the screen.

"I'm. Not. Telling. You," I reply, stressing each word between clicks of the video game controller. She is kicking my ass at NHL Live.

"Fine. Be that way," she says, slamming her thumbs into a consecutive series of buttons that makes her player steal the puck from mine, skate it the length of the ice and shoot it past my goaltender with little-to-no effort.

"Game," she says, tossing the remote aside.

"It's uh… It's my wrist," I say dramatically. "It's really sore. It's throwing off my game."

"You never had any game," she says, sticking her tongue out at me.

She picks up her open energy drink and taps her fingers against the can for a moment, then looks at me, like she's avoiding something.

"I think I saw Mariah yesterday. I'm not sure, so don't quote me on it, but just so you know, she might be back in town. I just don't want her to cause any problems for you. You're finally in a good place, physically and mentally. I don't want to see her scare Natalie off and have you practicing your stage dive while riding a motorcycle," Jana says, trying to lighten the mood surrounding the subject.

"Thank you," I say, scratching my chin. "I haven't heard from her since…New York. She didn't even try to contact me after the accident. Which is fine, don't get me wrong. I am just surprised."

"Maybe the message finally sank in," Jana added. "After what she put you through, you don't need her contacting you."

"Tell me about it," I say, tossing popcorn into my mouth.

"Does Natalie know about all that?" Jana asks with curiosity coating her words.

"About why Mariah and I broke up? No, I never told her. I mean, I didn't really think it mattered. Mariah lied to screw with me. I just don't see how it has any effect going forward. It doesn't change anything for me, and I certainly don't plan on going backward any time soon," I say. "Natalie couldn't be more perfect. Mariah was... I don't know. Call it a temporary lapse in judgment."

"For two years?" Jana says. "You had a temporary lapse in judgment for two years?"

I throw a handful of popcorn in her direction and she laughs a hearty, echoing laugh.

* * * *

I sit in the back of a car that pulls in to pick up Natalie at The Rock Room after her shift. It's late and it's dark, but I told her I was taking her somewhere, and I planned to uphold that promise.

She slides into the back seat next to me and crosses her seatbelt across her chest.

She looks at me and lowers her eyebrows, wagging her finger back and forth, which I recognize as the sign for 'Where?'

A half-smile grows at my lips as I shrug my shoulders. I know the answer. I'm just not going to tell her.

The car pulls to a stop outside a brick building and we exit the vehicle. The driver pulls away and I step toward the building, but she doesn't follow.

She's smiling but skeptical. She looks at me with her head tilted to one side and her eyes narrowed.

It amazes me how if you really pay attention, in just a few months' time you know exactly what someone is trying to say. I hold out my hand and she laces her fingers with mine.

As we near the end of the long hallway, I take a set of keys from my pocket and unlock the recording studio door.

She wants to know what we're doing. And I want her to know too.

I open the door to the sound booth and she hesitates. I take both her hands and I walk backward, leading her into the space. I purposely chose this area because its whole function is to cancel out noise. Natalie can't hear, but she can sense. Without looking, she usually would be able to determine if it was a large truck or a just a small car passing behind her, or if a she entered a room blindfolded, she would be able to tell if it was overly crowded or occupied by only a few people without looking. She's overly perceptive to what she feels. I wanted as few distractions as possible, and I couldn't think of a better spot.

She looks around then at me, still requesting answers. I hand her one, single folded piece of newspaper. She unfolds it and runs her fingertips over her own handwriting where she wrote *I'd love to hear your music someday* in blue ink across the top of the page the first time we'd spent time together at my apartment.

Showing her what I want her to do, I point to the floor then cross my legs and sit. She follows suit. I reach for my acoustic guitar and pull it into my lap. Her face has had confusion stamped on it since I picked her up. I pull the strap over my shoulders and rest the body of the guitar between my thighs. I hand her a second piece of paper which she unfolds, then flattens it.

Her eyes scan the page, reading the notes we wrote to each other during karaoke at Prophecies. She laughs, surely remembering the night and the laughs we shared. I point to one comment. Her bubbly handwriting reads—*I love music...really, really loud music. This is actually perfect. I can't hear it, but I can feel it.*

She smiles and looks at me from under brilliantly long lashes—the distinction between her two different colored eyes more prominent than ever—and she smiles.

I wrap my fingers around her wrists and place her hands flat-palmed against the front of the body of the acoustic guitar. Goosebumps cover her forearms as I strum a few notes across each of the six strings. She squeezes her eyes shut, but it's a good thing. She's happy. And I'm happy. So, I play her a full song.

She keeps her eyes closed from the first note of the song until the last. She opens her eyes and looks at me when the song is through. Moisture rests on her bottom lids. She's not sad, but touched. She may not have listened to my song, but she heard it, and there will always be a difference.

She places her hands on the guitar front once more, an indication she wants to hear, or feel, more. Instead I pull the guitar strap off my shoulder and put it aside. I place my hands at her elbows and pull her toward me, turning her body so her back is against my chest and she's sitting between my legs. She giggles in this odd mix of sounds and presses her hands over her eyes as if she's embarrassed and I smile too. I reach for the guitar once more but this time, I place her left hand on the neck and her right hand on the body, which sits between her thighs instead of mine.

I place her fingers against the strings and strum once, then adjust her grip slightly and repeat the chord. She moves her hands away from the strings but keeps her palms against the instrument, and I play her one more song, the vibrations from the guitar now running through her hands and stomach where the instrument touches her, as well as the vibrations from my voice and my chest, which lean against her back, and the sound reverberates through the floor we sit on.

She's feeling it from all angles, and I keep singing into her ear in a way that moves her hair with my breath alone, and though the efforts may be seemingly wasted, they weren't at all.

She reaches one hand up and places it on the back of my neck. With her body still facing away from me, she turns only her head until her eyes meet mine and she's pulling me into her, placing her lips against mine.

As gently as possible I slide the guitar to the side and wrap one arm around her waist, taking a fistful of the hem of her shirt in my hand. I move my other hand so it's against the back of her head in the exact spot hers is on mine.

She turns her body weight until she is facing me, straddling my legs so her chest touches mine. I take her bottom lip between my teeth. She backs away from the kiss for a moment, but skims her lips and tongue the length of my jaw line and stops at my ear. Her breath tickles my ear drum, and she bites playfully at my ear lobe. I swallow loud enough that I can hear it.

She moves her fingers into my hair and I press my lips against the front of her neck. I can feel the low groan leave her throat and it's a sound I want to hear again. She works at unbuttoning my shirt and I slide my hands up her back and unclip her bra. All in one motion she slides her shirt over her head, taking her bra with it. She leans into me and kisses me again, working her tongue against mine.

She is perfect and beautiful and captivating, and I know in this moment there is nothing I want more than I want her.

We have waited and been patient and something always seems to get in the way — but I have no interest in being patient anymore. The way I feel about her consumes me, telling me to keep taking it one step farther then another. I want to ask her how far is too far. I want to know what she is thinking more now — on this floor, in this room — than I've ever wanted to know before.

As if she is reading my mind, completely in tune with how I am feeling and what I am wanting, she takes the lead. She slides my T-shirt over my head, takes it in both hands and drapes it over my shoulders, using it to pull me in close to her once again. The areas where my skin was damaged and the scars at my abdomen and shoulder are exposed, but here, in this moment, I forget they exist.

I forget anything exists — except her.

I kiss her more fervidly than I have ever before and wrap my arms around her waist, lifting her body weight off me while turning her against the floor of the recording studio sound room.

She takes a few deep, audible breaths and runs her hands through her hair. Goosebumps cover her perfect skin, and her stomach muscles tremble. She's nervous, and I consider taking a step back, taking things slower. But she reaches up and unbuttons my jeans at the waist.

I follow suit, unbuttoning and unzipping as she tilts her hip bones in an inviting, persuasive manner, and I pull her free of her jeans.

She slides her fingers into my pockets and tugs downward, leaving me unclothed in front of her. She runs her fingers from the muscles in my shoulders down my abdomen all the way to my groin then scratches her hands down my back and pulls me forward, on top of her and against her and into her.

We are a tangled mess of limbs and skin and desire still lying on the floor of the recording studio, now half-dressed, and I can't think of a place I would rather be.

I hold her close to me, caressing her bare thighs with my fingertips and watching as goosebumps appear across her skin in the path my fingers make. My eyes find hers and I dive into them without blinking, not wanting to miss even a second of this night. I open my mouth like I have something to say, something long overdue, but I can't find the words. She's so beautiful, lying here next to me with her hair falling wildly down her back and across her shoulders.

I run my fingers across her temple, down her neck, and leave my hand there, running my thumb the length of her bare collarbone.

"I am in love with you. You know that?"

Her eyes brighten, her chest rises as she takes a deep breath and holds it. She places her hand over mine and nods an enthusiastic yes.

"What is the sign?" I ask. I want to tell her I love her in her language. I want to tell her I love her in every language.

She bites her lip, but then her mouth grows into a half smile.

She makes the sign for rock on — the sign every rock fan knows and every rock musician recognizes — her index finger and pinky pointed up to the sky while the middle fingers fold down, held by her thumb.

I know that sign. I've always known it. Rock, rock on, rock music — that sign is all inclusive, widely recognized. I've known it since before I knew her — since before I knew or understood any other sign language at all, but I'm still missing what it has to do with telling her I'm in love with her.

I raise an eyebrow at her, knowing this isn't the correct sign, but then she extends her thumb outward — just one motion more — creating the sign for I love you.

I mirror the motion, and move my mouth into a warm smile. I reach forward, placing my hand at the back of her neck and pull her in for a passionate, conclusive kiss.

Chapter Twenty-Five

"Damn, it is good to see you with a guitar in that hand," Cooper says as he enters the room. "You promise you're okay? I don't want to push you." He has genuine curiosity in his eyes.

"I'm okay, Coop," I say. "I'll admit that there was a time I was afraid I wouldn't be the same musician at the end of it all."

"I wasn't," he says. "I wasn't worried about that, not even for a second. I was worried about you, sure...but never the music."

I scrunch my forehead and look at him. He places his hand on my shoulder and continues speaking.

"Writing music and playing an instrument is what makes you a music *artist*, Xander. Doing it in a way that no one else can see or explain is what makes you a music *magician*. You've got music in you, kid, and magic too. Accident or not, that part of you remains intact."

I am speechless, having no idea what to say in response to the compliment he just gave me, but it doesn't matter. He snaps back into the businessman type we have grown used to and jumps right into the notes and heavier subjects.

There are just a few weeks left between now and the holiday show at CommOcean, and Cooper wants us to showcase at least one new song. We agree to work on one idea that has been coming together for us, and now that I can play, we can start perfecting the sound behind the lyrics and clean it up by the time the concert rolls around.

As he talks, my mind is elsewhere. I think about how I've felt over the last few weeks when I couldn't play. I think about the dark places I found myself in when music wasn't part of my daily routine. I think about the way it felt to wonder if I'd ever be part of it again. It didn't promote my healing to not have music. It hindered it. As I think through each of these points, I realize, it's not me I'm thinking about.

It's Julian.

Not having his spot in the band, not having the support of this group and the music as a stress reliever. That's not what he needs. When I told him that the band isn't what he needed, I was wrong. I just had to go through it myself to figure it out.

Cooper is talking about what we can do to give ourselves a stronger, better sound when my mind returns to the conversation, and I know what the answer is.

* * * *

The olive-green painted door creaks loudly on its hinges as Julian opens it. He's surprised to see me and looks over his shoulder, back into his home, before stepping outside on the stairway and closing the door tightly behind him.

"Hey, Xander," he says, "what...uhhh... What are you doing here?"

"I wanted to talk to you. I know I haven't been the most supportive person, and that's on me. I'm sorry for that. But we want you back in, man. It's not the same without you," I say. "We need you. It took us a bit to realize it, but you're in, if you want to be." I'm less than smooth with the words. They feel awkward coming off my tongue, but I've never been great at apologies or admitting I was wrong, and here I was, trying to do both.

He thinks about the offer longer than I thought he would. I more than half expected him to walk away from this apartment with me tonight and head directly to the studio to lay down a track. I figured he'd be that thrilled — but he wasn't.

"Julian?" I ask, probing for an answer.

"I appreciate it, Xander. I do. But I can't." He rubs his fingers above his eyebrow and looks anywhere but at me.

"You...can't?" I repeat at a loss for more profound words.

I scan over his worn sneakers, the purple-colored tiger tattooed to his calf, the tan cargo shorts and the black shirt he wears. He fidgets with his backward cap, his longer-than-normal hair peeking out under the band at his forehead. He looks like Julian. He sounds like Julian. But somehow, he's *not* Julian. There is something off, something different.

"Anything you want to talk about?" I ask.

"No," he says, too quickly. "I don't want to talk. Just go home, Xander." He turns away and places his hand on the doorknob.

"Julian," I say, and he pauses, but his back is still toward me, "whatever it is, whatever you're doing, let me help you through it this time. I can be there for you."

"You can't. Not this time," he says, never turning to face me, and disappearing to the other side of the door.

Chapter Twenty-Six

Kelly, who still works behind the bar but has recently been promoted to venue promoter, has booked a newer band to play The Rock Room tonight. She is good at what she does. Many bands that are well known now, started as nobody on this very stage — Consistently Inconsistent included. She loves to have a hand in getting bands booked and helping them get noticed, but this time, she took it a step further to get people in the building.

Celebrity bartending, featuring Consistently Inconsistent.

Blake, Theo, Dom and I arrive a few hours early for a quick bartending 101 tutorial. For someone who can strum a guitar while jumping around on stage and remembering hundreds of words to an ever-changing line-up of lyrics, I am extremely uncoordinated. I keep dropping bottles and spilling liquor as I pour into the plastic cups, while Blake gives even Kelly a run for her money. He's a natural, flipping bottles around and mixing drinks like he's been doing it for years.

"All right everyone," Kelly says and signs, simultaneously addressing the band and Natalie too, "go out for a bit, take a break, but be back here by five and not one minute later." Her eyes are trained on me like laser pointers as she emphasizes the words.

"Five-thirty then... Got it," I say with an enthusiastic thumbs-up. The guys laugh, but Kelly taps her foot and narrows her eyes at me. "Kidding! Kidding, man. Tough crowd." Kelly breaks into a smile and cuts us loose. Everyone else leaves The Rock Room but I lace my fingers into Natalie's and lead her backstage. I turn toward her, kissing her cheek, her jaw, the side of her neck, her collarbones. She drops her head back and my lips meet her throat and work toward her chest as I kiss downward toward her breasts.

I lift my head and bring my eyes to find hers, then take the bottom of her shirt in my fingers, but she places her palms on my wrists, stopping me from removing it.

I give her a curious look, and she waves her hands around the backstage area. *Kelly is still here, Xander. Someone could see us.*

Letting go of her shirt, I take a step away from her — respecting her wishes. She means well, always wanting to do the right thing, but all the good intentions fade. She smiles a brave grin, steps forward and closes the gap between us. She kisses my neck and bites at my ear, seemingly free of her initial reservations.

She reaches one hand behind my back, gathering the fabric of my shirt in her hand and pulls it over my head. I wrap my arms around her, lifting her off her feet and pull her in close to my bare chest. She presses her legs tight at my hips and around my back, as I take steady steps backward and sit on the couch at the edge of the room. She explores my tattooed arm — tracing the lines of the inked designs, the scars, the damage — exploring my skin's terrain, taking mental pictures of my body.

I slide my hands up the sides of her shirt and run my thumbs underneath the wire of her bra. Her skin is soft under my hands as I move them across her body to remove her shirt, but I don't.

Footsteps echo from the far side of the stage.

I jolt at the sound, and Natalie notices the shift in my body, both physically and mentally — the sudden stop, the unexpected jump. She's looking at me, but I'm staring past her, reaching for my shirt. She starts looking around, perceptive to both my body language and her own inhibitions. This is exactly what she didn't want.

I take a deep breath and hope it's not Kelly.

And it's not.

The man standing at the backstage entrance apologizes and turns away. 'No harm, no foul' comes to mind. I figure he will just turn around and be on his merry way and Natalie and I will pick up where we left off, but she stands, adjusts her clothing and chases after him. Her back is to me, and he's facing her.

They talk for a moment — only, they don't speak. They sign. And now I can picture it. She's sitting with her back to me at the coffee shop and he sits down across from her. Hours later, I'm in a hospital bed with casts on three out of four of my limbs and my pride as damaged as the skin that covers me.

My footsteps are heavy as I walk the length of the room and stand a few steps behind her. His attention shifts to me, and she turns to face me too. He extends a hand to me – an awkward introduction, but a genuine attempt at being a decent guy.

"How are you feeling?" he asks, as if we've been friends for years – and maybe we have been. He looks familiar. "Looks like you're progressing well."

His voice takes me by surprise. I didn't expect him to speak.

"Uhh, yeah. I can't really complain," I say in return.

"Well, that's good to hear. We are looking forward to having you back on stage here again soon," he says in way that is the epitome of small talk.

"You work here?" I ask, but I think I already knew. It has been a while, years maybe, but I know I have met him prior to this.

He looks at Natalie then to me. A sullen look crosses his already-downcast eyes as he realized, in that moment, that she has never talked to me about him.

"I own the place," he says, but the conversation is over and awkward, and he's looking for an out. "Anyway, I'm glad to see you are making strides toward a full recovery."

"I guess I just got lucky."

He glances toward Natalie one last time then to me.

"Yeah, I would say so," he mutters as he leaves the stage. Natalie doesn't remove her gaze from him as he walks away. As for me? Well, I feel for the guy. I know what it's like to stand on his side – to be the man that Natalie Montoy didn't choose.

* * * *

Natalie, though in the same room as me, behind the same bar, is light-years away. The moment Ethan walked in today, her mood shifted, and it hasn't reset.

I know Natalie cares about him. I could see it in her eyes when he walked in, and even more so when he left. I have those eyes memorized—the colors, the thoughts that pass behind them, the way they light up with excitement and the way they frown when she is disappointed in someone or herself, the way they shift when she feels embarrassed or uncomfortable. I know all her looks, all the feelings those perfect two-toned eyes can muster, and I couldn't shake the feeling of wanting to know if on some deeper level, she still had residual feelings for him.

The doors open and fans flock to the front of the bar. Kelly had the right idea—Consistently Inconsistent, as expected, enticed a lot of paying customers into the venue. The quick-paced environment paired with the band's lack of bartending experience—save maybe Blake—and overall contagious excitement from the fans was a much welcome and somewhat comical distraction, saving myself from my own imagination.

On some level, seeing Natalie and Ethan brought me back to the last time I'd seen him—the day of my accident. But on the other hand, I can see how far I've come since then—how far *we* have come since that day. I am happy and healthy and serving drinks to these loyal fans—*badly*, I might add—but that time of my life seems like a distant memory.

Blake stands beside Kelly and Natalie and says something that has half the bar laughing—and the girls too. The smile she wears, the light and worry-free expression on her face leaves a smile stamped across mine as I turn toward her and throw a wink her direction. She waves back, and I know we have made it all the way.

We made it, and it can only go up from here.

* * * *

My breath is visible against the cold air as we walk to my apartment, hand-in-hand under a black sky that holds millions of stars that can't be seen over the bright city lights. I wrap her in close to me and we slow dance on the sidewalk. There's no music and no need for it. Just her and me and the cool air as fall begins to come to a close and invites winter to take its place.

With my nose pressed into her hair, inhaling the strawberry scent, I find myself marveling that the two of us have overcome so much and become an important part of the other in just a short amount of time. I thought I knew what *having it all* was. I didn't know I was missing anything until she filled the void I had never been aware of. I may have taken the long way around, and even been lost a time or two, but I know now that this is what happiness *is*.

In many ways, we couldn't be more dissimilar, but then again, opposition is what makes two magnets find each other. We complement each other perfectly. She added some reservation to my recklessness, which was a much needed and welcomed change of pace.

We get home, shed our coats and I got us something to drink.

My freshly poured glass of whiskey sits next to her glass of red wine on the coffee table. We both settle in to relax and I turn on the entertainment news channel. Different stories flicker across the screen as Natalie curls up on the couch next to me, handing me my whiskey and taking her wineglass in her hands. Nothing noteworthy catches my attention, but just as I make the decision to change the channel, an unmissable headline fills the top of the screen. A red banner with white lettering reads, "Mariah Delani Postpones Spring Filming Start Date."

Tempted to ignore it, I almost click away — but the news anchor starts talking and I can't unhear what she says.

"Mariah Delani, director of the Havoc *series, announced that she plans to push back filming the third installment of the hit movie franchise into next summer, rather than the originally scheduled March start date. Delani revealed that she is pregnant with her first child and is about seven months along, her expected due date falling in the end of February."*

A photo of Mariah entering a black limousine takes up the screen. She's waving with one hand and the other rests on her surprisingly small, but evident baby bump as she positions herself into the back seat of the limo. Sweat pours from my brow, and the color leaves my face. The feelings are flooding, instant and hollowing. I don't want to listen anymore, but I can't tear myself away. I can't stop what is about to happen. This information is coming through like a freight train that can't be slowed. There is nothing I can do except sit here and take the blow.

My first reaction is to count backwards in my head — November, October, September, August, July, June, May…

"She did not release any information regarding the father, but as many of us know, Mariah Delani and Consistently Inconsistent front man Xander Varro were hot and heavy for a long stretch of time around then."

Pictures of Mariah and I from various stages of our relationship fill the screen. Hearing my name is excruciating but reading it in the subtitles is exponentially worse. My eyes dart back and forth across the screen at each picture they post, mentally calculating when they were taken, but again, the news answers the questions as I think them.

"This photo here was taken while Mariah was filming on a set in LA and Consistently Inconsistent was playing locally the same weekend. The couple was seen together in various locations across LA that weekend. If you are any good at math, I don't think this equation is too hard to solve."

I can feel Natalie's eyes on me, boring into me, waiting for me to say or do something.

She doesn't know what to do with this information any more than I do.

The news fades into a story about some topic I can't bring myself to pay attention to and Natalie reaches for the remote. She clicks the TV to a dead black and places it on the table. She's not touching me. She's not trying to get my attention, but I can feel her gaze on me, staring, waiting for me to do something.

I finally find it in myself to lift my head and meet her gaze, though I'm not sure I can handle whatever it is her eyes are currently saying. She reaches for a pen and sheet of paper at the side table and pens a few words, handing them to me with shaking fingers. *Could it be true?* is written in handwriting more messy and uneven than her usual lettering.

I read the words and stare at my reflection in the glass windows directly across from me.

"Yeah," I say out loud, accompanied by a long, exaggerated head nod.

Her bottom lip trembles and she moves her hair out of her face, leaving her fingers wrapped in the roots. Tears press at the corner of her eyes. I don't know what she's thinking. She doesn't seem mad — scared, maybe?

This is a chapter of my life that came before Natalie, one that I thought had come to a close—but this news twists the plot, redirecting my story entirely.

I'm overwhelmed, unable to think one direct thought without my mind going in a thousand different directions. Just when I thought I was fixed, I start unraveling. Things had been stable for only a moment, and now the ground under me is dismantled where I stand, leaving me no solid flooring to place my feet on.

"How could she not tell you?" Natalie signs in a quick, emphasized way, mouthing the words as she says them, a bit of sound leaving her throat as she expresses so much emotion in only a six-word sentence.

I run my hands down my face and push myself up off the couch. I walk away, leaving Natalie by herself in the middle of the room, left to wonder where I am going—where *we* are going—and what happens next. I return with an envelope and hand it to her with shaking hands.

Her eyes scan the ultrasound pictures, the dates in the corner of the black and white scan. She unfolds a piece of paper—the blood test results, all the things I knew about, but were then told that they had been fabricated. Now, I have no idea what to believe. And judging by her expression, she can't believe it either.

I never told Natalie there was ever a time when Mariah thought she was pregnant. I never told Natalie about the voicemail Mariah had left me. In fact, when it came to Mariah, I'd left almost all the details out altogether. I'd truly thought this was the right choice, the better way.

Tears fall from Natalie's eyes, down her jaw and drip to the hardwood floor. I step forward and she steps back, keeping the distance between us from closing.

Leaving my phone behind, she steps past me, making her way through my bedroom into the bathroom, and she closes the door behind her. My mind races as the lock clicks, wondering if there will ever be a time that this relationship doesn't take place on an obstacle course.

Chapter Twenty-Seven

Hours have passed and I still haven't made it to my bedroom. Instead, I sit on the floor in the corner of the living room, propped up against the solid wall behind me, looking out the floor-length windows. My breath creates a foggy cloud each time I exhale, and my forehead leaves smudges where it rests against the pane.

Every few moments I look at my phone, considering texting Mariah — or calling her, or emailing her — but I don't know what I'll say, so I refrain. Eventually contact has to happen, but when it does, I need my head fully wrapped around the whole situation, and part of me still feels like this is all one big, fucked-up nightmare.

All the members of the band members have contacted me. Cooper has messaged me. Kelly has messaged me — which means she saw the clip and is simultaneously texting Natalie. Jana's name is the next one to appear on the screen. I don't read the text, but I think back to not too long ago when she warned me I should bring Natalie up to speed on my history before somebody else did. I swallow back the regret and guilt that forms in my throat.

It is only a matter of time before my mother sees this circulating news clip and shows up here to lecture me in person. My *mother*.

This is the curse of the celebrity lifestyle — the dark, draining abyss that is never considered when fame and fortune are craved. It is not always smooth sailing, and when it's not, shortcomings are broadcasted nationwide. Anybody with a known name can do thousands of productive, successful things in a row before stepping out of line, but the moment they do, the action is magnified and displayed for the world to see.

Checking on Natalie crosses the traffic clogging up my mind, but my brain is disconnected from the rest of my body. I'm unable to force myself to stand up, move or make any decision that doesn't involve sitting on this floor, looking out of this window and drinking whiskey from the bottle.

The floor creaks as Natalie joins me. She slides her back down the wall, falling into a cross-legged position next to me. I don't object when she pulls my arm over her shoulders, resting her ear against my chest where my heart beats too fast.

"This can't be happening," I say out loud.

A marker rests in my pocket, as one so often does, but no paper is in arm's reach and I don't want to stand up — not with her this close to me.

"I am going to have to talk to her," I write on my palm, and hold it out to her.

"*I know*," she signs back to me.

I don't want her in the middle of this, but I don't want her anywhere else. I have needed her countless times but never more than I needed her right now.

She falls asleep there, next to me, and I know I should try to find sleep too. I wrap my arms under her legs and behind her back, lift her off the floor and carry her to my room.

I try to count sheep. I try to take deep breaths. I try to clear my mind and fall asleep, but I can't.

My eyes are trained on the bedroom ceiling for hours, wide eyed and unblinking, sleep completely eluding me. Natalie lies close to me, but I can't tell if she's sleeping or not. I roll over, pick up my phone and send a quick text that I truly wish I didn't have to send.

Can we meet up and talk?

I stare at the screen, waiting to see if Mariah will reply, but she doesn't.

At some point, fatigue wrestles out anxiety and my lids fall closed.

My phone rings, waking me, but I ignore it and try to find sleep again. The buzzing sounds once more, and I begrudgingly pick up my cell phone.

The text is from Mariah.

Chance's. 9:30 a.m.

Natalie is still sleeping and I don't want to wake her, so I dress and leave her with a gentle kiss at her temple.

* * * *

Mariah is already at Chance's when I arrive. As I open the door, Jana stares at me, worried. Her expression asks a thousand silent questions. I pull out the chair across from Mariah and my lips go dry. My palms sweat, and suddenly, no words exist.

"You wanted to talk, so *talk*," she challenges.

My eyes automatically fall to her stomach. Seeing the news on TV was something I didn't expect, but seeing her pregnant in front of me makes it all real.

"You should have told me," I say in a less-than-smooth tone. It takes everything I have to push the words over my frozen tongue.

"I tried to talk to you, Xander. Twice. You told me to go to hell. Don't try to blame me for your shortcomings. You didn't want to talk to me. You made that very clear," she says through a half smile, like she feels victorious in all of this.

"You told me you weren't pregnant." My top lip twitches.

"No, Xander, I didn't."

"Yes, you did!" I raise my volume and slam my fists against the table. Pain shoots through my arm, reminding me of my recent injury. I try to return my voice to a cool and collected pitch, but my words are shaking. "You said that you lied. That you weren't pregnant with my..."

My voice trails off before I finish the sentence.

"That I wasn't pregnant with *your* baby," she says. "I never said I wasn't pregnant. I just said this baby isn't yours."

Confusion floods my nervous system. I finally feel as if I can take a deep breath, but I forget how. My heart is beating like a drum in my ears. At first, I'm relieved, but part of me is still retracing my thoughts and steps.

"But…I did the math. We were still together." I say, unsure what to believe.

"We were. But…there was someone else. You were gone. You were on tour. I was…lonely."

I look away from her to the old, stained-tile floor. I couldn't believe it, and yet, I wasn't surprised at all. This revelation should be shocking, but somehow, I had known all along that Mariah wasn't capable of being faithful. I push my chair back, stand up from my seat and walk out of the coffee shop, the bells from the door ringing wildly behind me.

"Xander, stop!" Mariah yells from behind me.

"The actor…from the movie? The picture that I saw that you continually told me was nothing—"

"That *was* nothing!" she yells, interrupting me. "We were over, Xander. Even if neither one of us wanted to admit it, our relationship ended a long time before either one of us called it what it was."

"So that makes it okay? It makes it okay for you to get knocked up by some guy while I'm halfway across the country singing songs off an album I wrote for *you*?"

Tears fill her eyes and her bottom lip shakes.

"That isn't fair. I said I was sorry. I said that the baby wasn't yours and that I made mistakes," she says through tears. "I'm sorry your name was dragged into this. I didn't know the media would involve you."

"Of course they would, Mariah, because they thought we were together at the time you got pregnant, just like I did. But I was wrong—and so were they."

I turn my back and walk away, leaving her behind me to go home. Mariah and I haven't been together for months, and I have been fine with that, but it doesn't hurt any less when you find out someone you remained loyal to didn't respect you enough to do the same. Then again, there is a reason she is a part of my *past*, and now this can be too. Now that I know, now that she has come clean with me about being with another man, I can move forward with Natalie and my life and my music and concentrate on more successes and less setbacks.

I get back to my place, crawl back into bed next to Natalie and push back her hair from her face. She blinks the tired from her eyes a few times, then stretches and sits up.

"Are you okay?" she signs. I let out a short, loud breath and nod my head. I tell her everything, leaving nothing out, beginning to end, the way I should have from the start.

Chapter Twenty-Eight

Jana joins me and Natalie at the table at the side of Chance's, but she doesn't look happy, which is surprising to me, considering.

"You have *got* to be kidding me," she says, folding and unfolding the birthday card she holds in her hands.

"No." She slides the card across the table. "I decline."

"Jana, you can't decline. It's a birthday *gift*. No one declines a gift," I say, and Natalie giggles, sensing Jana's shock and stubbornness.

"*Xander!*" she hisses, lost between speechless and angry. "That's way too many zeros!"

A genuine, happy grin forms at my mouth.

"You've done a lot for me—for us." I reach across and take Natalie's hand in mine. "You deserve it, Jana. It's for school. Trust me. I tried to just pay a few semesters over the phone, but they just laughed and didn't believe me."

"You are in so *much* trouble," she says, but moisture glistens at the corners of her eyes. Happy tears, I hope.

"I'll try to look past your lack of excitement about the concert tickets for this weekend that are in there," I say as she stands from the table. She never has been a fan of my music, whether she will admit it or not.

"I *am* excited, actually. I even have someone in mind for my plus one."

I raise my eyebrow at her. "Anyone I know?" I add.

"Actually, yeah. Your physical therapist," she adds with a laugh as she leans in and hugs Natalie and me for her gift.

"Happy birthday," I say as she wraps an arm around my shoulder.

"It's the best one yet," she adds as she skips across the coffee shop floor tiles to help her next customer.

Apart from visiting Jana for her birthday, our afternoon was uneventful and relaxing which is an unusual combination for us these days, but much needed and welcomed. Natalie cooks dinner and I taste-test her new recipe, which is as delicious as always. As the timer counts down, she teaches me the next set of signs I planned to learn. I'm getting pretty good, I think. I understand a majority of what she's signing, even if I often confuse signs and do them wrong, but I'm making large strides toward being able to communicate with her when there is no pen or technology available, and I was falling in love with the language as much as I was falling in love with the woman teaching it to me.

She brews a pot of coffee with dessert and lets me sample a fork full of freshly baked pie. I smear a small amount of whipped cream at the corner of her lips and kiss it away.

Her lips turn to a smile against me, and mine mirror the image. There is a happiness between us that is beyond anything I have ever recognized, and I'm certain I don't deserve, but I'll take it. She's elated and I'm ecstatic, and together we are the very definition of warmth and affection.

There was simplicity and a complexity to being with her that always kept me on my toes, but I didn't have to think about. It just *was*. We just *were*.

Music was the first thing I ever knew I loved. It was a love I was born with, and I always assumed I would die with it too. Then I met Natalie, and I knew there was room for one more bond — one more true love. I think about it often, how I am so lost in her that I would give up the music if she asked, but I fall for her even harder knowing that she never would.

I run my fingers the length of her blue-black hair, twisting it in large, gathered amounts around my hand. I stare into her eyes and mouth the words 'I love you' and she silently mouths them back.

And it's enough.

It's more than enough.

There is a loud, impatient knock at the door. I want to pretend it's not there, but the rapping repeats.

I open the door and at the other side stands a breathless, overwhelmed Blake Mathews.

"We need to talk," he says, taking a deep, audible gulp.

He comes in and opens my laptop, opening to the webpage of the entertainment news station that aired the story about Mariah's pregnancy. He opens the link that connects to the story.

"Blake, no. We've seen it, okay? We don't need to do this again," I say, backing away from the screen.

"Xander, please. Just watch…and wait," Blake says through large, wide-open eyes. He's…sad? Disappointed? I don't even know how to describe it because the usual exuberant, overly enthusiastic Blake Mathews I know usually only exists at one side of the emotional spectrum.

He pauses the video and takes a deep breath.

"Watch right here," he says, pointing to the open door of the limo. He clicks 'play'.

Mariah waves and blows light, flirty kisses to the fans and cameras in the area. She leans into the limo, and as she does, another passenger assists her as she sits and places his hand on her stomach prior to leaning forward and pulling the door shut.

"Back it up," I say, and he does. When he clicks 'play' again, I see what he's seeing.

The person who shares the limo helps Mariah into a seated position and places his hand instinctively on her stomach. I missed it before, because I wasn't looking for it. But the man who helps her into the seat, the man who tries and fails to keep himself out of the camera's shot, also has a large, dramatic, purple-colored tiger tattooed across his calf.

I have always been a decent writer. Math was never my thing, but somehow, I can't stop doing it. Dates and times and specific memories and certain things either of them have said scroll continuously across my mind, and I keep calculating and recalculating and coming to the same conclusion.

Julian is the baby's father.

It's well past midnight and the world outside is dark and empty—parallel to how I'm feeling. I'm a mix of silent and angry and calamitous. The clip plays over and over and over again in my mind and I can't stop the repetitiveness. I can't stop it at all. I can't rewind. I can't move forward. I can't pause. The only functioning option is 'repeat'.

Rain slams hard against the windows. Natalie sleeps through the treacherous thunder, but I can't, and I'm positive it has everything to do with the internal storm and nothing to do with the exterior one.

I push the covers back and place my feet on the floor.

There is a relentless part of me that continuously cautions that every step I physically take forward is going to be a large mental step back, but I don't heed the warnings.

My steps echo as I walk down the stairs and through the lobby and out into the rain. The rain soaks me from head to toe, seeping through my boots and drips from my hair and into my eyes, disrupting my vision.

Making a left, I turn down the street I had every intention of finding, but I don't remember taking the step by step turns to get there.

There are three steps separating me from the olive-green door and I take them.

With the outside of my white-knuckled fist, I bang on the door, and there is no answer.

Harder, more urgently, I drum on the door, and this time, Julian whips it open, spewing profanities and anger until he sees me on the other side. He runs his hand across his forehead and cuts off his own sentence.

"Oh, Xander," he says with surprise in his voice and I think, somewhere behind those empty eyes, lays the recognition of why I'm here. He knows I've figured it out. He knows I know everything.

"How long?" I yell through the rain. I'm angry — beyond angry — and I deserve at least the answer to that question from a man I had once considered a band mate, a friend, a *brother.*

He begins to close the door, an attempt to shut me out and end this conversation, but I jam the toe of my boot between the frame and the door, interrupting its closure.

"Get the fuck out of here, man," he says, pushing me backward at the shoulders.

Catching him off guard, I slam my body weight into the door. The door flies open as the sky around us lights up from one, purple-white lightning strike.

I have one hand at his throat and one hand at his shoulder, pinning him to the wall just inside the door as the rainwater floods the entryway.

"How long have you been with her?" I say through gritted teeth and a pained jaw.

"Xander! What are you doing? Stop!" I hear Mariah yell over the earth-shaking thunder as she runs into the room. I don't listen, and she turns around and dials into her cell phone. I know the consequences here. I know this will not end well for me, but at that second, the answer to the question I asked was vastly more pressing than the outcome I was sure to face.

"The whole damn time," he chokes under the weight of my palm. I release the pressure, and the moment I step back and let my guard down, Julian's fist connects with my jaw, leaving my ears ringing and both my nose and mouth bleeding.

I wipe my sleeve across my face and turn toward the doorframe, spitting blood onto the cemented steps.

I came here for an answer, and I got one. I was living with Julian when Mariah first came along and now I know, even then, she was never faithful — and neither was he.

The puddles splash under my boot as I step outside onto the stairs and lift my face to the crying sky. The rainwater runs across my forehead, into my hair and thins the blood that runs from my mouth. My teeth and nose throb as I inhale deeply, trying to collect my thoughts. As my mind clears, my vision is blurred by the red and blue lights atop the police cruisers that appear at the bottom of Julian's concrete steps.

I am cuffed and shoved into the back of one of the cars. As it pulls away, I can see Julian wrap his arms around Mariah and place his lips against her forehead.

Chapter Twenty-Nine

"Did you want another one?" the man next to me asks, pointing to the tattoos that cover my arm. He's missing many teeth and smells like tobacco and liquor, but somehow those aren't his most noticeable features. He has what I would estimate as three dozen piercings sticking wildly out of every inch of his face. His head is shaved and he wears a large design at the side of his neck that is raised and red. It looks as if he recently allowed someone to use a makeshift branding iron against his skin.

"I know a guy who will give you a good deal," he continues.

I ignore him, stand up from the hard bench and make my way toward the vertical metal bars at the front of the holding cell. I wrap my hands around them and lean my forehead there. I welcome the cold temperature against my warm skin.

C'mon, Blake, I think to myself.

It seems like hours have passed since I had called him, though I'm sure that isn't the case. Between my previous lack of regard for the rules and Blake's short-fused temper and lack of filter in his younger days, we have earned so many trips to holding cells all over the country that I had lost count. But we had a pact.

When we say 'I'll always be there to bail you out', we mean it both figuratively *and* literally. I always help him out as soon as I can, so where the hell is he? I am not even sure what time it is at this point, but I hope he arrives soon. Cooper might actually fire me this time if I'm behind bars instead of at this morning's sound check for the CommOcean holiday show.

I have seen the view from this side of the cell more times than I care to admit. Before, being behind these bars didn't bother me. I welcomed it, even. But now I know I want this to be the last time. I wanted last time to be the *last* time. I'm not the same man I was before Natalie came into my life. I want to be better because she deserves better, but I continue to take steps backward. My chest tightens with guilt and embarrassment. *Natalie*. What is she going to think about all this?

A door opens somewhere in the distance and echoes down the white-tiled hallway.

Just by listening, I know one of the officers is heading our direction. *Footsteps. Keys. Footsteps. Keys.*

The officer pulls the key ring loose from her belt and inserts one key into the door of the holding cell. She opens the door, gestures for me to step through it and closes it behind her, locking the door and returning the ring to her hip.

I follow her down the hallway in silence. Her lips are pressed into a hardened line and she doesn't make eye contact with me. We stop at a desk near the front of the station. I lean backward to see if I can see Blake through the glass of the police station doors as she hands me my cell phone and other belongings over the counter.

"Thank you, uhh" — I look at her name tag — "Officer Jennings."

"Don't thank me. You might be asking me to put you back in that cell in a minute. She doesn't look happy," Officer Jennings replies.

"She?" I ask, and my heart falls into my stomach. Did Blake contact Natalie instead of coming here himself? I haven't even thought about how I was going to *explain* all this to Natalie, never mind *look* at her. I don't want her to see me like this.

I nod in Officer Jennings's direction and turn toward the exit. I press the metal bar and open the door. A cool, wintry gust of wind bites at my face. I step onto the cement and look to the bottom of the stone steps. Kelly stands there, leaning against the railing with her arms crossed and her face painted with an unamused, very angry expression.

"Kelly," I say with surprise in my words, "what are you doing here?"

She raises her brows and her lips separate in shock at the question.

"That's funny, Alexander. I was about to ask you the same damn question."

I shove my hands in my pockets and take the cement steps slowly, one at a time, until I meet her at the bottom.

"What the hell were you thinking?" Kelly asks. Her eyes darken and her nostrils flare.

"I wasn't, really," I respond, scratching my head. I look around at the very few cars in the lot, but no other person is in sight. "Is Blake here? Not that I'm not happy to see you, I just expected him, since I used my phone call—"

"I know you called him," she interrupts. "I was sleeping next to him when you called," she says. The threat of anger has left her voice now, if only for a moment.

"Ahh," I say. "Well it's about damn time." I laugh.

"This isn't funny, Xander, and I'm not here to talk about me." She crosses her arms and leaves all her weight on one hip. "What happened?"

I push my hair back with my hands, take a deep breath, and sigh as I let it out.

"I just felt cut to the core when I realized Mariah was cheating on me the entire time we were together with one of my best friends. He was my band mate, you know? I asked him to come back. I invited him back in. He played in that New York show with us. He looked me in the eyes and said *nothing* about being with her. I felt like there were ropes left untied and I needed to knot them. I just felt...betrayed."

"Betrayed," she repeats, sarcasm drenching the word. "How do you think Natalie feels?" she adds in a sharp tone that cuts right through my chest bone. I don't say anything because I have nothing worth saying. Nothing I say is going to matter.

"Let's go, Alexander. I'll bring you home." She walks to the driver's-side door of her car and opens it.

"Will Natalie still be there when I get there?" I ask over the car, but I already know the answer.

"If she isn't, do you blame her?" Kelly asks, shrugging her shoulders and dropping into the driver's seat, out of view.

I don't. I wouldn't. There's only one person to blame here, and as usual, it's me.

When we get to my place, I get out of the car and walk to the entrance of the apartment. I turn around, and Kelly rolls down the car window. She leans her head back against the seat, exhausted and frustrated, torn between wanting to be here for me as a friend but wanting to hate me as the cousin of my girlfriend.

"Kel?" I ask, in a subdued voice I hardly recognize. She rotates her head toward me. She's listening, but she doesn't say anything. "What happens now? Do I still have a chance at a future with Natalie?"

"I talked to her after you called Blake. I asked her if this was it, if this was the final time. She said it's not up to her, that she's not the one who has a decision to make. So, yeah, Alexander, I think Natalie still wants you as part of her future. But you have to stop living in the past."

The rest of the early morning hours pass before I even consider reaching out to Natalie, partly because it was the middle of the night but more so because I had no idea what I was going to say.

I sit at the counter and tap a pen against the granite. I run my fingers against the facial hair that covers my jaw. I tap the toe of my boot against the metal footrest of the stool I sit on.

I can't sit here anymore. Not alone. Not without Natalie at my side.

So, I do what I do best, and pen words on blank pages.

* * * *

I send her a text to tell her I'm outside and stand there, on the wrong side of the door, staring at the knob, mentally pleading for it to turn. I rock back and forth on the balls of my feet.

Just one more minute. If the door doesn't open in the next minute, I'll leave.

I count backwards from sixty. Fifty-nine, fifty-eight, fifty-seven…

When I reach zero, the knob has still not shifted. *Maybe just one more minute,* I say to myself, and restart from sixty.

I've lost count. I have no idea what number I had reached when the doorknob finally turns.

Natalie stands on the other side, and the moment I see her every muscle in my body unwinds, tendon by tendon, a calming effect that only she is capable of creating in my otherwise-hectic life.

I want to believe that on some level, she's happy to see me too. She hasn't turned away yet or slammed the door between us, so I've already gotten farther than I had anticipated.

She places one hand against the door and leans her weight into it. I can see in her eyes that she's hurt and confused and angry, and even with all the pent-up negative energy coursing through her system, in that second, she is still perfect.

I reach into my pocket and remove a white, unsealed envelope and hand it to her. She takes it from me and turns away but doesn't close the door. Her back is to me, and I know exactly what she's doing. She doesn't want me to read her emotions as she reads my words.

I hear the rustle of the paper as she unfolds it and lets the envelope float to the floor.

I watch as she reads the words, words that I read over and over so many times, ensuring they were enough, that I can practically recite it as she reads.

Natalie,

Have you ever wondered why the band is called Consistently Inconsistent?

Believe it or not, the name idea came from my mother. Blake had a really hard life growing up and eventually, he moved in with us. We were mirror images of each other. We either brought each other way up or anchored each other down. We were either excelling and doing well or hit a new low. There was no in-between.

I guess some things never change.

There was a stretch of time when we both had our grades up, we were getting paid to play small gigs, we both were doing okay...until we weren't. We got in trouble for underage drinking, and shortly after that our grades declined and we had letters sent home from school.

She sat us at the counter and slammed the school letterhead down in front of us and she said "I can't keep up with you two – just when I think I can let my guard down and trust that you both are maturing, you pull stunts like this. Inconsistency is just about the only thing you two do consistently."

And so, the name was born.

We, as a band, don't answer people when they ask where the name comes from. Though the story isn't nearly as exciting as people want to believe it is, it's a story we keep close – a secret only we know.

But I don't want to keep any secrets from you, in any capacity. Not anymore.

I tend to ride a train that only goes downhill and makes stops at bad decisions. I am far from perfect, but you make me want to be. I have asked for exponential chances over the years from various people, and I am often given them. I have never been less deserving of another do-over than at this moment, but I'm asking.

I'm asking you to let me try again.

What I have realized is this… In our time together, I've learned the signs for colors and days of the week and meals. I've practiced the signs for answers to everyday questions. I've mastered the sign for 'I love you'.

History repeats itself — mine, for sure. So, I should've known, from the beginning, that there was a sign I was going to need, and I should've been practicing all along.

She flips the paper over, looking for more, but that's it. The end. No signature, no further words. The very second she turns to me and her eyes meet mine, I lift my fist and run it in a repeating circle over my chest — hopefully, a well-timed, well-executed attempt at the sign for *'I'm sorry'*.

Her eyes fill with warm tears and her bottom lip quivers.

She places her hand on the edge of the door, and I'm sure she's about to close it, leaving me on the other side. But she doesn't and I'm glad. I have no intention of ever letting outside people or problems get between us again — not this door or anything else.

She reaches forward and takes my hand, pulling me across the threshold and closing the door behind us.

There is something about Natalie Montoy that just leaves me weak at the knees — and everywhere else. My heart rate slows to an unfindable, almost nonexistent beat and my once-clenched fists fall loose-fingered. That's the effect she has on me, and I hope I never get used to it.

I place my palms at her jaw line and wipe her tears away with my thumbs. I press my mouth to hers with a kiss that crashes over us with the force of hundreds of apologies and thousands of 'I love yous' and she returns the impact with all the forgiveness she has to offer.

I release her hair from the tie that was holding it back. It cascades around her shoulders and down her back. She steps backward, taking me with her toward the couch, though our locked lips never separate.

She pulls me against her and falls backward onto the black couch cushions, taking me with her, pulling me on top of her, over her body.

We are a mess of strewn clothing, bare skin and tangled limbs.

On a day that could have ended with us lost without each other, we lose ourselves in the other and search for our way back.

I catch a glimpse of the clock and wish I hadn't. I have to be at sound check, but I'd rather stay here with her.

I point to a nonexistent watch at my wrist and she nods her head.

I walk to the door and turn to face her. I spell out the word 'concert', since I don't know the actual sign but have mastered the alphabet.

Our show is tonight, and last I checked, she and Kelly were going with Jana and her date, but that may have changed since the previous night. I wanted to make sure she was still coming.

She nods and smiles at me, then leaves me with a lingering kiss over the threshold of the door.

* * * *

"There he is," Blake says, as I enter the backstage area of CommOcean. "I was kind of starting to think you were still stuck behind bars."

I laugh, though I shouldn't.

"Well," he continues, "I for one am looking forward to the dark, angsty album that is sure to come of this breakup."

I pull my guitar strap over my shoulder and shake my head. "Sorry to disappoint you," I say sarcastically, "but we are still together."

"Shit," he says, wide-eyed and in disbelief. "Coop!" he yells, and Cooper sticks his head out past the backdrop at the edge of the stage. Blake reaches into his pocket, pulls out a twenty-dollar bill and holds it out to Cooper. Cooper approaches with a victorious smile on his face, places the paperwork he was reading under his arm and all in one motion takes the twenty from Blake, shoving it into his pocket.

"Let me get this straight," I start as I scratch my chin. "You two are making bets on if I get dumped or not while my ass sits in a jail cell?"

"That's an accurate assessment," Cooper admits with a laugh. "But hey, I was right. I knew she'd stick around. That girl loves you for reasons I have yet to figure out." He lets out a light laugh and puts his nose back in the papers as he leaves the stage.

"In all seriousness, though, are you okay?" Blake asks, plucking a few notes on his guitar as he tunes it.

"I don't know what I was thinking, man," I say. "Right now, I literally have it all, and I almost threw it away over two people who haven't been in my life for months. In a way though, I feel like last night offered some kind of closure. Julian isn't going to be part of this band. Mariah isn't going to be messing with my life anymore. We can finally cut ties and move on, going separate directions, and now, with a clearer head, I realize I'm okay with that."

Last night was the final time I'll spend any time in the past, and from now on, I'll concentrate solely on my present and future with a woman who not only has patience with my shortcomings but makes me want to be a better person.

I can hear the beat of the drums from the other side of the backdrop. Blake and I join Dom and Theo on stage and strum a few chords of the new song we planned to debut tonight. With every chord I play, I realize how grateful I am to be healed and healthy and able to wrap my hand around the guitar neck. I am lucky to play tonight, not only to an audience who has never lost their faith in us, but also for a woman who has never lost her faith in me. I am appreciative to have a band that wants to work hard and be successful and has a bright future ahead with nothing or no one holding us back.

Chapter Thirty

The lights are shining bright and brand new over a never-performed-on stage. Under the lamps, I almost forgot that it is winter and we are outdoors. We take the stage and the over-packed crowd lets out a collective yell that echoes against the dark winter sky.

"Bostonnnn..." Blake says into the microphone in a long, drawn-out, exaggerated tone that only exemplifies the crowd's cheers. "How are we doing tonight?" he yells at a more amplified volume.

I smile widely and look around. Through all the performances over all the years at all the venues, I don't think I've ever witnessed a larger crowd. I am almost overwhelmed for the first time in a long time. A crowd this loud and this full takes me back to the very first time we performed, when Kelly helped us get a spot as an opener at The Rock Room and our careers only went up from there.

We run through the beginning of our set seamlessly—no faults, no issues, which is always a concern in a brand-new venue.

I can see where Kelly and Natalie stand from where I play, and every time I look for Natalie, she is looking at me too. Over the years, I've perfected the art of not letting anything interrupt or pull my mind away from the music while I'm on that stage—until now. She distracts me in a way I couldn't hope to explain, but it isn't unwelcome. Thousands of eyes are on me in this moment and the only ones that matter to me are hers—completely different colors but equally perfect, looking past who I've been and standing beside who I will be.

I am in love with her. Whatever comes next for her career or mine or the music or anything life throws our way, I have her, and that will always be more than enough.

The energy from the crowd is contagious, as they reach their hands toward us their liveliness flows from their fingers into our veins. Every musician can look back and pinpoint their best shows, their strongest performances, and this was one we won't soon forget.

I step to the front of the stage and speak with my lips close to the microphone.

"All right, Boston. You guys… You guys are unreal." I'm slightly out of breath as I address the crowd, but that is a sign of a great performance. "We have something new for you tonight. Your ears will be the first to hear this new track, and we hope to have more for you very soon. We hope you love it. Here it goes. This one is called *Letters That I'll Never Send.*"

Blake leads us in and Theo lays out a thick melody on his keyboard. I tap my foot, counting myself in, and think on the opening lyrics.

Picked my favorite salutation
Penned the words I couldn't say
Had the address all filled out
Never sent it, but it's the thought that counts.

It's a slower, heavier song than we are used to playing, but the lyrics are entirely about having good intentions, even if you don't always follow through on them. I am singing the words, directly to her, only to her, regardless if she can hear them.

The words are for her. They have always been for her.

Blake sings the bridge consisting of the words *'And I haven't had a chance to meet my neighbor opportunity, but she still waves when she drives by'*, while Dom and I drop out of the song completely, leaving only Blake's voice and Theo's amalgamation of high and low keyboard sounds that echo through the temporarily quiet crowd.

As the song comes to a close, the house lights turn to a blue that floods the whole stage. Theo, Dom and Blake leave. I walk off stage and take a sip of water, but return to center stage, by myself, and find my microphone again.

"This next song, you've heard it a thousand times and seen us play it at every show, but maybe not quite like this," I explain. "There is someone I want to introduce you all to, and she's going to leave the crowd and come up here to join me on stage for this one."

Every head in the crowd turns and faces the side of the venue I point to. I can see the color leave Natalie's face and panic take its place when all eyes are on her, and she assumes I have said something to draw attention to her or introduce her to this rambunctious crowd. She hates the spotlight. She hates the attention. Even from here I can sense her sigh of relief when Kelly starts her walk toward the stage and Natalie realizes I wasn't pointing her out at all.

She bites her bottom lips and shakes her head at me, and I smile in return.

"Boston, this is Kelly. Kelly, well, this is Boston." The crowd erupts and she waves to them. "Kelly is proficient in American Sign Language and she's going to join me up here and sign this song for you."

The response from the crowd is encouraging and inviting.

"In the spirit of doing something new, I'm going to show you guys something I've been working on. This is not something I've ever done for a crowd before and I'm not sure I'll ever do again. But, do one thing a day that scares you. Am I right?" The fans yell and scream in response. If I wasn't ready before, I am now.

"Theo?" I say into the microphone and he steps back onto the stage. "Can I borrow this?"

I point to the keyboard, and the crowd continues their motivating antics. They want to hear it, and I want to show them—but there's one person's approval in particular that I want.

Natalie has been asking for this since we first met, mostly because she knows it's one of the things that scares me most, but now I know—the thing that frightens me the most is not having her, and everything else is a distinctively distant second.

She presses her hands over her mouth and hops up and down in excitement.

I press the keys down and listen to them resonate through the sky. The acoustics are different in an outdoor venue, and the music has a different sound played on the keyboard as the primary instrument, but somehow, it works. I sing and Kelly signs and Natalie gets a private, personal show among a crowd of thousands of strangers.

I lower my head, close my eyes and belt out the words to the slow burning, intense bridge of the song as Kelly signs a beautiful accompaniment. When I lift my head and open my eyes, Natalie is no longer in view. I search around different parts of the venue, but she's not there.

We close out the song, and I look around, trying to find Natalie.

And I do.

She's directly in front of me, standing on the floor in front of the stage. I kneel at center stage and lean into her. She wraps her arms around my neck and I pull her up, kissing her smiling lips as the confetti cannons explode around us, millions of multi-colored strips of paper swirling around us in a color-filled blizzard.

She doesn't care about the attention.

She doesn't care about the crowd.

She disregarded those inhibitions to be with me, everywhere, every time, in front of everyone.

But now, in this second, there is me and there is her, and even though there is a thick applause and a loud, riveting crowd, I only see her — and the rest is just background noise.

Epilogue

"It has been one year, three hundred sixty-five days, since the motorcycle accident that I would say made me a very lucky man on two accounts. One, it didn't kill me. In retrospect, I got off relatively easy. Two, it brought you back to me and was a reminder of how short life truly is. I don't want to waste even one more second of this too-short life without you by my side."

I would imagine that there are probably signs I missed as I tried to sign out the words and phrases, but judging by the tears that fill her brilliantly beautiful different-colored eyes, I think she gets the point. When I finish my thought, the officiant, who is also fluent in ASL, asks Natalie the question all our guests have been waiting for.

"Do you, Natalie, take Alexander to be your lawfully wedded husband?"

I watch her hands, waiting for her to sign a response, but she doesn't. And for one second, I panic. I take a deep breath and hold it.

She stares deep into my eyes, and a nervous but knowing grin grows across her blushing cheeks.

"I do," she says.

She *says*.

Two small words that have more impact than any verse or chorus I could ever hope to write.

Two small words. One incredible voice.

I didn't expect it. I didn't see it coming. That was the moment everything changed forever.

Want to see more from this author?
Here's a taster for you to enjoy!

Each and Every Summer
L A Tavares

Excerpt

Weston

The campground was quiet. Not silent, but quiet. Silence on the grounds was a rarity. Birds chirped and critters snapped twigs and crunched leaves as they ran through the abundant foliage, sounding off their small, happy-to-be-out-of-hibernation squeaks. The fire Weston Accardi kept lit continuously, day and night, crackled and popped as it chewed into the pieces of wood he fed it.

Soon the soundtrack of the campground would transform from its current nature-inspired sounds to a blend of noises that belonged to the incoming camping families. Children would run and play, shrieking at decibels specific to summertime. Their laughter and yells would echo through the plush pine trees as parents unpacked the camping gear and essentials from the overloaded trucks to prepare the site that they would call home for the duration of their stay. Music — both played through Bluetooth speakers and strummed on old guitars — would travel from the dirt driveways beneath each RV and become one with cloudless blue sky above.

Each currently bare site would have a tent or RV secured on it, and every available rental trailer or cottage would have people occupying them. *Every single one*, Weston thought as he thumbed through countless pages of reservations. He'd requested the bookings be printed and delivered to the site he'd claimed as 'The Owner's Headquarters' during the off-season renovations. The rest of the employees had WiFi access within the offices and laptops or tablets to view the information and spreadsheets, but Weston found nostalgic peace of mind by holding the printed reservations in his hand the exact way his father before him had done while sitting in the very same chair. A half-grin slid onto Weston's cheeks. He was pleased with the turnout of reservations for the grand reopening of Begoa's Point Family Campground. His father would have been too, had he been alive to see it.

Weston tucked the most recent reservation listings into the worn-out openings of the accordion-style folder and tossed it inside the door of his RV, which was situated in a wooded area well away from the hustle and bustle of the main grounds. When his parents had owned the campground more than fifteen years before, they had chosen a site at the center of the grounds directly within earshot of anything and everything going on within their property's perimeter. They'd preferred it that way — involved, hands-on. In many ways, Weston liked that too, maintaining full control, but when the sun went down, he preferred a hushed space to retreat to in order to separate himself from his work and enjoy the serene nature that surrounded him.

"Achilles." Weston followed the call with a quick, wet-lipped whistle and a pat of his palm against the thigh of his cargo shorts. He grabbed a leather leash from the picnic table with a clink as the metal clasp sounded against the tabletop. The dog's ears perked up like antennas receiving a signal. His tail picked up speed, wagging in long, swift motions that swept the sand off the patio mat that covered the land just outside the RV. "Want to go on a run?"

The dog leaped from the shaded dirt area he could usually be found in — a spot he'd claimed to hide away in from Maine's hot summer rays. He darted toward his owner and pushed his large head into Weston's hips with a force that almost knocked him over.

"I'll take that as a yes." Weston used his palm to ruffle the fur between the German Shepherd's ears. Achilles bounded around in circles with an impressive agility comparable to that of a show dog. With his energy and antics, no one would guess he was missing part of his hind leg. Then again, like pup, like owner. Most people hardly noticed that Weston was an amputee as well. He was a man who ran multiple miles per day, every day, with his dog stuck to his side. He walked all over the campground and was hardly ever seen in a golf cart unless there was an emergency that he needed to handle sooner rather than later. He maneuvered around using his left leg prosthetic as if it were his own natural limb.

Weston stretched out his back and his existing leg before clipping the dog's leash around his waist. The dog usually ran free, but the leash stayed on Weston's person in case the need arose for him to use it. Weston took off down the winding dirt path into a long trail of cookie-cutter cottages — empty now but soon to be filled with families ready to embark on their summer camping adventures. There would be some newcomers, but most of the reservation list was composed of returning families from his parents' time of owning and operating the same campground prior to its untimely closure.

He and Achilles ran uphill, turning a corner to jog past the recently updated tennis and basketball courts, as well as a newly renovated shower and bath house. A custodial worker waved as Weston came around the bend of the road and jogged past.

"Good morning, Larry!" Weston called. Larry tipped his hat in Weston's direction. Weston had made it a point to learn the name of every employee—a rule of his father's that he'd inherited and valued. He continued his journey down the pathway toward the beachfront bar and restaurant, stopping where Mark Jenson was readying the place for the upcoming grand reopening. The outdoor bar itself was a new addition, built while the cabins and sites were being remodeled, but Mark was an original employee. A longtime friend of Weston's father, Mark had run the bar and restaurant during Begoa's Point's first run and had agreed to come back to manage the new facility.

"Morning, boss." Mark moved large boxes of glasses from the ground to the bar top as the sun beat down on the tiki-themed hut while he worked. He wiped his brow on his forearm. His sweat-soaked shirt clung to his skin at his chest and back. "What are we having today?"

"The usual will be fine." Weston slowed and came to a full stop. Achilles followed suit, coming to a halt, then lying down in the small bit of shade the bar provided.

Mark grabbed a silver bowl from a below-bar cabinet and filled it with water before stepping out from the service area and coming around the bar to serve it to Begoa's Point's most prominent VIP. Mark stayed on one knee for a moment, scratching below the dog's chin. Achilles stood and started lapping water from the bowl, leaving more water on the ground in a messy puddle than he'd swallowed.

Mark returned to his position behind the counter, filled a cup with ice and water and slid it across the bar into Weston's hand.

"Where are you headed to today?" Mark leaned into the bar.

"All over the grounds, I think. The usual path." Weston paused to take a sip of the ice-cold water. "At least as far as the marina. I just want to make sure everything is ready to go for the opening."

"That's what you said yesterday." Mark raised an eyebrow. "Then again, it's what you will probably say tomorrow and the day after that too."

"I like to be prepared." Weston sent his now-empty plastic cup back across the bar.

"You will be. You are your father's son, after all. I wouldn't expect anything less."

Weston looked at Mark, analyzing the new lines that sank into his skin, but other than a few signs of aging, Mark looked almost the same as he had when Weston's parents had owned the campground before its closure, leaving Mark and many others without a job.

"Thank you for coming back, Mark. This place wouldn't be the same without you, even after all these years. I'm sorry we ever put you out of a job in the first place." Weston turned his eyes downward in sadness.

"It's not your fault, Weston—"

"It is, actually," Weston interrupted, adjusting his ballcap, with his gaze still glued to the floor. He watched the dog, if for no other reason than to avoid Mark's eyes. "You know it and so do I."

"It's not. You knock that off right now." Mark's voice teetered on scolding, and he wagged one aging finger in Weston's direction. "You know that your dad used to come down to the old bar every night for last call. *Every* night. He sat on the same barstool each time, and you know what he told me?"

Weston shook his head. He had been only seventeen when his parent's ownership had come to an end, so he'd not reached the legal drinking age where he could spend those waning nighttime hours with his dad, occupying Mark's bar stools. His 'no' wasn't an entirely honest answer to Mark's question, however. He knew what Mark was going to say — what his dad had used to say — but he wanted to hear it. If he couldn't hear it from his own father, Mark's affirmation was the next best thing.

"He said it was his dream to see you run this place. So maybe it didn't happen as he'd expected, but it's happening, and you should be proud of that. You're not a kid anymore, Weston. You've grown and should be so proud of who you've become. Your father would be."

"I remember that. He used to come down here every night but never had a sip of alcohol." Weston smiled at the seemingly small memories of his father, but they were anything but insignificant. They were everything.

"I remember watching you run around these grounds, from learning to walk all the way to chasing after the girls on the beach in your teenage years." Mark continued to speak, but Weston's mind was elsewhere, time-traveling down a winding path to his childhood.

It was a humid day, the kind where it was too sticky to do anything except sit around and complain about how hot it was.

"Give me your change," Charlie said, reaching across the table for Weston's quarters.

Weston grabbed the coins off the table and held them in his sweating palm, pulling them out of his best friend's reach. "You just had two ice creams. What do you need now?"

"Fried dough, of course. I'm just fifty cents short. Come on. I'll share it with you."

Weston handed over his quarters begrudgingly, but he couldn't resist fried dough any more than the next kid could. Charlie sprinted to the ordering window.

Charlie returned to the table, but just as he did, his mother beckoned from the beach.

"Be right back, Wes. We're number one forty-eight." The red color of his skin peeking out from the edges of his tank top led Weston to believe it was time for Charlie to reapply sunscreen.

"Numbers one forty-seven and one forty-eight," the snack bar attendant yelled from the pick-up window. Weston stood and headed toward the counter. Just as he did, a young girl with a mess of deep brown curls made her way there. The attendant handed two large, golden-brown fried doughs out of the window and they both headed toward the table where the cinnamon and sugar – the best parts – were kept.

The girl waited, rocking back and forth.

"Go ahead." Weston slid the shakers toward to her. "You ordered first."

She smiled and flipped the cinnamon shaker, brown dust falling to cover her plate. She followed with the sugar shaker, but no matter how much she tried, nothing came out. She looked at him and gave an embarrassed frown.

"It's not empty." Weston looked at the shaker. "It can be tricky, though. Sometimes the powder clogs the top. Let me try?"

She handed over the shaker. Weston tapped the container on the tabletop three times then flipped it over, hitting the side. A fractional amount of powder come out, and the girl giggled.

Weston undid the top, wiped away the excess confectionary powder with a napkin and pressed the lid back on. He picked it up once more and shook hard.

The top popped off, covering his fried dough in a small mountain of white powder. A cloud of sugar flew through the air and stuck to his black shirt and hair. The girl laughed so hard that she snorted.

Weston nodded, accepting an embarrassing defeat, then started laughing too. He picked up the fried dough and held it at an angle, allowing some of his sugary mess to fall over onto her piece.

"Thank you." She was still laughing as she walked away with her fried dough plate in hand.

Weston kept his gaze down the beach, imaging that younger version of himself as his adolescent years flashed before his eyes. He shook the memories away and returned his attention to Mark. "I was only chasing after one girl."

"Whatever happened to her, anyway?" Mark grabbed a towel to continue his cleaning.

"She got away." Weston slapped the bar top with his palm and winked before turning away and heading back to his predetermined path. Achilles bounded to his three legs, following behind him without being told.

The path came to an abrupt halt at the end of the shuffleboard courts and immediately turned to acres and acres of sandy beach at the lake's edge. Weston continued his jog, both his real foot and his prosthetic one kicking up sand as he ran down the untouched beach. Achilles kept pace, his paws stirring up a dusting of sand alongside Weston's. They ran the length of the main beach area, past the snack bar and mini-golf course, then turned left before finding a dirt pathway that led into the marina. He slowed as his feet hit the wooden dock. The structure, which extended into the lake, creaked under his weight. He kicked off his shoes, taking a seat on the edge of the dock and dipping both his feet into the water, only feeling the lake's cool temperature around his right ankle. Achilles sat next to him, proud and tall, as if the multiple-mile run had taken nothing out of him.

"We did it, Achilles." Weston wrapped his arm around the dog's shoulder blades. Achilles licked the side of Weston's face, stopping the salty sweat from dripping past his ears. The dog lay down next to Wes and inched forward, trying to reach his tongue into the rippling lake.

Weston removed his prosthetic and pushed himself off the dock, submerging in the water. He resurfaced and used one hand to balance on the wood. Achilles paced the edge of the dock, deciding between jumping in after him or remaining dry.

Weston used his free had to slap the water. "Get in here, boy!" Before he'd finished the command, Achilles dove in, splashing Weston upon entry and paddling toward him. They swam around, cooling off in the cold lake. Weston pulled himself back onto the dock then helped Achilles up next to him. The dog braced himself and shook, water spraying from the ends of his fur and further soaking Weston in the process. Achilles lay down once again at the edge of the dock, his front paws dangling over the wooden edge. Weston looked out over the unoccupied lake.

"This is what we've been waiting and working for. We counted down the moments to the grand reopening and it's finally happening." Weston stroked wet fur out of the dog's face. "Tomorrow is officially camping season, boy. Memorial Day. Best day of the year, if you ask me."

Home of Erotic Romance

Sign up for our newsletter and find out about all our romance book releases, eBook sales and promotions, sneak peeks and FREE romance books!

About the Author

When it comes to romance, L A doesn't have a type. Sometimes it's dark and devastating, sometimes it's soft and simple—truly, it just depends what her imaginary friends are doing at the time she starts writing about them.

L A has moved to various parts of the country over the last ten years but her heart has never left Boston.

And no, the "A" does not stand for Anne.

L A loves to hear from readers. You can find her contact information, website details and author profile page at https://www.totallybound.com

Made in the USA
Columbia, SC
12 March 2021

34367576R00198